Cooper

RICH
Girl
PROBLEMS

A Millionaire Wives Club Novel

The Ex Factor
Millionaire Wives Club

Published by Kensington Publishing Corp.

RICH *Girl* PROBLEMS

A Millionaire Wives Club Novel

Tu-Shonda L. Whitaker

KENSINGTON PUBLISHING CORP.

www.kensingtonbooks.com

KENSINGTON BOOKS are published by

Kensington Publishing Corp.
119 West 40th Street
New York, NY 10018

All Kensington titles, imprints, and distributed lines are available at special quantity discounts for bulk purchases for sales promotion, premiums, fund-raising, and educational or institutional use.

Special book excerpts or customized printings can also be created to fit specific needs. For details, write or phone the office of the Kensington Special Sales Manager: Kensington Publishing Corp., 119 West 40th Street, New York, NY 10018. Attn. Special Sales Department. Phone: 1-800-221-2647.

Kensington and the K logo Reg. U.S. Pat. & TM Off.

ISBN-13: 978-0-7582-8375-7
ISBN-10: 0-7582-8375-X
First Kensington Trade Paperback Printing: July 2014

eISBN-13: 978-0-7582-8377-1
eISBN-10: 0-7582-8377-6
First Kensington Electronic Edition: July 2014

10 9 8 7 6 5 4 3 2 1

Printed in the United States of America

To Cairo, who always answered the phone and stayed up with me—no matter the time—until I got it right! May God continue to bless you, may all of your dreams come true, and may your steps continue to align and lead you to greatness!

Acknowledgments

First and foremost I thank God for all of His many blessings!

To my husband and my children: You are truly the loves of my life! I do it all for you and I wouldn't have it any other way.

To my parents: Thank you for always having my back and for being my number one cheerleaders. There's no way I could do any of it without you.

To my family and friends: Your love and support is endless and I thank you for that.

To my agent, Sara Camilli: Thank you for being the best that any author could ever ask for!

To Selena James and Dafina Books: I thank you for all that you do, for I may have written the manuscript, but together we made this book! The best is truly yet to come!

And saving the best for last, the readers, the bookstores, social media friends, librarians, and libraries: I am humbled by your continued support of my work. Many of you have been there from the beginning, and eleven years later you're still here and I thank you for that. You all are truly a blessing to me. Please e-mail me at tushonda111@aol.com, follow me on Twitter @tushonda, instagram tushondalwhitaker, or Facebook at Facebook.com/tushonda.whitaker. Oh, and if you love reality TV as much as I do, then join my Trashee Tea Time Facebook page.

Best always,
Tu-Shonda

You've been misled.
Karma isn't a bitch.
Reality TV is . . .

CHAPTER 1

BRIDGET

Season Three

Hmm . . . Seems it's that time of the year again for us peons to all sip our beer and dream it's champagne, finger our glass pearls and pretend they're the sea's offspring. Why? Because the rich bitches of *Millionaire Wives Club* are *baaaaack!* And if we are to be anything like America's top rated reality show, then we'd better get it together.

Oh, wait. I didn't introduce myself. I'm the executive producer and show's creator, Bridget Palmer, once known as Sister Mary Frances. Long story.

But more to the point, and just so you understand my role, I'm the shopkeeper.

The shot caller.

The true baller.

And these slores keep me loaded, locked, and stocked. I have four homes. A penthouse suite in the Trump Tower of midtown Manhattan. Another in Holmby Hills, California. An Aspen ski resort, and a five bedroom flat in the Seventh District of Paris, France, of course.

I have a fleet of antique cars.

Two Picassos.

And several bank accounts, all courtesy of these conniving

whores—who want us all to think they are June Cleaver-esque mothers, stellar wives, philanthropists, and the empresses of goodness.

Bull. Shit.

I'll tell you what they are.

A bunch of frauds.

Jedi mind tricks.

The messiest slores I've ever met.

All with a bunch of fuckin' problems they manufacture for themselves. And as soon as the press gets wind of their un-timely disgrace . . . what do they do? They race to their publicists and assistants to hide their pending divorces, midnight brawls, summer flings, pesky skeletons, unexpected firings, drunk and druggy children, mothers in rehab, and any other inconvenience that has muddied their red bottoms and dared to fuck up the faux lives they have worked so hard to make us to believe.

And why are they in such a hurry to do this?

Because for the last two seasons, these girls have fallen vic-tim to the curse of reality TV, sold their souls to the devil, and sucked his dick during commercial break.

Take Milan. She wanted desperately to play the part of the angelic, sweet and sensitive, stand-by-her-man kind of woman who'd been wronged by love. When all she was, was a shifty bitch who'd spent all of her junkie ex-husband's money and left him broke, busted, and disgusted. Then she turned to Kendu, a conveniently wealthy football star who was also her costar Evan's husband. Let's not leave that out. Poor, sick, and twisted Evan, who, after learning of Kendu's affair with Milan, killed herself. Leaving Kendu free to not only marry Milan but also to happily raise Evan's daughter with Milan as if she were their own.

Now Chaunci, I'll give her some credit. Her mission was to be authentic. *Real,* as she liked to call it. *Real* as in the single mother and self-made editor-in-chief of her own *Vogue*-esque magazines and publishing company, who always spoke her mind. That kind of *real*. Yet what the cameras revealed was that this bitch was a real gnome. And underneath that frozen smile was a cold, unemotional, unforgiving, unable to commit, I-don't-know-my-daddy, catfightin' drama queen.

And Jaise, better known as Madame Bourgeois, would've never dreamed of auditioning to be an emotional bag lady. She had too many diamonds for that, spoke flawless French, was too cultured, and could point out prized antiques with her eyes closed too damn well to be deemed an emotional wrecking ball. But that's exactly who she was. A whiny trick who was dying to have a man. Got one. Married him. Yet failed miserably at being his wife. And that son of hers . . . Sweet baby Jesus. He was an oversexed and irresponsible maniac who made babies with every goddamn hood rat who came his way.

Then there was Vera. The oncologist's wife who tried her best to be the girl next door. But there was this tiny little problem with being cultivated in the projects. Yet Vera prided herself on being in control. So pulling out Vaseline and giving speeches on how she didn't bring knives to gunfights, and how she could carry a razor blade in her mouth, pressed against her cheek, and cut a bitch down in two seconds flat was never supposed to be revealed on TV. Being a reality TV star—for Vera—was never about being a reality TV star. It was truly about having a season-long infomercial for her tri-state full-service spa and hair care salons. Nonetheless, with her "darling I-ain't-the-one personality," discovering her husband had a son she didn't know about, and subsequently filing for divorce on national TV . . . well . . . that just made her famous for the very thing she didn't want to be famous for. And now she was the quintessence of what every talentless little girl wanted to be: a reality TV star.

If only this could be as sweet as it was meant to be. As sweet as the first time someone said he was a fan and nervously asked for their autographs. As fabulous as the exquisite designer gowns, rare jewels, and platinum clutches they worked the red carpet in.

The epitome of rich bitch candy.

But.

The reality TV gods either had fucked up or were fucked up. And since the gods had delivered on this cast's prayer of lights, camera, and action, the cast had no choice but to deal with what they'd prayed for.

I smiled as I stood behind the velvet rope and stanchions, among the screaming fans and hungry paparazzi, watching a single limo arrive at the gates of Manhattan's Metropolitan Club for the network's season premier party.

The limo driver opened the back door. A single stiletto stepped out, followed by another, and immediately a series of camera flashes sizzled through the air like electrified kisses as reporters vied for prime position.

The limo driver closed the door and there was only Milan standing there. I turned to one of my most trusted cameramen, Carl, and said, "Where are the rest?"

"I don't know. No one's heard from them."

I pulled in a deep breath, eased it through the side of my lips, and cast an intense gaze over Milan, as she smiled and made love to the cameras. "Carl. Put that fame whore back in her car. Then you are to find the others, and I mean it!" I flipped my crimson-colored hair behind my golden shoulders, shook off the pricks of stress, and said to myself, "No worries, Bridget. We'll find them."

CHAPTER 2

VERA

Action!

The swoop train of Vera's black rhinestone-studded Louis Vuitton gown swayed in the autumn breeze as she quickly clicked her Eternal Borgezie Diamond Stilettos out of her Fifth Avenue apartment building and over to her black Phantom, where her driver awaited her. "Good evening, Mrs. Bennett." He smiled as she glided into the backseat and he closed the door behind her.

"Good evening, Richard," Vera said as she melted into the soft leather and stared out the window.

Half of my shit? Mine?

Vera sank into vision of Taj sitting across from her and her attorney at the arbitrator's table earlier today, while his cocky lawyer argued that Taj was entitled to half of her millions—millions that she'd broken her back to make. She'd slaved in the kitchen creating hair products while simultaneously building and branding three tri-state full-service spa and hair care salons, brick by brick.

"We feel this is only fair," Taj's attorney had said, causing Vera to peer at them, cross her thick mahogany thighs, and be convinced that Taj was ridiculously stupid, in spite of his years of medical training. Specialized oncology studies. Researching cancer cures. Uncovering how to love her. How to make her scream his name and call him Daddy in the wee hours of the morning. Be her best friend. Her only child's father. Know her favorite foods. Favorite color. Deepest secrets. What made her cry, laugh, and think. In spite of all of this if that highfalutin' Negro—who sat there in his gray pinstripe and handmade William Fioravanti suit, looking finer than black china—thought for one minute that she would let him pimp-slap her by snatching half of her shit then he had to be the dumbest motherfucker alive.

Fuck. That.

And she couldn't bear another thought that told her to calm down and think this whole situation through. As far as Vera was concerned those were the same thoughts that kept her up most of the night and caused her to run her hands across Taj's cold and empty side of the bed, stroke between her thighs, and cry while moaning his name and mourning his absence.

"Richard, I need to make one stop before we pick up Jaise."

"Where to?"

"Five-fifty-five Park Avenue."

The evening midtown traffic whipped past Vera in streaks of blurred colors as Richard swayed in and out of the congestion of the traffic and within minutes, was parked in front of the building where Taj lived. Taj had owned this apartment since before they met, and after they married, he'd rented it out. He had moved back in a year ago, shortly after they'd separated.

"I'll only be a minute," Vera said, as she eased out of the backseat and into the building. She nodded at the doorman, flashed a smile and waved the electronic key at security before catching the elevator to the penthouse suite.

The elevator doors opened and let her off in Taj's foyer. Vera's heart raced like a '57 Chevy and felt due to break through her chest cavity at any moment. She took in a deep breath and walked into the living room. Her eyes bounced from the fifty-inch plasma television on the wall, to the custom made glass case that housed Taj's collection of signed baseballs, to the original and signed Malik Whitaker paintings on the wall. Tears filled her eyes as she spotted a framed picture of her and Taj on the fireplace mantel.

You'd better not fuckin' cry!

You've loved this motherfucker for eleven years and he's reduced your relationship to half of yo' shit? You'd better not shed a tear.

Fuck. Him.

"Taj!" Vera called. "Taj, I need to speak to you right now!" She stormed into the kitchen.

Nothing.

The bathroom.

He was nowhere to be found.

"Where the fuck are you?" She hurried into his empty bedroom. Stopped and sniffed. "Imperial Majesty. Two dabs."

Tears beat against the back of her eyes. "You have lost your fuckin' mind! Here I am feeling hurt and unsure so I come here to talk to you, and this is what I get? Some bitch's perfume running through here! Now I see clearly, motherfucker. Not only are you snatchin' my fuckin' bag, but you've also been up in here fuckin' some bitch!" She spun on her heels. Her eyes scanned the room in a whirlwind. "And this bitch has the audacity to wear the same perfume as I do!"

Vera's six-inch pencil heels beat against the bamboo floor like angry wind chimes as she rushed into the living room, placed her platinum clutch on an end table, and walked over to the fireplace. She grabbed the remote off the mantel and turned the fireplace on. Red, orange, and yellow embers sparked and sparkled over the logs. A growing fire ensued.

She reached for Taj's gleaming gold-tipped baseball bat that hung on the wall, took it down, and tapped the tip against her right palm. "So you want half of my shit because you want to lie around, fuck some trick, and have me finance it! Did you really think I'd let you pimp me and that I'd let the shit go down quietly?" Vera reared the bat back and struck the center of Taj's glass case, sending a downpour of glass and baseballs to the floor. "Always collectin' some shit! Is that what I was? Is that what our child was? Part of your fuckin' collection?!" Vera yanked each ball from the floor and hurled them one by one into the fireplace. The fire crackled and hissed as it opened up and welcomed the balls in.

"Here I've been loving you!" She walked over to his collection of jazz albums. "And you took the love I have for you, laid it on the bed between you and some ho, and together y'all trying to screw me?! Oh, hell no!"

She sailed his albums like Frisbees into the fireplace. Immediately, they warped, melted, and married the flames. "You think you can just spit on my feelings, motherfucker!" Tears streamed. "And I gave you everything. Every fuckin' thing!" She knocked his paintings off the wall. "All of me! My time. My love. My emotions. My secrets." She flung her tears into the air. "When we got married, I wrapped up all of me and left it at the fuckin' altar. I became one with you. With yo' ass. But that wasn't good enough for you. And to top the shit off, you expect me to accept some *son* you just found out about! How the fuck am I supposed to do that, Taj?! When I haven't even gotten over the death of *our* son! I don't want a replacement! . . . Oh my God! That's who you're fuckin' . . . that little bastard's mother?! Dion?!" Vera hesitated and a vision of Dion riding Taj's dick, Vera's favorite position, pillaged her mind. And no matter how she tried to shake the thought, the vision wouldn't let her go and forced her to stand there and in her mind's eye see Dion screaming Taj's name while he demanded to know his favorite thing: "Whose dick is this?"

The vision faded.

More tears streamed as Vera took Taj's collection of baseball cards and sent them to a charred grave.

"So I see, you just take everything that I've given you and present yourself as a full package to some dog-ass trick! I don't think so!" Vera ran over to Taj's tower of hip-hop CDs, took position, pulled the bat back, and aimed for a home run. "Hell no!" She shed more tears and wiped the sweat that had gathered on her forehead. "I promise you, you gon' learn today about fucking with me!" She picked up the bat and hammered his CD player.

Sweat rained down her temples and her eyes swelled as she raced into the kitchen, grabbed a knife, and returned to the living room.

She slashed the brown leather sofa with hard and heavy strikes. "Here I thought we were best fuckin' friends. You were my man! My husband! And now there's some new bitch on the horizon?!" She moved over to the chaise lounge, lunged, and landed the knife deeply into the leather, freeing bursting bubbles of white foam. "You were supposed to be my man, motherfucker! Whether we were together or not! You didn't have the right to run off and fuck some slut! How could you do that shit to me, Taj?! Me? Vera? Really? For some side pussy? For money?!"

She walked over to his collection of African masks and Thomas Blackshear busts and sent them one by one to their burning grave.

"What happened to 'I'm sorry, Vera?!' " She stormed into the kitchen. "What happened to 'What could we do to make this right'? Had me lying and shit on my show!" She reared the bat back and destroyed half of the cabinets, kitchen chairs, and two of the table legs, which caused the table to topple over and fall to the floor. "And now motherfuckers are leaking reports about me, thinking I'm crazy! And that I lied on the reunion, saying we were back together when we weren't! Where'd they get that from, Taj? How would they know the truth? 'Cause they got it from yo' ass!" She took the bat and swatted it across the counter. All of the appliances and the dishes bounced off the walls and smashed into the sliding glass doors that led to the balcony.

"You couldn't act like a fuckin' adult!" Vera moved on to the bedroom, swung the bat, and cracked the plasma television in half. She ripped down half of the electric blinds and broke the lamps. "You had to wage war!"

She gathered the Rolexes and his collection of gold coins from his dresser and tossed them into the fireplace.

She returned to the bedroom, opened up the closet, and found hanging on the back of the door the same suit that Taj had worn earlier that afternoon. She carried it to the living room and tossed it into the fire. "Fuck you and that suit!" She stormed back and forth from his bedroom to the living room, each time taking handfuls of his handmade Italian suits and custom made shoes, to be devoured by the fire. Once his closet was empty and the only things left were a few lonely hangers, she dusted her hands, took a step back, and stared at the built-in fish tank on the wall above Taj's king-size bed. Exotic and rare saltwater fish swam in a three-hundred-fifty-gallon tank that had been specially designed to look like the ocean floor.

"You wanted to wage war . . ." Vera picked up the bat, swung it back, gathered strength from what felt like the depths of her soul, and crashed the bat into the fish tank.

Nothing.

She regrouped. Wiped sweat from her brow and tears from her cheeks. Took a step back and went for a grand slam.

It still didn't crack.

Shit!

She lifted her arms again, and just as she decided that she would beat it until it opened up and let the bat in, the glass shattered and a surge of water rushed out of the tank like a tidal wave, drowning the bed below and sending the fish flopping to the floor. "Welcome to the battlefield, motherfucker!"

Vera lifted her swoop train as water inched beneath her

feet. She closed the door behind herself, stepped back into the living room, and admired how she'd redecorated the place.

She couldn't help but smile and congratulate herself on soothing the part of her heart that she thought for sure had withered to shit and died at the arbitrator's table. Now all she needed was to find a way to appease the iron fist that had crept up on her and had wedged into her throat.

After a few more moments of admiration she walked over to the elevator, stepped in, and watched the apartment disappear behind the wood panel doors.

"Where the hell have you been?" Jaise quipped as she entered the backseat and sat next to Vera. "Do you realize we are late as hell?"

"I know. I meant to call you. I had a stop to make."

"What stop?" Jaise sniffed. Squinted. She lifted her eyes to the car's ceiling and then lowered them and landed them on Vera. "What. The. Fuck. Is. That. Smell?"

"What smell?" Vera frowned.

"You know what smell. And why are you sitting over there looking like a two-dollar tramp who just escaped from a tittie bar? What is wrong with you? What is wrong with your makeup?" Jaise curled her upper lip. "Did you look at yourself in the mirror? You look like Lauryn Hill's stylist fucked you up, and with the exception of that dress, which is I'm-in-the-building fabulous, you look casket ready."

"Jaise, please. I stopped by Taj's before I came here."

"What the hell were you doing with Taj?"

"I needed to stop by his place to have a li'l conversation with him."

"And?"

"We had it. And now we have a li'l understanding."

"Well, you need to stay away from any understanding that involves your makeup and hair looking this fucked up. This is not how we do things."

"Stop exaggerating."

"I'm not exaggerating. And what are those li'l nicks and scratches on your arm?" Jaise ran an index finger up Vera's right arm. "You been in a fight? Or did Taj slam you against the wall, yank your hair back, and do you real good? You know that make-up-break-up sex is the best. Did I ever tell you about that time . . ."

"Jaise, it was nothing like that." Vera frowned, took out her compact, popped it open, and did everything she could not to reveal the shock she felt. All the sexy, bouncy curls in her hair lay limp on her bare shoulders. Her mascara resembled war marks. Her eye shadow had inched from her eyelids and was smeared across her eyebrows. Her lipstick ran a trail down her right cheek. One of her false lashes dangled for dear life and the other was simply missing. Tears filled her eyes.

"Exactly!" Jaise said. "Now do you see? You can't step onto the red carpet looking like who shot John, fucked up, and let his ass live."

Silence.

Jaise carried on. "Can you imagine the looks on the faces of that countrified Chaunci and sleazy ghetto trickafied Milan if you stepped onto the red carpet looking like this? Oh no, honey."

"Richard," Vera called.

"Yes, Mrs. Bennett."

"We need to make a detour."

CHAPTER 3

BRIDGET

The evening sun gently bowed and made way for a crisp fall New York City night. Two six-foot-tall, robust, olive-skinned men, dressed in black top hats and tails, standing on opposite sides of a massive black-and-gold-trimmed iron fence, slowly pulled the immense gold handles and brought the ultraexclusive and private lawn party into full view.

An eighteenth-century Manhattan mansion served as the backdrop, with glittering white lights wrapped around four colossal columns that lined the veranda.

On the left of the sprawling and verdant garden was an all-glass, L-shaped bar that glowed with a hue of blue. To the right were white-linen-covered chairs and matching round tables; mini white trees with crystals dangling from their branches served as the centerpieces.

Glowing white lanterns hung from white painted bamboo poles that separated the buffet station, the dance floor, and the makeshift stage where Jonathan Butler and his jazz band performed.

There were white-gloved butlers serving champagne and hors d'oeuvres. The guests—A-list celebrities, politicians, and Fortune 500 bigwigs—were all dressed in white.

And then there were the bitches, center of the red carpet and posing for pictures that were sure to hit the Internet at any moment and appear on the front pages of every fashion and gossip magazine across the nation by morning.

"Ladies! Ladies!" A *Page Six* reporter's voice rang out among the crowd. "Where's Chaunci?"

Everyone turned toward Milan, given that these two were the best of friends. "She'll be arriving at any moment." Milan smiled. "She's just running a little late. Which I'm sure my costars, Jaise and Vera, can certainly understand, being that they just showed up ten minutes ago. Isn't that so, girlfriends?"

Jaise flashed a quick peek of her pearly white teeth. "We're not late. We're fashionably on time."

"Speaking of fashion," a *Life & Style* reporter jumped in, "what are you wearing?"

Each was adorned in an exquisite gown and limited edition stilettos; the designers "Gucci, Louis Vuitton, and Yves Saint Laurent," eased from their full, glossy lips and into the air with glee.

"Ladies!" an *Elle* reporter yelled. "How do you respond to the criticism of reality TV? Tell us, what can we expect from this season?"

Hesitating, their glances bounced from one to the other. Their eyes told that they had no idea what to expect. Hell, I knew better than anyone that the wonderment of what would happen from one season to the next had mind-fucked them with no orgasmic reward since the first episode.

After all, season one was about their struggle to play nice and hide the knives they'd tucked away in their expensive clutches. Season two was about stepping over and pretending the unexpected skeletons that had fallen at their feet didn't exist. And, well . . . herein lies season three. . . .

"Ladies! Come on, give us something!"

After an awkward silence, Jaise smiled and took a step forward. Her platinum rhinestone-studded Louis Vuitton gown glimmered into the night. She looked toward the reporters and said, "You can expect us to spend more quality time together. Build a solid, sisterlike bond. We're truly dedicated to showing that reality TV isn't just about catfights and drama. There's substance. There's friendship. And we have it."

Impressive. A smile ran across my face. Apparently she was jockeying for the peacemaker's spot. *How interesting.*

The paparazzi carried on. "Ladies! Who's the new girl?"

"Excuse me," Dominique, the cast's publicist, interrupted. "Thank you, everyone, but that will be all for the evening. We must get to the party."

The two olive-skinned men assumed their positions and closed the iron gate, leaving a lonely choir of screaming fans and overzealous reporters to shoot questions and snap pictures behind us.

The cast walked to the end of the red carpet and into the center of the party. The emcee, Danny, with overly bright blond highlights in his gelled back hair, was clearly uncomfortable in men's clothing, hence the reason he was dressed like nineteen-eighty-fuckin'-five in a velvet lime green bolero tuxedo jacket trimmed with black stitching, matching ultratight tuxedo pants, lime green patent leather shoes, and a humongous rope chain and blinging crucifix hanging around his neck and highlighting his hairy chest. Nasty. Obviously, he had hope that *Miami Vice* was making a comeback. Danny gave short speeches about each cast member, thanking them for being number one the last two seasons.

Thankfully, the guests overlooked Danny's disgusting-ass appearance and serenaded the cast with a gracious round of applause.

Once the fanfare ended, Vera and Jaise headed to the powder room, while Carl and I stood next to Milan. "So, Milan," I said.

"Yes?" She turned toward me.

"Where's Chaunci?"

"I don't know," she said without hesitation. "Did you call her?"

"I don't call. You all are to be where I tell you to be when I tell you to be there."

"Well, obviously she isn't here, now is she? And instead of being so focused on Chaunci, why don't you ask those two phony tricks?" She pointed in the direction Vera and Jaise had gone. "Ask them why they showed up two hours late. Unless of course you three arranged that grand entrance."

"Me?" I said. "This is reality TV, darling. I would never arrange anything." I gave her a wide grin. "So, no, that fierce entrance had nothing to do with me, but I loved every minute of it. Those two know how to arrive. Wouldn't you agree?" I put up a hand for a high five, but instead of her hand greeting mine, she sneered.

Slut.

"No, I don't agree and I especially didn't appreciate being herded back into my limo and made to sit there like a child until the teacher's fame whores arrived." She surveyed me from head to stilettos. "And it's my expectation that that will not happen again or you will be minus a reality star."

My, my, she seems confused. "Or I'll be minus a what?" I blinked. "You wouldn't be threatening to quit so early in the season, would you? After all, this is only the first episode. At least allow me to record you for two or three more shows so that when I sue your ass you won't be completely broke." I nodded at the butler and he handed me a glass of champagne.

Silence.

Thought so.

"I'll tell you this," Milan said, clearly changing her sarcastic direction. "If Vera and Jaise say something offensive tonight, it will be a situation." She twisted her lips and her face confirmed that she was looking for a reason to set shit off.

Oh, please.

She continued, "And being that this is a nice place, I would hate to tear it up. Now answer this question, Bridget. Who's the new girl? I've heard reports that whoever she is, she's getting paid more than us."

"How ridiculous!" I assured her. "You, Chaunci, Vera, and Jaise are the highest paid reality stars on any network. Period. Trust me. What the new girl gets paid is the least of your worries."

"And what the hell does that mean?" Milan eyed me suspiciously.

"It means you'll have to wait and see who she is. She'll be introduced soon enough."

She sighed. "As long as she knows her place and understands there's a pecking order around here, then I have no problem welcoming her to our team. Otherwise, I'll turn her ass into fodder for the tabloids and toss her to the side with those two other phony bitches."

"Speaking of phony bitches," I mumbled, and nodded my head toward Jaise and Vera. "Look who's coming our way."

Jaise and Vera approached, each with a glass of champagne.

"So, Bridget," Jaise said in a playful British accent, "do spill the tea, dahling. Who's the new chick?"

Vera sipped and then said, "I've been meaning to mention that a very reliable source called me this morning and said it was Kim Kardashian." She paused, obviously for effect.

"What? Are you serious?" Milan said, put off.

"Ohhellno." Jaise quickly dropped her fake British accent. "Whatthefuck? Let me explain something here. I don't do ghetto and I don't do Beverly Hills trashy." She dropped her voice an octave, leaned in, and attempted to whisper to me, "Seriously, Bridget, Vera, and I have already made allowances for the hood-rich and classless mismatched within this cast and now you really expect us to run around town with the most passed around blow-up doll in America? I don't think so."

"Hood-rich? Allowances? And classless mismatched!" Milan gasped. "If anybody is mismatched here, it's your son and his multitude of baby mamas! So the last thing you need is to make any allowances for me or Chaunci!"

"Oh, Milan, please," Jaise said flippantly. "Who would stoop so low as to talk about a twenty-year-old child? Now if I spoke about your hundred-pound, six-month-old with the crooked-ass eye, you'd have a problem with that. So I suggest you leave my baby the hell alone!"

"You know what, Jaise? I'm going to just ignore you before I end up beatin' your ass." Milan guzzled her champagne.

"Suits me. Anywho, Bridget, will you just tell us who she is?"

"No." I smiled. "But I will say this: That speech you gave on the red carpet about friendship and you all being like sisters was absolutely wonderful. So elegant and so graceful."

Jaise smiled as she looked toward Carl, who had the camera pointed her way. "I meant what I said. Someone has to be the bigger person here. And I truly believe that Boom Kiki and her gang learn best by example." She smiled at Milan. "By the way, Boom Kiki, where is your gang?"

"Boom Kiki?!" Milan snapped. "Boom Kiki would be the ass who stayed with a man for seven years who used her as a punching bag. Oh wait, that would be you. So Boom Kiki must be the one whose fiend-ass mama tossed her in a garbage bag." She looked over to Vera.

I swear the look Vera gave Milan, with one eyebrow arched and the other dipped low, made me want to clutch my pearls and piss in my pants. I looked at Carl and mouthed, "Zoom in."

Vera dusted invisible wrinkles from her midthigh, strapless, royal blue, hourglass-fitted cocktail gown that hugged her double D's and wide hips like expensive paint. "Obviously, since the last time we saw one another was at the reunion, you've gotten a few things fucked up. So here's what you need to remember. I'm not the one. And unless you want me to slap the shit out of you, you'll shut the fuck up! 'Cause unlike Jaise"—she looked into the camera—"for me this season is not about getting along and showing more togetherness. For me, this season is about giving it to whoever brings it, whenever and wherever they bring it—"

"Pardon me," Jaise interrupted. "You two might want to put that on pause; there's a reporter coming this way. So smile, ladies."

Click!

Flash!

"You ladies look fantastic!" the reporter complimented. "Do tell. When did you decide to mend your friendship? Last we left off, you three were definitely at odds."

"Well . . ." Jaise smiled. "I think we've all grown up a bit, and given that most of us here are mothers and so many women look up to us, we thought that we'd be a little more tolerant of one another. And once we did that, the friendship just seemed to fall in place."

"Isn't that interesting?" The reporter pointed his digital recorder toward her. "So then you're not upset that Milan tweeted a blind item this morning to guess which of her costars was no longer allowed in Bloomingdale's because she'd written one too many bad checks? And when one of her followers tweeted your name, Jaise, Milan responded with a smiley face. That doesn't concern you at all?"

Jaise's eyes looked as if she'd entered another zone. "Bitch, you did what?!"

"Is that your statement?" The reporter beamed.

Jaise quickly whipped back around toward him. "Umm, no." She smiled. "Here's my statement: What happened on Twitter is of no moment to me. Milan already explained that someone hacked her account. So that's water under the bridge. Isn't that right, girlfriend?"

"That's exactly correct." Milan smiled.

"Great! Can I get a picture of you two together?"

"Of course," Jaise said, and she and Milan posed with arms slid around the back of one another's waists.

"Thank you, ladies." The reporter nodded as he walked away.

Jaise practically broke a heel stepping out of their embrace. "Ugh, I think I need a bath." She flicked invisible dirt from her shoulders.

"Fuck you!" Milan said.

Jaise whipped around. "You have absolutely no class. I wouldn't fuck you with somebody else's dildo."

"Ladies," a voice poured over their shoulders.

"Yes." They all turned around, wearing Barbie doll smiles, only to greet two uniformed NYPD officers.

The lead officer took a step forward. "Which one of you ladies is Vera Bennett?"

Vera smiled. "I'm Vera Bennett. May I help you with something?"

"Ma'am," the lead officer said, "you're under arrest. For criminal mischief and trespassing. I need you to place your hands behind your back."

Shut. The. Front. Fuckin'. Door. "Oh, my!" I gulped down the rest of my champagne in one shot.

Jaise looked panicked while Milan looked to be in shock.

My heart raced and my inner thighs tightened. I smiled at Vera and said, "That's it, Vera! Bring it home!" I shivered in excitement. Dear God! I swear Vera knew how to take shit to new heights every fuckin' time! And to think I couldn't wait to introduce them to the new girl and get their reactions! But this topped it all! *Thank you, Jesus. This right here . . . is cum worthy!* I shivered again, had a moment of silence, and then did my best to collect myself, as every reporter in the place, along with some I knew for sure were not on the guest list—but had somehow eased their way in—hurried over and began flashing their cameras and shouting questions, while everyone else was virtually on pause.

"Hurry, Carl, over here!" I popped my fingers and pointed at my other cameramen. "And you, over there! You make sure you zoom in, goddamn it! And you pan around and get the guests' reactions!"

Vera took a step back, and judging by the look in her eyes, a thought danced before her. She looked into the distance and then back at the officers. "You came here to arrest me? Really?" She looked back into the distance and said to no one in particular, "So this punk motherfucker called the police on me?"

"Vera," Jaise whispered. "Does this have anything to do with the conversation you had with Taj earlier this evening? Did you kill him?"

"Ma'am," the lead officer spoke again, "I'm going to ask you one last time to place your hands behind your back."

Vera shook her head. "Oh, that motherfucker will pay for this." She handed Jaise her purse and her blue diamond earrings, necklace, and matching bangles. Afterward, she placed her hands behind her back and said, "Let's go."

All I could do was smile. I promise you, I loved this dramatic whore!

Jaise looked over at the officers. "You have to be mistaken! And what the hell is your problem, coming up in here like this?! This is not proper conduct!"

"Ma'am," the lead officer said to Jaise, "I'm going to ask you to be quiet and to take a step back."

"Excuse you. You don't speak to a lady like that! Now my husband is Captain Bilal Asante and I demand that you get those cuffs off her!" She grabbed the officer roughly by the chin and snatched his face toward hers. She squeezed his cheeks. "Now you listen to me—Ahh!" She screamed as the officer quickly grabbed her arms, spun her around, and slapped cuffs on her wrists. "You're under arrest for disorderly conduct! And assault on an officer!"

Jesus, Mary, and Joseph, I so love these whores!

"I didn't assault you!" Jaise wiggled and screamed. "I'm not some common damn criminal! Bridget, call my attorney and have him meet us at the station!"

Oh, hell no. This will make a much better episode if you two stay there over the weekend. "Of course, Jaise. I'm on it. Carl," I directed, "follow them."

Once the iron gates closed behind them, I clapped my hands. "Perfect. Fuckin'. Scene. Fuckin' fabulous. Orgasmic!" I leaned in close to Milan, whose mouth was hung open in astonishment, and spoke in a low tone. "Now I need you to take it home! Here's your chance to outdo them. Look into the camera and own it. Swear that you called the police on her and had her arrested. Make up some shit. Anything. I got it! Say that Vera was the one writing bad checks."

"Why would I say that?" Milan asked, and had the nerve to sound as if what I'd just suggested was beneath her. "I don't like her, but that's going a little too far."

"And this is why you'll never have a spin off."

"That's fine," Milan said, as she patted the sides of her shoulder-length hair and spoke into the camera. "I would never lie on someone and wallow in their moment of distress. And, yes, as far as I'm concerned, those two bitches got what their greasy-ass hands called for. And I'm not surprised that Vera had a warrant. Look at her. Think about where she came from. The trash. And Jaise. I'm sure she'll do just fine in jail. It'll take her punk ass no time to become some dike's wife. However, I will not stand here and pour piss in an open wound. I simply won't do it."

I clapped my hands and smiled as I turned around and looked toward the guests, who all were still in shock. "No worries, anyone!" I said, as I made my rounds. "No worries. Vera and Jaise will be fine. Please. Let's get back to having a good time. After all, I have a wonderful surprise for everyone!"

Some of the guests left, but most took my advice and carried on. I made eye contact with Danny and nodded, which was the cue he'd been waiting for.

"The moment we've all been anticipating has arrived,"

Danny said, as he stood on the makeshift stage. "May I have everyone's attention please?"

The crowd grew silent and Milan paid particularly close attention. For a moment, I didn't think that she was breathing.

Danny continued, "As you know, everyone has been champing at the bit to see who the new Millionaire Wife is. Well, I'm here to tell you she's beautiful. Stunning. A mother. Rich. Very rich. The bride of oil tycoon Zachary Dupree—"

Milan looked perplexed. "I know damn well this is not some old whore with worms, Bridget. Isn't he like seventy . . . or eighty?"

I didn't answer her; instead I looked over at the reporter who quietly stood next to Milan and hung on her every word.

"Without further ado," Danny carried on, "it is my pleasure to introduce the newest member of the *Millionaire Wives Club,* Journee Dupree!"

"Wonderful!" I yelled as the crowd and I broke out in rambunctious applause. At six foot one, she wore fabulous python skin Prada heels with straps that snaked up her calf.

Journee didn't walk. She sauntered.

Back straight.

Head held high.

Pelvis thrusting.

Glowing maple skin. The exact color that I loved in my men.

She was fabulous and served everyone in the place Parisian runway. With hair flowing over her shoulders, she worked the stage in a sparkling cream Prada gown that stopped midway up her thigh and complimented every one of her size-six curves. She walked up to the mic and said, "You all are way too kind, but I thank you nonetheless. I'm sure that I will bring everything that you have ever dreamed of to reality TV." She gave a small Miss America wave as I joined her on stage, and together we answered reporters' questions and posed for pictures. A few minutes into the sunlight of her superstardom, I leaned in and said, "Journee, I'd like to introduce you to Milan."

"Of course," she said, her eyes slowly rising from Milan's stilettos to her mink lashes.

"But"—I lightly grabbed her forearm, stopping her mid-step—"I must caution you before we walk over there, please don't think that you'll be holding any afternoon tea-esque conversation about the children, the husbands, Italy, Chanel."

"Why not? There has to be an effort to be friendly."

"Friendly?" I all but laughed. "With that girl? That expectation is awfully high, darling. And given the Milan I know, that will never happen. She is the epitome of unfriendly. She can be nasty. Very nasty . . . You know, Journee, if this were anyone else, I wouldn't tell them this, but I think you ought to know."

"Know what?"

"When Milan found out you were the wife of Zachary Dupree, she classed you immediately as an old whore with worms."

"She did what?"

"And then she laughed."

"Laughed?"

"Cackled. Like trailer trash with too much time on her hands. So you see"—I looked her straight in the eyes—"Milan is a jealous, pussy-poppin' madwoman. Believe me. I've worked with her long enough to know. Don't misunderstand me though. I'm not saying not to be nice. I'm simply saying to watch yourself."

We resumed our walk over toward Milan, and once we arrived Milan turned and smiled at Journee.

"Milan," I said, "this is Journee Dupree."

Journee held her hand out and Milan accepted her gesture. *How sweet.*

"Journee, it's truly a pleasure," Milan said, as her eyes darted back and forth between Journee and the camera pointed at them.

"Yes, it is," Journee said. "I'm sure we're going to have a fabulous season."

"I was thinking the same thing," Milan agreed.

Journee continued, "As long as everybody stays in their lane and I don't have to cuss a motherfucker out, then I'm sure we'll be fine." She gave Milan a look that confirmed she had heard right. Then she looked from side to side. "Now where are the other ladies, Vera, Jaise, and Chaunci?"

Milan blinked. "Rewind. As long as who stays in their what? You won't have to what?"

Journee smiled. "Oh, forgive me. Did I say that too fast? What I said was: As. Long. As. You. Stay—"

"I heard what you said!" Milan said. "Now hear this! I don't know where you get off—"

"I watched the show," Journee interjected. "Both seasons. And I already know you throw the rock and your girlfriend Chaunci hides your hands. But, just so you know, the day that your rock hits me, I'll be sure to make you choke on it."

Boom!

"However," Journee batted her lashes, "I don't believe in violence. So, I'm just letting you know the rules for us getting along famously. Now where are the other girls?"

"Chaunci didn't show up," I said. "No worries though. My lawyers and I will be dealing with her by morning, and the other two are in jail."

"Jail?!" Journee said in disbelief.

"Five-0 carted Vera and Jaise out of here a little over an hour ago. It was one of the greatest spectacles I'd ever seen! You were in the mansion awaiting your introduction at the time."

"Hold it!" Milan said. "To hell with the other girls; let's get back to our situation at hand. Let me inform you how things work around here. There is a pecking order and you—"

"Pecking order? Really?" Journee chuckled. "How cute. Do tell; is that your rendition of shade? Girl, please. Your kind is not for me. I have my own league; real bitches do real things."

"I don't know who the fuck you think you are!" Milan said.

"Journee Dupree, bride of billionaire Zachary Dupree. And that worm is richer than both you and your pet unicorn, Chaunci, put together. So you two sad, desperate, and pathetic thots better run along. " She flicked her wrist.

Dear God, I was about to drool.

Milan pointed in Journee's direction, yet looked into the camera, "Somebody better get this bitch. Because she's obviously new to this and Bridget forgot to tell this hoe the rules. Rule number one: don't come for me. Rule number two: don't break rule number one. 'Cause if you do, you'll end up tagged and body bagged."

"Hilarious!" Journee's platinum and diamond bangles clanked as she clapped her hands. "You tried it. But clearly you're doing all of that talking to punk out of getting your ass beat. "

Milan took two short breaths and did her best to collect herself. "You know what? Let me leave here before I forget all of my anger management techniques." She tucked her clutch beneath her arm and stormed away.

I smiled as I handed Journee a glass of rosé. "You know, Journee, the viewers will love you. So welcome, my dear, to the *Millionaire Wives Club*. Where bitches reign supreme. Ratings rule everything. And love . . . is a whole other story on another goddamn channel."

CHAPTER 4

VERA

Three Days Later

Vera slowly opened her eyes and realized that since Friday she'd watched three sunrises slither through the tiny barred window in the cell she shared with seven women. One who had a full beard, mustache, and pissed standing up and leaning over the toilet like a man. Another who dug into her wrists and sliced her skin with her fingernails; two who cried all weekend; one who hid in the corner, dripped snot and moaned through meth withdrawal.

Jaise side-eyed everydamnbody. She had been threatened with not one, but four beat downs and a coma. Then there was the fan, who screamed for two hours straight about how much she loved the show but hated both of their raggedy asses.

Dear God.

The smooth mulberry silk of Vera's cocktail gown was stained and ruined with indentations and snags from the rough concrete bench where she sat next to Jaise, who whispered in a panic, "I have got to get the fuck out of here or go crazy." Tears filled her eyes. "I haven't slept in three days! The bitch over there told me she wanted to smell my panties. I've got sores on my ass and I just can't. I can't help you anymore, Vera!"

"Help me?" Vera said, taken aback.

"I can't do this with you. You're in this ghetto shit a little too deep for me. I never expected to go to jail behind trying to save your ass. I need to—"

"Shut. The. Fuck. Up." Vera squinted as she pushed her face into Jaise's and said in a low yet stern tone, "Let me get your ass together real quick. It's your own fault that you're in this motherfucker in the first place. You're married to a damn cop, so you knew better than to put your hands on one. Then you do it the same weekend that your husband is away at a law enforcement retreat, where he can't be reached, and now we have to sit here all goddamn weekend. You want to blame this shit on me? Here's what I need you to do: turn yo' ass the other way before I forget that you're one of my best friends and clothesline the shit outta you!"

"Trouble in TV land?" the fan yelled. "Y'all bitches finally see in each other what the fuck I see when I watch y'all on TV!"

Jaise jumped up. "You know what—!"

"Bennett, Asante!" the correction officer yelled into the cell. "Step to the front. Time to go!"

"Thank God!" they said simultaneously as they rushed toward the electronic door and watched it slide back.

"Bye, bitches!" the fan screamed. "Better hope I don't see your asses on the schreetz". The electronic door slammed and reduced her voice to a muffle.

The officer escorted Vera and Jaise to the processing clerk, who shoved a plastic bag with their belongings into their hands and asked them to step on the opposite side of an electronic door that slid closed behind them.

"My shoes are not in here," Vera said as she rummaged through her bag and looked over to Jaise, who pounded on the door demanding to get the processing clerk's attention.

"Half of my shit is missing!" Jaise screamed. "And where the hell are my shoes?!"

"You know what," Vera spun around and yelled at Jaise, "If

you get arrested again you'll be in there by your damn self! Fuck the shoes!" She stormed out of the precinct with Jaise pissed off, yet following behind. They walked directly into an unexpected mob of reporters, a smiling Bridget, and television cameras.

"Over here, baby girl." Vera's Aunt Cookie grabbed her hand, while Jaise's driver rushed to her, tossed his blazer over her head, and made a mad dash for the car.

Jaise and her driver peeled off and one of the *Millionaire Wives Club* vans rushed behind them.

Aunt Cookie, however, posed for pictures and strolled her size-sixteen hips through the mob of paparazzi over to her pristine '74 candy-apple-red-and-white ragtop Eldorado. Vera yanked the handle, got in, and slammed the door. The paparazzi flashed their cameras into the purple-tinted window.

"Make that the last time you slam my damn door," Cookie said as she slid the key into the ignition and started the engine. The hydraulics made the entire car bounce and raise three feet off the ground. The black velvet dice that hung around the rearview mirror swayed from side to side as Cookie reached for a cigarette in her ashtray, lit it, and took a pull.

Vera did all she could not to stare in the direction of the reporters, but she needed something to focus on, especially since she knew it was only a matter of time before her aunt went on a rampage about her being in jail. She settled for a snag in her dress.

Cookie placed the car in drive and took off for the West Side Highway.

One . . .

Vera flipped down the visor and took a deep breath as she spotted Bridget and one of the cameramen following behind them in a dark blue van. She quickly flipped the visor back up and took a quick peek at Cookie, who turned off the first exit and a few seconds later was double parked in the street.

Two . . .

Cookie took a long and deliberate pull of her cigarette, blew a small stream of smoke from the side of her ruby red lips, and ran an index finger across the slicked edges of her lace front.

She mashed her cigarette in the ashtray, leaned back in her seat and snorted. "I have half a mind to take my hand and back smack, sumo-flex, and clothesline the shit outta you!"

"Aunt Cookie—"

"Shut up! Now tell me, who in the hell gets arrested on a Friday? A Friday, Vera? How goddamn slow can you be? Must be that damn crack and dope fiend shit ya mama was smokin' comin' back to haunt you! 'Cause, yeah, I raised you, but you didn't get this dumb shit from me! I don't know what you workin' wit'!"

"Aunt Cookie—"

"Didn't I tell you to shut up?! Now answer me this. What have I always told you? Huh? What?"

"Not to get arrested."

"Hell no!" Cookie mushed Vera on the side of her forehead. "Now say some dumb shit like that again and see what I do to you! You know I have always told you that if you gotta bust ass, then bust ass Monday through Thursday! But what did you do?"

Vera hesitated. "I—"

"You went and got your ass locked up on a ma'fuckin' Friday! Leaving me with that spoiled ass, pain in the ass daughter of yours! And you know my weekends are tied up. After I raised you, me and kids got a goddamn time limit. Called an hour. Now I love Skyy, but she talks too damn much. You don't know how many times I wanted to yell 'Shut the fuck up!' But I didn't. I was close. But I said a damn prayer and Jesus helped me get through the goddamn weekend! 'Aunt Cookie this. Aunt Cookie that.' I promise you, Vera, I wanted to slap the vocabulary outta her ass. Children in my day didn't talk that damn much! I swear it's that private school you got her in. All this damn money you got done messed her up. She needs a broke ass-beatin'. That's what she needs! Too damn grown!"

"Aunt Cookie, she's just seven."

"I don't give a damn! When I was seven, I knew how to shut the hell up. And don't interrupt me again. Now. Make this your last time I have to come and get your crazy ass out of jail on a Monday morning. Are we clear?"

"Yeah."

"Now, where are we going?"

"I need to make a stop—and I also need to use your cell phone."

The rubber soles of Vera's forest green prison slippers slapped against the bamboo floor of Taj's private medical practice as she walked in and slammed the all-glass entrance door hard enough to make the pane shake.

The people in the lobby—patients and two secretaries, one standing and the other sitting behind the desk answering the phone—all froze. Bridget all but lost her balance as she and Carl rushed in behind Vera, who stormed past the secretaries and down the hall into Taj's office.

Where the hell is he?

Vera's eyes scanned the black-and-white framed family photos that hung on the walls and surrounded Taj's medical degree and license. She whipped toward the door where Taj's secretary, Miranda, stood.

"Mrs. Bennett." Miranda's voice quivered. "Dr. Bennett is in a meeting with some of the other doctors and nurses. Please—"

"Miranda." Vera popped her lips and cocked her neck to the right. "I advise you to get the fuck out of my way."

Miranda stepped back.

Vera pushed past her, charged down the carpeted hall, and

stopped at the closed double doors of the conference room. She placed her hands on the nickel-plated handles, twisted them, and swung both doors open.

All heads turned and seemed stuck Vera's way. The only one looking the opposite way was Taj, who pointed to a Power-Point of a cancerous cell. "So you see," he said as he turned around and locked eyes with Vera.

"Oh. No. The fuck. You didn't," Vera said. "You had my motherfuckin' ass locked up!"

"Can everyone please excuse us?" Taj said, and his staff gathered their things to leave.

"Oh, you don't have to go no-motherfuckin'-where, 'cause I won't be here long!"

The staff gave one another uncomfortable grins and glances.

"Vera," Taj called, and she hesitated. "Stop. It."

They locked eyes once more and after a few seconds of loaded silence, Vera screamed, "Don't 'Vera me,' motherfucker! You have lost your rabbit-ass mind! Now we can do a whole lot of shit to each other, but jail? Really? Oh, you have taken it to a whole other level! You had five-0 roll up on me—and then they cuff me on *national* TV? Seriously?" She glances at the camera and then back over to Taj.

"Vera," Taj said, loosening his tie as a road map of thumping veins webbed their way up his thick neck, "I need you to step into my office."

"Oh, what? You're embarrassed? I don't give a damn! You should've thought about that before you called the po-po on me!"

"Listen, you need to stop. Now, I will leave here in a few minutes and meet you at our house."

"Our house? We don't have a house!"

"I will meet you at your house."

"Really? How the hell are you going to get there?" She

pointed to the picture window where a tow truck had raised Taj's silver Lamborghini Veneno onto the flatbed.

"What the fuck?!" Taj rushed over to Vera and yanked her by the forearm with one hand and with the other hand pushed Carl and the camera pointed at them out of the way. He charged out the back door and into the parking lot.

Aunt Cookie rolled down her tinted car window. "Keep it clean, Taj. Let her arm go. 'Cause I don't wanna have to put no sauce on you." She pointed a hand like a gun and blew at the invisible tip.

Still clutching Vera by the forearm, Taj ignored Cookie and instead ran over to the tow truck driver. A burly black woman with an attitude, her blond hair dyed the wrong shade for her maple complexion; she jiggled keys and walked toward the driver's side of the tow truck. "That's my damn car! Take it off your truck right now!"

The driver ignored him as she got into the truck and slammed the door in his face.

"Vera, get my damn car!" Taj demanded.

Vera snatched away. "Do you have amnesia? That's my goddamn car! Motherfucker's in my name!"

"It was a gift for my birthday. Now get my shit off that damn truck!"

"Hell no. That's my shit—and I'm selling the mother-fucker. You better get yo' pretty cop-callin' ass a cab, get on the goddamn bus, or hitchhike! Punk, snitchin'-ass beyotch! Better make sure that's the last time you call the po-po on me!" She turned on her heels and slid back into Cookie's car. The tow truck pulled out of the parking lot, Cookie popped the hydraulics and screeched out behind it, leaving Taj and the camera crew engulfed in a cloud of fumes.

CHAPTER 5

JAISE

*B*reathe . . .

Jaise sat in the back of her snow white Rolls Royce, feeling smothered by the lingering stench of the cell she'd been in all weekend.

Exhale . . .

Before she left home she'd had a bath for an hour and cooked a soul food feast for two hours, hoping that the stale and musty scent of the inmates and the damp concrete would go away.

It didn't.

It was everywhere. In everydamnthing. The new Prada jeans, white lace blouse, and black strappy Manolos that her stylist had picked out and dropped off this morning for her to wear.

Even the fried chicken, the rice, the peas, the sweet corn bread, mashed potatoes, collard greens, and apple turnovers that she cooked all reeked of hell.

Her only vice that seemed able to save her life and help her get her thoughts in order were her Virginia Slims Menthol Lights. She pulled her vintage mirrored cigarette case from her purse and tried to open the clasp. She fumbled. The case slipped from her hands, hit the carpeted floor, and popped open.

Fuck.

The case was empty.

I thought I had at least one cigarette left.

Jaise ran her hands frantically across the floor and under the seats.

Nothing.

Shit.

Did I smoke the last one this morning?

Damn.

She leaned against the butter-soft leather seat and glanced in the rearview mirror at her driver, who she just realized was staring at her, and judging by the look he gave her, he must've thought she was crazy.

Maybe I am . . .

Jaise and her driver shifted their eyes from one another's reflection and looked in the opposite direction.

Relax . . .

Five minutes into warring with her thoughts, Jaise watched her husband, Bilal, pull into the parking lot in his navy Escalade and park next to the *Millionaire Wives Club* van, where Bridget and Carl sat taping her.

"Okay, Jackson," Jaise said to her driver, "I'll have Mr. Asante drop me. I'll see you later this evening perhaps."

"Have a good day, missus," Jackson said, getting out of the car and opening the door for Jaise. She smiled and nodded good-bye. When Jackson pulled off, Jaise walked over to Bilal.

Showtime!

He stepped out of his truck and she reached up, sliding her arms around his waist and kissing him. Usually kissing her six-foot-four, beautiful, honey-colored husband, with Egyptian eyes etched into his clean-shaven face, calmed her. But not today. She was anxious. Nervous. And she prayed like hell that Bilal couldn't tell.

They ended their kiss. "Babe, how was the retreat?" she asked.

"It was cool," he said, short, curt, unimpressed by her question.

She pulled in a heavy breath and released it in a smile. "Okay, well, I'm glad we're here today."

"Yeah?" He arched a brow.

"Yeah. Hopefully, the counselor will help us get back to the way things once were."

Bilal let Jaise's words dangle in the air as he walked toward the glass door with the name of the practice, New Beginnings Counseling Center, etched into it.

Jaise followed him as he walked into the waiting room, took a seat, and immediately began to leaf through a *Black Enterprise* magazine. She sat next to him and her eyes combed the antique coffee table and she guessed that it was at least a hundred years old and worth over a thousand dollars. She smiled. She loved antiques. Their richness, the stories they held, their ability to withstand the test of time, no matter how battered and bruised they were.

She nervously crossed her legs to the left, then to the right.

I need to tell him about my weekend.

No. Now is not the time.

She eyed Bridget, Carl, and the camera pointed her way.

I'll tell him off camera.

Her eyes swept over Bilal, from the low waves in his hair, to his large hands that held the secret to how she liked to be held—a firm grip around the hips and pulled closely to his chest. She studied his athletic frame that lionized his sex appeal and smiled as her eyes drifted down to his feet, which lived up to the big dick myth.

"Mr. and Mrs. Asante?" The secretary interrupted her thoughts. "Dr. Johnson will see you now."

Bridget and Carl positioned themselves in the far corner of

the doctor's office to ensure the camera had the best angle, while Jaise and Bilal walked in after them.

Jaise smiled at Dr. Johnson and said, "You have such a beautiful office."

"Thank you," said Dr. Johnson, a tall and lean maple-colored woman with a close-cropped haircut and broad shoulders.

"The antiques in the lobby are so grand," Jaise carried on, shaking the doctor's hand. "That coffee table has to be at least a hundred years old. If you're ever thinking about selling it, please give me a call." She handed the doctor her online antiques business card.

"Thank you." Dr. Johnson placed the card on her desk and pointed to the black leather love seat. "Have a seat please."

"We certainly will." Jaise smiled as she and Bilal sat facing the doctor on a red, oxford leather chair.

"What brings you to couple's therapy?" Dr. Johnson tapped the tip of her pen on her notepad.

Bilal sat quietly as Jaise hesitated. "We're separated. I want my husband back home, but first we need to learn to communicate. It's a struggle. Most times we end up in an argument and neither one of us wants that."

Dr. Johnson looked over at Bilal, whose eyes and facial expression revealed a thousand thoughts—but his mouth didn't say a word.

Jaise continued, "We love each other dearly."

"Okay." Dr. Johnson nodded. "Tell me, was communication always a problem?"

"No. Until about a year ago, our life was perfect."

Bilal cut his eyes at Jaise, yet still didn't say anything.

The doctor continued, "Tell me about that. What made it perfect?"

Jaise grabbed Bilal's hand and held it. "Well, let me start with telling you about my first husband, Lawrence, so you'll understand why my marriage to Bilal was perfect."

"Please do."

"Well, I married Lawrence when I was seventeen and the best thing that came out of it was my baby."

"Why did you divorce?"

"Because he got the bright idea that he should beat the hell out of me. And that I should let him do it."

"So he was physically abusive?"

"Yes. And before you even ask, my father did not beat my mother. He didn't beat me. No one ever abused me sexually or any of that other sick and twisted shit that people always assign to battered women. I'm not a victim either. I don't subscribe to that. Lawrence kicked my ass because he thought he could. I fought back, but next to cuttin' and killin' that motherfucker, there was no way I could beat a prizefighter."

"You don't have to curse to make your point, Jaise," Bilal interjected.

Jaise turned to Bilal. *Relax.* She let his hand go and turned back to the doctor.

"How long were you with him?" Dr. Johnson asked.

"For seven years. After that, it was just Jabril and me. I dated a few men here and there, but they were all a mess. When I started to give up hope, I met Superman." She placed her hand on Bilal's right knee and squeezed.

"How'd you meet?"

Jaise chuckled. "He arrested my son."

Dr. Johnson looked puzzled. "How old is your son? I thought you referred to him as a baby?"

"The baby's twenty." Bilal smirked.

Jaise looked at Bilal, raised one brow and dipped the other. *Breathe.* She glanced at the camera and mustered up a smile. "Dr. Johnson, I had my son when I was seventeen. I was pregnant when my father forced me into a shotgun wedding. And, yes, my son's twenty."

"With two kids," Bilal added.

"What the fuck is your problem?" Jaise asked.

"I'm just helping to give the full picture. That your son's a man. Not a baby."

"He's twenty. That's hardly a damn man."

"I was a man at twenty."

"This is not about you—and furthermore, Mr. Man-At-Twenty, you didn't have a daddy or a mama who gave a damn!" She read Bilal's face, which momentarily revealed he was shocked she took it there." *Whatever.* She carried on. "I love my son and I will not toss my arms in the air and watch him fall simply because you were the great American dream at twenty! Fuck. That."

Bilal scoffed. "I never said I was the great American anything and I am definitely not saying he has to be."

Dr. Johnson interjected, "Mr. Asante, what would you like to see from your stepson?"

"I'd like to see him be more responsible. Take care of his own children and not depend on his mother so much."

"What do you think of that?" the doctor asked Jaise.

"I think it's ridiculous! Jabril can't afford to take care of children right now and Bilal knows it! Not too long ago, he was picked up for not paying child support! It's not as if he has a job and can help himself."

"He quit!"

"His supervisor was nasty to him, *Bilal.*" Jaise clenched her jaw. You know what, Dr. Johnson, Bilal just doesn't like my son!"

Bilal scoffed. "That's the first thing that you've said since we've been here that is the truth, I don't like him. I don't like what he's become. He's lazy and if he can't afford to take care of his children, then he needs to stop making them! He's disrespectful—"

"He's not disrespectful! You're the one who told him that you were going to kick his ass!"

"I meant that. The next time he gets up in my face when

all I'm trying to do is help him, I'm going to bust. His. Ass. So you might as well mark the date"—he pointed to a pen and a pad on the coffee table—" 'cause that's a promise."

Jaise turned to the doctor. "See, this is why we can't communicate. Because he makes everything about my son. That's *my* son, and a mother knows her child. I cannot and will not wash my hands of my baby. Ever! And I need my husband to support me!"

"Never." Bilal shook his head. "I'm never going to support a twenty-year-old being a baby or a screwed up man."

Jaise looked at Dr. Johnson. "So you see, he sets limits and conditions on loving me."

"I didn't hear him say that," Dr. Johnson said. "He appears to be expressing his frustration. I think—"

"Apparently you don't think I'm frustrated as well!"

"I hear frustration coming from the two of you, but—"

"For you to say you don't see him setting limits and conditions on loving me—I resent that."

"Support and love are two very different things, Mrs. Asante."

Bitch, please. "You can't be serious with this. Support and love are on the same level. You cannot have one without the other." Jaise turned toward Bilal. "Just like I needed you to support me Friday!" She pointed in his face. "You knew it was the first day of taping and you knew I wanted you there! Instead you went to that damn, stupid-ass retreat! I had to go to the taping by myself and then I had to spend the rest of the weekend in bed and feeling miserable. Why? Because apparently I'm the only one invested in trying to save this marriage!"

Bilal stroked his chin the way he always did when he was pissed. He sat up straight and looked Jaise dead in the eyes. "This is why we have problems—because you're a liar! Why would I care about the first day of taping when I told you I didn't want to be on TV? But, noooo. What did you do? You renewed your contract—"

"I didn't know if you were coming home or not. Hell, you're still not home, and there was no way I was giving up my job—which happens to be on TV—not knowing for sure if you planned on divorcing me."

"Would you like your husband to come home?" Dr. Johnson asked.

"I want to do whatever pleases him, but I will not beg him."

"I didn't ask you to beg him. I asked you if you wanted your husband to come home."

"He doesn't want to come home."

"You don't want me to come home. While your mouth is saying you want to be my wife, that's not who you really want to be."

Jaise felt like he'd just kicked her in the gut. "Who the hell do you think you are? You don't psychoanalyze me! "

"You need to stop lying, Jaise, and just tell the truth!"

"I'm not lying."

"Then why don't you tell us what really happened this weekend?!"

Silence.

"Mrs. Asanti," Dr. Johnson called for Jaise's attention.

Jaise stuttered, "I . . . umm . . . umm—"

"I got this," Bilal said, pulling out his cell phone and reading from his screen. "Captain Asante, your wife was booked this weekend. We released her this morning."

Jaise's heart dropped to her feet.

"Is that true, Mrs. Asante?" Dr. Johnson asked.

"What the fuck do you mean, is it true? You know what? You've been siding with his big ass since we've been here. I didn't come here for this shit!" Jaise jumped up from her seat and yanked her purse off the coffee table. "I came here because I thought you were the best, but I see that you're just as fucked up as he is! Since you think his ass is so great, you marry him! 'Cause I'm done!" She stormed out of the doctor's office and into the hallway, with Bridget and Carl on her heels.

"Jaise! Jaise!" Bridget called, as Jaise paced along the hallway, calling her driver and demanding that he come and pick her up right away. "Can you at least tell the camera how you feel?"

Jaise spun around. "I came here with my heart in the right place and with every intention to get my marriage back on track, get my husband back home, and this is what the fuck I'm greeted with? Blame? My son made out to be some kind of villain? That's *my* child! He needs me and I'm not going to coddle some grown-ass man because he is in competition with a kid. Ridiculous. And that bitch"—she pointed toward the doctor's office door—"is the absolute worst. All she did was listen to him. I could barely get a word in. This was supposed to have been for both of us, but obviously that whore has seen him on TV and, doctor or not, she wants to ride his jock. Well, have at it!" Jaise dusted her hands, as she watched Jackson pull up, park, and take his position outside the back passenger door.

"And, yes, I love him and I want him back." Jaise cleared her throat. *I need a cigarette.* "But if he can't remove his ridiculous ass conditions and stop demanding that I abandon my son, then fuck him! My son doesn't need a father. I got this. When Jabril gets out of hand, I know how to deal with it." She looked up at the doctor's door. "You see that motherfucker is still in there, so obviously he doesn't give a fuck about me, or she's in there sucking his dick! Now I need to go 'cause I need a cigarette and I need to leave here before I completely lose it!"

CHAPTER 6

JOURNEE

Journee, dressed in a midthigh, green, blue, and white plaid
and pleated Catholic school skirt, a starched white cotton
blouse with a loose plaid tie hanging around the unbuttoned
collar, leaned against her husband Zachary's bedroom doorway
and watched him drop the needle on the vintage record player,
filling the room with the sounds of Sarah Vaughan. "I've been . . .
waiting . . . on you," he said, "wondering . . . what took you so
long."

"I was praying."

"About . . . what?" he asked, his raspy voice sounding as if
he'd lived one too many lifetimes.

That by the time I arrived you'd be dead. "About so many different things, Granddaddy."

"Different things—*like what?*"

*How today is the four-year anniversary of the day the doctor told
me you had three days to live. So I ran home, planned our wedding
and your funeral, had Ralph Lauren hand make you a dual purpose
suit, only for you to live four years past that diagnosis and continue to
be the perverted and stubborn motherfucker your five ex-wives before
me all said that you were. But, instead of being a rich and happy
widow, I'm now a pissed Catholic schoolgirl every other Monday; an*

underage slut the last Thursday of the month; and every first Sunday,
I'm an eighteen-year-old nun trying to find my way, all to the back-
drop of Sarah Goddamn Vaughan and your fucked up, perverted, pe-
dophile fantasies.

"Journee . . . did you . . . hear me?"

"I heard you, baby. I was only praying that you would be
my granddaddy forever. And thinking about how much I've
missed you since last night."

"If you missed me . . . so much, then why are you . . . so
late? Eight o'clock in the morning is when . . . you're supposed to be here. Not eight-twelve. Eight. I've stopped and
started . . . this record three times. And I don't like waiting."

Me either. And I've been waiting a lot longer than twelve minutes.
I've been waiting for four fuckin' years. "Oh, Granddaddy," Journee
whined. "Don't be upset. It'll only aggravate your heart."

"Come . . . here."

Journee hesitated. For a moment, she considered walking
away and leaving him sitting in his wheelchair. She didn't. Instead, she pushed aside her feelings of disgust and found com-
fort in the thought that one day she'd be able to cremate his
black ass and blow him away.

Her five-inch, black Mary Jane pumps tapped against the
wood floor as she stepped over to him, stroked his cheeks and
placed her hands on his feeble shoulders.

Her eyes swept over his wrinkled caramel skin, from his
wide and flared nose invaded with oxygen tubes that snaked
down the creases in his neck, to his sunken chest, connecting
to the large steel tank strapped to the back of his wheelchair.

Journee ran her hands over his bald head and rested them
back on his shoulders.

His quivering lips kissed her right arm. Then her left. He
ran his hands over the wet spots his kisses left behind, clutched
her wrists and snatched her down to his chest. His arms shook,
but his hold was strong, evidence that once upon a time he was
a strapping man who stood upright and didn't take kindly to

anyone disobeying his orders. "Where the fuck were you?" he demanded. "And don't tell me you were praying!" He tightened his grip. "You were supposed to be here at eight o'clock and you're late."

"I overslept, Zachary, baby. I was up late last night. Bridget and the cameras were here having a tour. You're hurting me."

He let her go. "Did you . . . fuck one of them?" He squinted as he looked her over.

"What?"

"You heard me! Take your panties off!" he demanded.

"Zachary!"

"I need to smell 'em! Right . . . now."

She looked into his wild and wide round eyes and knew that if she turned on her heels, there wouldn't be much he could do. But she opted not to. Instead, she smiled, slid her black lace panties from between her legs, down her thighs, and handed them to him.

He unfolded them, sniffed lightly and slowly licked the seat. Her salty flavor teased his tongue. "You've really been a good . . . girl . . . with this pussy?" He smiled.

"Yes, I keep telling you that, Granddaddy." She lifted his hand, took his left index finger, rubbed it over her clit, and placed it against his lips. "All yours, baby." She turned around and placed her ass in his face. He licked between the slit and smashed both cheeks together.

"Jiggle it," he demanded.

She obeyed, jiggled her ass in his face as he pushed his tongue deeper between her slit, tossing her salad until she dripped stickiness across his lips. The heated wetness of his tongue swimming on the underside of her nectar caused her to close her eyes and envision him being forty years younger.

Tall. Robust. Sensual.

His lips, popped, pulled, and tugged, as he bit one cheek and then the other.

"Mmmmm, eat it up, baby," Journee moaned. "I want that

dick. That big dick, baby." She hissed as she imagined he had a dick with immeasurable inches preparing to take her to a place beyond space, and just as she was ready to leap toward the sky, he spun her around and she looked into his face, her eyes dropping down to his diaper.

Dear God.

He roughly unbuttoned her blouse, revealing the double D's he'd paid generously for. He licked one quarter-sized chocolate nipple and then the other. Journee eased one nipple into his mouth and he latched on with lollipop pulls and tugs.

He moaned, switched nipples, and Journee pushed her breast as deep as it would go into his throat. She closed her eyes again, slowly slid her fingers between her wetness and played in her pussy.

"That's it." She sighed as she circled the tip of her index finger over her swelling and slippery slope. She could feel her juices gathering and sliding between her thighs like smooth cream. Electricity shot through her body as she imagined again that he was the man of her dreams.

Six feet.

The color of light and sweet coffee, with a cleft chin.

Broad shouldered.

He continued to suck, rotating from one nipple to the other, and she continued to twirl her pearl.

He panted.

Her heart raced as she envisioned her invisible man and his thick dick at the tip of her cherry preparing to burst through and free her fuckin' misery.

"Almost . . . Almost . . ." she whispered as he moaned and her fingers reached toward bringing her sweetness home.

Her flesh dripped.

He moaned.

Almost there . . .

She groaned.

Almost . . .

He shivered and let her nipples fall from his lips, but she continued to work her clit, washing it in her sea of wetness. Her heart thundered. Her stomach tightened and her fingers squeezed her clit, forcing her juices to explode and leave sweet and gummy remnants between her thighs.

She opened her eyes. Zach's sleeping head lolled back and there was a drizzle of drool easing out the side of his mouth and a light snore sounding as if it poured from his nose.

Dear God, please kill this motherfucker by midnight.

CHAPTER 7

CHAUNCI

The afternoon sky was a perfect pale blue as Chaunci stood on the edge of the pier and stepped into the boat she'd chartered to take her up the St. Lawrence River to Millionaire's Row, a stretch of private New York islands.

Chaunci held the hand of the hat-tipping captain while he assisted her to her seat, a pilot style reclining white leather chair with a retractable sun visor.

She placed her Louis Vuitton signature tote in the chair next to her, crossed her legs, slid her marble brown Moss Lipow sunglasses up the bridge of her nose, and listened to a message on her cell phone. "This. Is. Bridget. Apparently you are confused by your current situation. This. Is. Not. The Chaunci Show. You don't get to disappear for an entire weekend without taping. No one's heard from you and this is unacceptable. Now unless you want me and my team of attorneys to sue your ass, then I suggest you call me back or this will not be pretty."

Click.

Chaunci slid her cell phone back into her purse and stared at the reflecting sun rays in the water.

This was supposed to be a hit it and quit type of thing. One sea-

son. Two seasons tops. Just long enough to solidify my brand's place in the rat race, so that when people saw my name and my face they'd know everything I touched turned to gold. The Oprah effect . . . or something like that. . . . I never considered that things would turn left.

She looked up from the water and reclined her seat.

A series of headlines rushed into her mind.

Why am I always on the cover of some skanky tabloid? Why is everyone wrapped up in me, my eight-year-old daughter, and my fiancé, Emory's, life? Why would anyone give a damn if I'm a millionaire and Emory is a regular Joe with a cleaning business? That's my affair and should be no one else's concern. . . .

Chaunci shook off her thoughts and sat up in her seat. She reached for her cell phone and checked her e-mail. She had four from Bridget and one from the network's president. She deleted all five without reading them and placed her phone back into her bag.

She reclined her seat.

To think I was pissed about Idris saying our daughter, Kobi, couldn't be a part of the show this season. I hated giving in, but I knew he was right. Reality TV was ruining her life. Our daughter had a horrible school year. Her grades were bad; she was teased and bullied. We pulled her out of one school, placed her in a more exclusive school, where all the New York A-list celebrities sent their children, and she cried that she missed her friends.

I couldn't win.

She sighed again.

Thank God that Idris put his foot down and decided against her being on the show. And I'm glad I let her go and spend the summer with him and his wife . . . that bitch . . . and her kid . . . in South Africa. Kobi needed that. I needed that.

And fuck Bridget.

Yes, I escaped this weekend. I damn sure did. I chartered a jet and flew to the south of France. Auvergne. A remote and quaint village where no one knew my name, knew my fame, or knew anything about this damn reality show. All the locals knew about me was that I was a foreigner there to visit. They wished me a good time, recommended the best wine, and after that they all left. Me. The. Fuck. Alone. I was able to sit in my villa, put my feet up, look out the eighteenth-century window at the green rolling hills, and pretend that all that mattered in the world was my moment and me.

And no, I didn't tell anyone where I was going. Hell, the tabloids seemed to pull the most private moments of my life out of thin air. I needed to steal some quiet time for me.

I swear I hated going back home. Because as soon as the jet landed there were reporters at the hangar snapping pictures, salivating, and screaming that they'd heard I was in South Africa having a secret affair with Idris. Stupid. Dumb. Ridiculous. Nonsense.

I kept my composure though, smiled, and merely said, "All you need to know is that I had a wonderful time. And, no, I was not in South Africa."

But I was back in the good ole US of A. The home of the free, the brave, and the do whatever the hell they wanted to do to the rich and famous. Why? Because these people, these fans, and these reporters all felt entitled to my life and my business, with the fucked up philosophy that I signed up for this. And, yeah, maybe I did, but not to this extent.

Every day I had to defend what I'd worked hard for—my money, my empire, and my reputation—because someone felt they had a right to tear apart my life based on the fact that they saw me on TV every Thursday night.

I'm not some low-grade with no skills and no money of her own. I didn't get upgraded by a hard dick. I worked hard. I don't need this goddamn show. I got this. I run my own company. I have my own staff. I sign my own checks and I get to say what I'll tolerate, which is the exact reason why I'm going to see this resurrected bitch and let her know that just because she returned from the dead in a ball gown and some fly-ass stilettos doesn't make her beloved. And she will not be haunting my life.

"We're here," the captain said as he extended his hand to help Chaunci onto the private island's dock.

"Thank you." She flashed him a quick smile. "I'll only be a minute."

She clicked her heels up the cobble stone pathway and stepped onto the veranda of the French chateau and rang the bell. A few seconds later, a short and matronly white woman answered the door. "Good morning; may I help you?"

Chaunci pushed past her, charged into the grand foyer, and said, "Tell that bitch that I said to get down here right now!"

CHAPTER 8

MILAN

Milan's hazel eyes danced as she sat on the carpeted floor in her son's Thomas and Friends train-themed nursery and watched him coo and burst into wet giggles. He bounced in his jumper and each time he caught a glimpse of himself in the mirror, laughter shook his body, his dimples sank into his milk chocolate cheeks, and the ebony coils in his wild afro spun into a tizzy.

"That's Mommy's baby!" Milan laughed as she pointed to the mirror on the jumper's toy deck. "Yes, yes, that handsome face is Mommy's man. I just love you. I just—"

"Have. You. Lost. Your. Mind!" Bridget shook her head. "What is going on here? Why are we lost in drool and giggle land? This is unacceptable!"

Milan tossed a snide look over at Bridget, who now stood slicing a hand across her throat, a signal for Carl to cut off the camera. "Gather your things, Carl." She dusted her hands. "We're done here!"

"What's the problem *now*, Bridget?" Milan rose from the floor, slamming a hard hand up on her hip.

"You can't be serious." Bridget paced. "You simply can't be. Because I know damn well that you've been warned not to play with my money. I told you that. The network executives have told you that. And what do you do?" She stormed toward the doorway. "You bring us into the goddamn nursery as if your baby has the Midas touch for ratings or saving your dead-ass career!"

"You are *waaaay* out of line—!"

"And so are you! And if you have plans to stay on the *Millionaire Wives Club,* then I suggest you get the nanny in here so she can help you get your thoughts in order!" Bridget stormed down the stairs and into the foyer with Carl lugging his camera equipment behind her.

"You know what, Bridget?" Milan charged into the foyer. "You have the right idea—get the fuck out! This is my house and the only bitch allowed to act crazy up in here is me! And then you cussed and carried on in front of *my baby*! Oh, hell no! Understand this. You might sign my checks, but I help create yours, so as far as I'm concerned, we're on equal footing and you don't own me. This is my damn life and that's what people want to see! Or is this *not* reality TV?!"

Bridget's eyes narrowed as she snatched a packet of papers from her purse and shoved them into Milan's arms. "That script is your damn life. You had a choice of being a down-low lesbian, having an affair with some young buck, popping a Molly, or having a goddamned drinking problem! Instead, you indulged in a bunch of bullshit, as if someone wants to see you play the impeccable mommy and the stellar fuckin' wife! Clearly, you've forgotten what low level you came from! You were once Kendu's mistress. Had the hottest story line on the damn show and now you've turned into this?!"

"I never agreed to be scripted!"

"It's simple then; if you don't want to be scripted, you're fired! And *yes,* this is reality TV. Not some Tyler Perry sitcom! It's not okay to be boring as fuck! And to think I had Kim Kardashian and God lined up!" Bridget shook her head. "No one on this show wants to see you play with your baby!"

"Then fuck them!"

"Excuse me." Alana, Milan's assistant, wrung her hands and said nervously, "I'm really sorry to interrupt, but I just wanted to let you know, Mrs. Malik, that the driver is waiting and your flight to Miami leaves in an hour."

"Flight!" Bridget screamed. "To Miami?!"

Milan turned toward her assistant. "Thank you, Alana. Now please excuse us." Alana nodded as she scurried out of the foyer.

"What *the hell* are you going to Miami for?!" Bridget questioned.

"To be a fuckin' stellar wife and fuck my husband!"

Bridget laughed emphatically and then said into the air, "Sister Mary Frances, this ho is out of control!"

"Ho? Don't let my boring ass slap the shit out of you!"

"Do it. Then at least we'd be able to record some action! Now I tell you what." Bridget stabbed an index finger toward Milan. "If you get your ass on that damn flight go to Miami, when you come back you will be replaced! And I mean that! Because I have had it with you! This isn't Burger King and you *will not* have it your way. This is the *Millionaire Wives Club,* the *hottest* reality show there is, and I run this! And I will have you replaced in five minutes flat! Trust me, there are a lot of rich bitches dying to suck on this candy! Now what I suggest you do is cancel that damn flight and get to planning a party. Invite every rich bastard you know and by the time the night ends, somebody better get to fightin', and I mean it! Or your ass is finished!" Bridget turned to Carl. "Let's go! I need to call in a few replacement wives for an interview." Bridget shot Milan one last look before shoving her purse strap up her arm and slamming the door behind her.

Milan stood completely still as her eyes jumped around the room, landing on her Louis Vuitton suitcase. Instantly, her skin felt electrified as the hackles on the back of her neck stiffened. She walked into the family room, stepped over to the fireplace mantel, and in one swift motion sent the candles and the family pictures that decorated it flying into the air. The candles rolled across the room as the silver frames crashed and sent shards of glass to the bamboo floor.

"Fuckin' bitch!" Milan screamed at an invisible Bridget. "I can't stand your ass! You don't ever tell me what to do! Do you know how many women are trying to be me? And you're trying to script me! You must be crazy. To hell with the *Millionaire Wives Club*! How about this: I quit! I'm done with this shit. I got my man and my child and I don't give a damn about anything or anybody else—"

"Mrs. Malik," Alana peeked into the foyer and said anxiously.

"WHAT?!"

"I just wanted to remind you that the driver is waiting and your flight leaves in a half hour."

Milan froze.

Fuck! Fuck! Fuck!

She rushed up the stairs, kissed her baby, left instructions with the nanny, and quickly returned to the foyer, where she picked up her suitcase and opened the front door. Just as she placed one red bottom on the walkway, she sucked in a hard breath and shoved it out.

Shit.

She turned back toward the door and walked into the house. Dropping her suitcase to the floor, she grimaced at her assistant. "Cancel my flight and get me the best party planner in New York on the phone!"

CHAPTER 9

JOURNEE

The invasion of 24, Faubourg perfume drifted through the salon as Journee stepped into the room and immediately zoomed in on Chaunci. The crisp menthol from the silver-tipped and ultrathin cigar she smoked eased into her chest and smoothly filled her lungs. She exhaled a cloudy veil and drifted into a twelve-year-old memory. . . .

"I just wanna get out of here—" Chaunci had said nervously.

"Would you relax?" Journee had replied.

"I can't." She quivered.

"Listen to me." Journee shook her by the shoulders. "Those niggahs think that we are so in love with their asses that we would never take them. Fuck that. And fuck them. I'm tired of sitting up in this trap while this motherfucker's high and shit. Listening to him lie about how he has a billionaire father who hates his mother and who won't have anything to do with him. How he's in the streets hungry and hustling while his father is rich enough to own the goddamn streets. Do you think I wanna keep listening to that bullshit? Hell no. And if he does have a billionaire father and I find his old ass, trust I'll know exactly what to do. But until then, I'm done. I don't know about you, but I didn't leave the strip club to chase lies, food stamps, and a hard dick."

"Me either."

"Exactly. And if it wasn't for you being the lookout and me driving the getaway car, their asses would've never pulled off that bank heist. Now, I've already washed and packed up the money. It's in the backpack by the bed. You ease into the other room, take it, and I'ma meet you at the train station."

"Where are we going?"

"New York."

"New York?! I don't know shit about New York!"

"Well, you will today. I'ma cook this shit up, skin pop those two bitches, and at the first nod, I'm out. Now go!"

"What. The. Fuck. Are. You. Doing. Here?" Journee asked as her memory and the veil of cigar smoke evaporated.

Chaunci arched a brow. "We need to talk. Now."

"I don't have shit to say to you." Journee flicked ashes into the crystal ashtray that sat on the lava fireplace mantel. "So I couldn't imagine what the hell you have to say to me. Not unless you wish to discuss how you have to be the stupidest bitch in the world to have come here, knowing that what you did requires me to scalp your ass and drown you!"

Chaunci looked toward Mary, the house manager. "Are you going to ask your maid to leave or should I do it?"

Journee laughed snidely. "Prime time has really injected you with one big-ass set of camera balls. But camera ball bitches get their asses beat when they step into the street with that shit. So unless you want me to gank you, I suggest you understand this: You don't give orders around this motherfucker. I do. Understood?"

Chaunci responded by having a seat on the white chenille sofa.

Journee turned toward Mary. "Be a dear and give us a few moments alone."

"Certainly, Mrs. Dupree." Mary smiled nervously as she

stepped over the threshold and closed the hand-carved double mahogany doors behind her.

Journee sat on the white Queen Anne chair adjacent to Chaunci. She took another pull off her cigar and released the smoke through the right corner of her glossy lips. "I'm giving you five minutes to speak and after that you'd better hope that I'm kind enough to let you live."

Chaunci rolled her eyes and flicked her wrist. "The time that I need to speak depends on how long it takes you to understand what I have to say. So I suggest you get it the first go-round. On the air we'll pretend to be friends, but when the cameras go off, we don't deal with each other. Point blank. Period. And when the season ends, you are to exit stage left."

Journee chuckled. "Fuck you. Fuck TV. Fuck that show. Fuck that fake-ass rep you're praying like hell that I don't blow! Did you forget that twelve years ago you took the money and never showed up at the station?"

"I waited for you at that station for hours."

"Liar! You didn't wait at all!"

"I waited too damn long and when you didn't come, I left. Hell, I was scared! I was seventeen. On my own. And caught up in a bunch of dumb shit! And besides, once I found out where you were, I sent you your portion of the money!"

"Yeah, five years later and a quarter million dollars short!"

"It wasn't short!"

"Bullshit! You know it was short." Journee stabbed an index finger into the air. "Your ass is lucky you're alive. Trust."

"Look, I'm really trying to be diplomatic here."

"Diplomatic? Bitch, you might get away with most of America believing that. But I know your thieving ass like the back of my damn hand and you can't script me nor scam me into ever believing that your ass is diplomatic. And another thing: If you think that I'll be pretending to like you and lying for you—"

Chaunci leaned forward. "Lying for me? This is not about

you lying for me! This is about playing your position and understanding that if I go down, you're going down with me, Mrs. Dupree. Now unless you want to be cell mates, I suggest you get your script together."

"Cell mates? Bitch, kiss my ass. That shit doesn't faze me."

"Well, it should."

"The statute of limitations says that it doesn't."

"Statute of limitations . . ." Chaunci slid back on the couch, crossed her legs, and swung them nervously. Then, as if a bolt of lightning had struck her in the chest, she lunged forward. "What the fuck?! There's no statute of limitations on murder! Did you conveniently forget that those two junkie motherfuckers botched the robbery and dropped a body?!"

Journee hesitated and drifted back into her memory. . . .

"Hurry, hurry, hurry!" Journee screamed as she tapped her foot on the gas and positioned her hands on the steering wheel to take off. The guys, Xavier and Aaron, jumped in the car, but the security guard was on their heels and able to snatch Chaunci by the hem of her ski mask and yank her back into his chest.

Without blinking an eye, Aaron burned a hole in the side of the security guard's head, and as his blood and brain matter splattered on the ground, he fell back onto the concrete with Chaunci's black ski mask fisted in his hand.

"They didn't botch the damn robbery! Your man saved your ass!" Journee reminded her.

"Look. It's only the two of us left. Xavier is in prison for life and Aaron died of an overdose. As far as I'm concerned, there's a special part of hell for a set of motherfuckers like that. They lied to us and convinced us to leave the strip club. I married Aaron's ass and he didn't have shit! And had he not died with a plastic dick stuck in his arm, God only knows what kind of mess I'd be in still, trying to get away from him. And I *will not* lose what I've worked hard for because yo' ass is pissed off!"

"You didn't work hard for shit! You robbed a bank and that's what cut your ass a break!"

"Journee—"

Journee stood up and pointed in Chaunci's face. "How about this: I don't fuck with you and you don't fuck with me."

"I'm trying to help you understand—"

"I don't need you to help me understand shit!" Journee charged toward the double doors and snatched them open. "Get out!"

CHAPTER 10

VERA

Twenty Four Hours Later . . .

10 a.m.

Taj—

Don't even go there.

Vera sat in the VIP room of her exquisite Manhattan spa and hair care salon, doing her all to shake off her thoughts.

She lay across the sleek black leather chaise and soaked in her surroundings—from the candelabra chandelier to the soft pink walls, the white leather chair attached to the soapstone shampoo bowl, the black leather sofa lined with black and white leather pillows, and a mirrored Hollywood vanity where the likes of Oprah Winfrey, Beyoncé, Janet Jackson, and Rihanna, just to name a few, had all sat and adored the hairstyle Vera's gifted hands had blessed them with.

She sighed. Looked at the clock.

10:02.

Maybe I should call him. . . .

She sat up.

Hell no, I shouldn't.

A lump settled in Vera's throat.

Don't drop a tear.

You have to get it together.

She closed her eyes and did her best to soothe her thoughts. At least she didn't have a client this morning and could have a few minutes to herself.

"Put the table over there."

Vera was jarred by the unexpected voice she heard coming from the doorway. She looked toward the door and watched the camera crew and Jaise step into the room, directing an entire wait staff where to place a vintage folding table and chairs. Bridget, Carl, and two others from the camera crew also made their way into the room and began recording.

"No. No. Not there," Jaise said. "In the center of the room. I told you, yellow floral linen." She huffed. "I guess white will have to do."

Vera sat up.

She must be crazy.

Vera looked over at Jaise as the wait staff covered the table with crisp white linen and then moved on to set the table with platinum silverware, Gucci china, and champagne glasses.

Jaise walked back to the door. "Let's go!" She popped her fingers, as more staff filled the room. "Put the food here. Please don't drop it."

Vera watched platinum trays covered with matching domes being placed on the table. The sweet smell of honey glaze, cinnamon, nutmeg, strawberries, freshly baked bread, and vanilla icing filled the room. "Umm, excuse you." Vera looked over at Jaise. "I think you're at the wrong address because the last time I heard anything from you, you said we were through—"

"Not now, bitch. Don't piss me off and make me order everything back out the door. Let me finish getting this set up and then you can talk shit."

Well, damn. Vera's eyes scanned the table as the staff removed the domes and revealed piping hot cinnamon and raisin biscuits, blueberry muffins, banana bread, freshly baked scones, strawberry and cheese crepes, sweet potato cake pops, chocolate chip pancakes, freshly made whipped apple butter, and lemon, pineapple, cheese, and apple fritters.

"Put the mimosa over there," Jaise continued.

The trick has been up since midnight smoking cigarettes and kneading dough. Every dish on that damn table represents a problem. She will be here all damn morning. I can already tell.

Finally the room was set up and looked more like a southern café than a high-end salon.

Jaise smiled at the staff and clapped. "This is beautiful." She pointed to the well-dressed table. "You can leave now. I'll call you when I need you to return."

Jaise quickly took a seat and immediately started eating. She looked over to Vera, who remained on the chaise. "Didn't I warn you not to piss me off!?" Jaise kicked her heels off under the table and stretched her toes apart. "I have been up since midnight, cooking all this shit for you. Now come on over here and eat. Because as you can see, I am starving and I have got to feed this size sixteen, honey. Let Milan and that other skinny bitch, Chaunci, starve. Chaunci, claims she went on a diet and lost fifty pounds, but I know she got her stomach chopped up."

"Hence the reason she looks anorexic," Vera added and looked over and into the camera.

"Exactly. But me, I'm a grown-ass woman who likes to eat. And yo' li'l chubby ass know you like to eat too. Now come on; what are you waiting on?"

Vera looked over to Jaise. "I lost weight. I'm now a fabulous size twelve, heifer. And that's not chubby."

"You say fabulous. Everybody else says plus size. Now come on over here."

Vera shook her head. As much as she wanted to be by herself, she was happy to see her friend. They hadn't spoken in two days—too long. And the last time Vera had heard anything from Jaise was by way of a voice mail. . . .

"I want all of my shit back. Everything. The Stuart Weitzman limited edition clutch and the matching heels I gave you for your birthday. The pink diamond and platinum Tiffany bangles I gave you for Mother's Day. And the Judith Leiber and platinum Pandora friendship charm I gave you just because. I will send my courier to come and collect my shit. I'm done with you. Don't call me again, bitch. I don't do hood rats; I don't do jail cells; and I already told Bridget, do not expect me to film with you. . . ."

Yet here she sat, bare feet and a mouth full of freshly baked strawberry and cheese crepes. Vera walked over to the table and sat down. She sipped a glass of mimosa and looked down at a piping hot plate of fritters. "You are so wrong for this!" Vera reached for the plate. "You know apple fritters are my favorite. And you had the nerve to put extra honey glaze on them! I should fight you!"

"Would you just eat?" Jaise reached for a blueberry muffin and loaded it with butter. "Now"—Jaise took a bite—"should I pour my heart out first or do you want to proceed?"

"Well, I—"

"Vera, wouldn't you think that I should go first, being as though I'm obviously stressed the hell out?" She pointed to the food. "You are not the only rich bitch with problems." Jaise's eyes turned teary.

Vera grabbed a napkin and dabbed Jaise's tears. "I'm listening."

"Just when I didn't think that things could sink any lower, Bilal is fucking the therapist."

Vera dropped the napkin. "Say what? The therapist? What therapist and when did they start fucking?"

"Right in the middle of our couple's counseling session."

"What—"

"Something told me from the moment I walked into the room that that ho would be a problem."

"I can't—"

"Not once during the entire session could I get a word in

edgewise. Nothing but Bilal this and Bilal that. And I'm looking at her like, what the fuck, bitch!"

"Jaise—"

"Seriously, who does that?!" Jaise said.

Vera agreed, "Therapy should be back and forth communication—"

"Not with this bitch. She twisted my words around, and everything I said, she assigned it a double meaning. Had Bilal looking at me like I was fifty shades of fucked up! His big ass sitting there with his arms folded across his chest, sneering at me like I'm the damn problem and that trick has suddenly helped him see the light!"

"Jaise—"

"I swear I couldn't say a word. I had to leave."

"Leave?"

"Leave, bitch. And Bilal's high yellow ass didn't even come behind me. I knew then that he was about to lay his dick on her couch. That fuckin' dick eater!"

Vera's mouth dropped open. This was insane. She looked over at the tray of blueberry muffins and they were all gone.

"That skinny bitch," Jaise carried on, reaching for the banana bread. "And if there's anything I hate more than Bridget"—Jaise looked directly into the camera—"it's a skinny bitch."

"Jaise—"

"Don't worry about me though. Because I know Jesus. And I have taken the time out to get to know myself." She sipped her mimosa. "I don't do negativity. I went out and purchased me a few self-help books, watched a few episodes of *Super Soul Sunday,* got my chakras aligned, and I'm living my life like it's golden. Doing me. Fuck therapy. And most of all, fuck Bilal."

"Really?"

"Hell, yes. I've signed myself up for Zumba class. I'm going to lose some of this weight. I did me a profile on eHarmony. I'm going to get me a little boy toy who doesn't talk the hell back. I'll be starting yoga next week—Wednesday. I'm taking back my life. Next week Thursday I'm getting me a colonic. And I'm flushing the shit down the toilet and the toxins away." She reached for a pineapple fritter. "Now what's going on with you?"

"I—"

Jaise pounded a fist on the table. "Hold up. Wait a minute! Why is there a viral video of you having Taj's car towed? Why are you in everybody's Facebook status? And why is the number one hashtag on Twitter, 'You better get yo' ass on the bus?' Now, Vera. I'm only telling you this because I love you and we're the best of friends, but you'd better get your damn mind right, because that shit you pulled on Taj was dead wrong. Unnecessary and so un-lady like. You tore his place up and now you had his car towed? Maybe you need therapy. Just don't go see the bitch that I did." Jaise's eyes welled with tears again. "Because if you do, her skinny ass will be licking around the head of his dick. I promise you that. Now what are you going to do? Give your man away to the enemy or be his damn wife?"

"I—"

"You need to stop being so damn selfish and let him be a man. Men need to express themselves too. You can't always shut them up and overtalk them. And back to what you did at his office parking lot. My God. I was so embarrassed. You were incredibly ghetto. Real hood and projectish. Showed exactly where you were from. And your aunt—"

"Wait a damn minute now, Jaise. Your food isn't that damn good where I'm going to sit here and let you talk about my aunt."

"Look, I love Aunt Cookie too, but let's face the truth. She is too old to be that ratchet. And the last time I saw Aunt

Cookie, she had on a pink pleather catsuit, platform heels, and feather earrings. My God. The devil is a liar."

"Jaise, I think we'd better move on. Now, as far as Taj is concerned, I'm not pushing him away. I had to check that ass. He'd lost his damn mind and I had to help him put a LoJack on it. Because I'm a good woman and if he doesn't get his act together, then he will lose out on me. So you worry about Bilal and your dick-sucking therapist and let me contend with my husband and my business."

"Excuse me, Vera."

Vera looked over to the doorway where her assistant, De-Andre, and an unfamiliar man with frizzy brown hair and emerald green eyes stood. *DeAndre knows I don't do walk-ins.*

"DeAndre, can the gentleman wait in the lobby until after we speak?" Vera asked.

"I tried to tell him that, but he insisted on following me."

The man stepped into the room and handed Vera an envelope. "Vera Bennett."

"Yes."

"You have just been served." He quickly exited the room and walked swiftly down the hallway. One of the cameramen flew after him as Vera stood in complete shock. A few moments later, she pulled a stapled packet of paper from the envelope and scanned the pages. "Oh, my God." Her heart raced. "Here this motherfucker goes again!" Vera snatched her Louis Vuitton bag and rushed out of the room, leaving a stunned Jaise sitting there with a mouth full of cheese crepes.

CHAPTER 11

MILAN

Milan sat on her snow white Lola leather sofa, her eyes roaming the white leather walls of her great room, as she soaked in the question the *Sister 2 Sister* magazine reporter had asked her. "How has your life changed since reality TV?"

A simple, standard, and ordinary question that could easily be answered a million different ways that would all allow her to flee from being seen as messy. But, up until last season, before Vera came along, Milan had been the top reality star. Now she played second fiddle. The girl whom all of the blogs had cast as last season's bore. A one-hit wonder.

That bothered her.

She had to get her shit together.

Now.

Right now.

She refocused on the reporter and crossed her legs. "The truth is, reality TV hasn't really changed my life . . . much." Milan swept her wavy mane over her shoulders. "But if I were to name one thing that's changed since I've been on television, I would say that the number of angry, obsessed, and jealous bitches who live to vilify me—*every chance they get*—has grown."

The reporter, Shakira Montgomery, a butter-colored black woman with an orange hue to her skin, raised a brow and then quickly lowered it.

"Tell us, why do you think that?"

"Think? It's not a thought." Milan frowned. "You read the blogs, the tabloids, *TMZ, E! News.* You watch the show. Just Friday, I met my newest costar, Journee Dupree, and this witch was filled with such venom and rage for no reason at all."

"Have you two ever crossed paths before the show?"

"No. Never."

"So what do you think that was about?"

"Jealousy."

"Jealousy?"

"Of course. I'm beautiful. I'm married to an incredible man. I'm the mother of his son and I know for a fact that whenever you meet a woman and her approach is really odd and teetering on insane, and you have never met this person before—it is a direct reflection of their own insecurities, which unfortunately causes them to display undeniable jealousy."

"So are you saying your newest costar is jealous of you?"

"I'm saying that Journee Dupree is one of many."

"Really?"

"Yes. Really. But it's not as if I've never experienced this before. All of my life I've dealt with black women and their shallowness. That's why, with the exception of Chaunci, black women and I don't get along."

"Did you say shallowness?"

"That's exactly what I said. Perhaps you would call it something else. But having grown up experiencing girls and now women upset with me because I have and have always had coal black, naturally wavy, thick, and extremely long"— she made invisible quotes—"good hair—as they call it. Or because I have no back fat, have never weighed more than one hundred and fifty-five pounds, have flawless honey-colored skin, or because my eyes are green in the summer and gray in the winter. I don't know what you would call it, but I call it shallow . . . and ignorant. It's as if they think I personally selected my gene pool. My mother is African American and my father is Italian, African, and Dominican, so black women need to stop throwing jealous tantrums when they see a naturally beautiful sister who doesn't need a perm, a weave, a diet, or colored contacts."

"And why do you believe these feelings exist within our community?"

"Because most black woman are insecure."

Shakira hesitated. "Insecure?"

"Insecure. You see them. There used to be a time when plastic surgery was the exclusive fountain of beauty for white women and now black women are off to the races and slicing themselves up. Getting their noses done, injecting their lips, their breasts, spending hundreds of thousands of dollars on somebody else's hair to weave into their heads. Gross. Getting their breasts done, butt injections, and their skin bleached. As if any of that makes them fabulous. Truth is, they look hideous." Milan flicked invisible lint off the crisp white, midthigh, sleeveless dress she wore. She crossed her legs. "Look at Lil' Kim. Prime example of self-hatred. And Nicki Minaj calling herself Barbie. How laughable. There are too many black women not celebrating their own beauty; instead they are basking in ignorance."

"Could it simply be you are someone they look up to? After all, you are on television and you're married to a very successful black man. You seem to have a wonderful life that I'm sure a lot of women would love to have."

"Listen, I understand that I am the epitome of beauty and I keep the girls striving, but if their version of admiration has to be attached to the pure hatred that I've experienced, then they can keep it. And, yes, I have a great man, a wonderful nine-year-old stepdaughter—who by the way is spending the summer in South Africa with her best friend, Kobi. I have the most adorable six-month-old son, and a great life, but do you want to know why?"

"Yes, I'd love to."

"Because I'm not some angry bitch, like my costar Vera Bennett for instance, who doesn't understand that you have to put in work to keep your man."

Silence. Shakira appeared to sort through her thoughts, and just as she seemed to have something more to say, Kendu stepped into the room, holding a suitcase. "And speaking of your man, here he is."

Milan looked up and over at her husband, Kendu, who stood six foot three with a perfect athletic body, his skin kissed by the prettiest dark chocolate, and his almond-shaped eyes seeming artistically etched into his beautiful face. He walked over to Milan, and as the photographer snapped a picture, he leaned in and graced her with a soul-stirring kiss. "I love you, Mrs. Malik," he whispered against her lips.

"I know you do." Milan wiped her gloss from his lips with the back of a thumb. "But I love you more."

"I'm getting ready to leave for LA, baby. The convention starts tomorrow and I need to get prepared."

"Do you have everything you need? I didn't get a chance to finish packing your suitcase."

"It's cool. I have everything."

"Are you sure?"

"Yes, baby. I'll miss you." He leaned in and gave her a peck.

"Don't miss me too much." She smiled. "I'll be there in three days to make all of the homesickness go away."

Kendu stroked Milan's hair. "I can't wait." He looked at the reporter. "Sorry to interrupt."

"It's no problem," Shakira said. "But would it be okay if I asked you a question before you go?"

"Of course." Kendu nodded.

"Can you tell us what you think of your wife's success as a reality TV star?"

"I think it's hot. I love to see my wife do her thing. Sometimes she has more fans running up to her than I have."

"Does that ever bother you? Or do you ever find yourself feeling a little overwhelmed by your wife's success? The world seems to love the reality show she stars on and she's always on the news, in the tabloids, the blogs. That's a lot. What do you make of all of that?"

"I'm very proud of my wife. She's a wonderful mother to our children and a great wife to me, and her being a star doesn't interfere with that. Besides, there's a difference in being a reality TV star and a sports legend. One goes down in history and the other fades after a few seasons."

Milan felt an invisible drop kick to her chest.

Kendu smiled. "It's been great talking to you, but I have to get going."

"Thank you." Shakira extended her hand. "I appreciate your time."

"You got it." Kendu accepted her gesture before leaning in to Milan, kissing her once more, and then heading out the door where his driver awaited him.

Milan peered at the space where Kendu had stood, doing her best to swallow the kick stuck in her chest. She turned to Shakira and mustered up a blush. "My husband is such a great man."

"Your husband is quite a hunk. How do you feel with him thinking your fame doesn't match up to his and will end after a few seasons?"

Milan frowned. "Don't twist his words, because that is not exactly what he said. He was simply stating the difference in being a sports star and a star on reality TV. I thought he made an excellent point."

"Okay. Perhaps he did. Now, let me ask you this. It's no secret that Kendu is the hottest thing on ESPN. There hasn't been another football player as great since he retired, and I'm sure that a lot of women are trying their best to get his attention. Does that make you feel the least bit jealous?"

"Never." Milan batted her lashes. "I am not in the least bit intimidated. I know how to keep my man happy. I cater to him. I don't emasculate him, and whenever he's away on business—which is quite often—I always fly on the third day to wherever he is and please him in whatever way he wishes to be pleased."

"You sound very confident."

"Why wouldn't I be? Kendu sees no one else but me. I'm not afraid to go the extra mile, unlike some of these black women who claim they love their men but have a ton of restrictions."

"Restrictions?"

"Yes. They won't suck. They won't swallow. They don't do anal. All they do is lie on their asses and bore the hell out of their man in missionary position. All three holes should be for your husband's satisfaction and if they're not, then you are wasting your man's time. And he will stray and he will run into the arms and the legs of someone else. This is why I'm writing my book, *Choose to Be Happy.*"

"Oh, you're writing a book?" Shakira asked, surprised.

"Yes, I am."

"Congratulations. And what will you be writing about?"

"Helping my sisters find their way to happiness." Tears welled in Milan's eyes and she dabbed at the corners with a Kleenex. "I honestly want to see them get it together."

"You seem awfully passionate about this subject."

"I am. There are just too many of our sisters with the angry black woman syndrome. Screaming they don't need a man yet dying on the inside for one. Pushing all of our good black men away and into the arms of our Caucasian sisters. And when black men turn to white women, do you know where that sends the average black woman?"

"Where?"

"Off to the prison yards standing at the gates and waiting for the electronic doors to slide open so they can be patted down and escorted to the playground of jumpsuits and numbers."

"That's quite an interesting perspective."

"There's no other perspective to have. Why do you think we have black women with four and five baby daddies? Sleeping with all of these men and with no condoms, as if they are exempt from AIDS. Can't keep their legs shut to literally save their own damn lives. Sending the AIDS cases in our community soaring."

"So black women are responsible for the AIDS epidemic?"

"There you go again, twisting words. That's not what I'm saying, so please don't put words in my mouth and don't put that in the article. I'm talking about the angry and irresponsible black women. The grease-eatin' ones, some with double chins, some rail thin, polyester hoarders, the ones who go to the liquor stores and choose names for their children: Alizé, Hennessy, Hurricane Hulk, and Chardonnay. Or the ones who go to the used car lot and name their children: Mercedes, Porsche, Jaguar, Lexus, Coupe de Ville. My Gawd." Milan fanned her face. "These are clearly the last days."

"How do you think this affects their children?"

"I feel sorry for their children. And God forbid if their mothers don't like their fathers. Who do you think they take it out on? They take it out on these babies, and before you know it, child protective services are raising their kids with my tax dollars. And don't even get me started on the subsidized housing and the welfare checks that these triflin' women sit on their behinds all day and collect, instead of getting a job. I truly want my sisters to understand that happiness is possible, but they have to start with loving themselves and embracing who they are."

"So are you saying that it's the poor black woman who's angry?"

"Don't be ridiculous. I wasn't born with a silver spoon in my mouth. I've had hard and trying times. Why would I blame it all on the poor? I know plenty of rich black women who are angry. Look at my costar Jaise. She's quite wealthy and she is the nastiest and most ignorant woman there is."

Shakira raised both brows. "Really?"

"Yes. And her son, *Jabril,* is a disgrace." Milan shook her head. "His mother is ruining him. And the way that Jaise is enmeshed in his relationships is so . . . so . . . off. Borders on sadistic, but I'm not one to spread lies and gossip. However, I will say this—their relationship gives you pause and makes you wonder what really goes on when the lights go out at night. I don't believe in talking about other people's children—even if they are unemployed, with no skills, have an arrest record, and two children with two different baby mamas. All of 'em packed up and are living in Jaise's home. She may as well be running a shelter. But I digress. I was simply using Jaise as an example of an angry black woman who's rich and can't keep a man because her attitude is the pits."

"Isn't she married?"

"Yes. But they're still separated. And leave it to Jaise, when she's completely done with her husband, he'll be gay. Chased right into the hairy chest and arms of some down low brother. I only want what's best for my sisters, which brings me back to the reasons I'm going to be writing my book. It will teach self-love. The power of forgiveness. To never settle. To always keep your eyes on the prize. And to know that a good man will stay with a good woman and he will marry her. But the only title an angry black woman will ever hold is baby mama." Milan wiped her eyes and looked over at Shakira, who watched her in silent amazement. "Shakira, are you with me?"

"Oh, yes. I just wanted to be sure I got everything."

"I certainly hope so."

"I believe I did. Is there anything else you'd like to add before I go?"

"No." Milan smiled. "I believe I've said it all."

"I believe so," Shakira agreed as she and the photographer

quickly gathered their things. "Thank you so much for the interview."

"You're welcome. I can't wait to see this in print," Milan said as she walked her company to the front door, where a sudden shadow of nervousness covered her. She did her best to inconspicuously soothe her disquiet as she slowly looked from side to side. Nothing.

"Take care, Milan," Shakira said as she and the photographer waved and disappeared down the tree-lined Westchester street.

Breathe . . .

Milan stepped into her foyer and as she turned to close her door, she locked gazes with a stranger in the distance and her heart stopped.

CHAPTER 12

CHAUNCI

Chaunci came just short of spilling her iced caramel macchiato all over herself as she planted her pencil heels in a sudden stop.

Maybe I didn't get off on the twenty-seventh floor. Her eyes scanned the massive lobby. It looked faintly familiar.

She faced the camera and squinted. "Did we get off?" She paused. This cameraman was new to the show and he'd never been to her office. He was simply following her lead.

She glanced over at the frazzled woman sitting behind the sleek red counter, wiping tears away.

Is that Julie?

Why is she crying?

That can't be Julie because this is not my office.

Chaunci's eyes swept the brick wall behind the counter where the logo for her publishing company, Morgan Enterprises, usually hung. It was no longer there. All of the walls were bare and there were men in blue T-shirts and matching Dockers coming and going, brushing past her and barking orders about where to place things. She watched two of them pick up a long, wide sign that read "Preston Publishing" and hang it on the wall behind the crying and frazzled woman.

I'm in the wrong place.

Chaunci turned toward the door when she suddenly heard, "Ms. Morgan!" from behind her. "Where are you going?!" She whipped back around and the crying woman, now standing, pointed at her.

That's Julie. Am I going crazy?

Julie, Chaunci's protégée and front desk receptionist, a usually happy, overzealous, overtanned twenty-three-year-old, wiped tears from her beet red face. "You're just going to leave?!" Julie screamed. "I can't believe I looked up to you. I thought you were honest! Truthful! I considered you to be like family!"

Chaunci walked over to Julie, placed her clutch purse and her macchiato on the counter. She reached for Julie's hands and enclosed them between her palms. "Jules, I need you to calm down and tell me what's going on here."

Julie babbled, "Some man walked in here like he owned the place—"

"What man?"

The babbling continued. "And these men! I told them to stop, but they ignored me and they kept moving things!"

"Who gave them permission to do that, and where did they take my things?"

"And Harry . . ."

"Harry? The mail clerk?"

"Yes. He clutched his heart, saying he had too much child support for shit like this! I thought he was going to die! Dear God! I just knew he was dead when he passed out!"

"Passed out?"

"And I feel horrible because now everyone suspects he's on the down low all because I called the paramedics, and they ripped opened his shirt and he was wearing a purple lace bra beneath it! Everybody's gone crazy!" she screamed. "I called my daddy and he told me to get back to Iowa immediately. But I don't have any money! I can't believe you would do this to me!"

"Julie—"

"Good morning," drifted over Chaunci's shoulder. "It looks as if my business partner has finally arrived."

Chaunci dropped Julie's hands and turned to her left. Her eyes rose from a pair of black Tanino Crisci loafers to a hand sewn, ash gray Italian suit that lay perfectly over the six-foot-two, athletic frame of a broad-shouldered and bronze-colored man with sea green eyes, a full stubble beard, and a casual, short-cropped haircut. With his hands in his pants pockets, he leaned against the door frame of her private office.

"Who. The. Fuck. Are. You?" Before he could answer, Chaunci looked at Julie. "Call security!"

The unknown man walked over to Chaunci and without hesitation said, "Don't ever speak to me like that again, and especially in front of an employee."

Chaunci shook her head and blinked. "What? Rewind. Stop the goddamn press! Employee? Are you fuckin' crazy?!"

"I think you should calm down and we should discuss this in my office." He pointed over to the door where her private office used to be. She noticed her nameplate, which used to hang on the door, was gone. She walked over and ran a hand across the empty space.

"Where the hell is my nameplate?" Chaunci said, more to herself than to him. She peered at him. "I don't know who you think you are—"

"Thoughts are not definitive. And I am *definitely* Grant Preston. The Third."

"Well, Grant Preston. *The Third*. You have me, Chaunci Morgan. *The First*. Fucked up. Because you don't have an office up in this bitch! And I don't take kindly to random *motherfuckers* raiding my business. Now I don't know if you are off your medication, you need some, or you have escaped from some damn mental institution, but I can assure you that your crazy ass will be dragged out of here in handcuffs!" She rushed back over to the counter and pounded both fists on it. "JULIE!"

"YES!" Julie jumped nervously to attention.

"Knock off that damn crying! I told you to call security!"

"I did!"

"Then where the hell are they?!" Out of her peripheral view, Chaunci spotted her missing sign being carried by two movers. She ran over and blocked their path. "Put that down! Where the hell is SECURITEEEEEE!" She stomped her feet.

"We're right here, Ms. Morgan!" The lead security guard pushed open the glass door as he and another guard rushed in. "What's going on?"

Chaunci's eyes popped out. "That's a good goddamn question because I don't know what's going on! All I know is that that asshole"—she pointed—"has demolished my office. Stolen my things! Those two monkey asses are carting my damn sign out of here! My secretary has lost her ever-lovin' mind, and I have no idea where my other employees are!"

Grant interjected, "After the mail guy passed out and the paramedics seemingly forced him out of the closet, I gave our staff two days off and instructed them to come back on Thursday. I thought it would give us a couple of days alone to discuss some things. Julie insisted on staying, so I let her."

"Are you insane?! '*Our* employees'? There's no '*our* employees'!" Chaunci whipped back toward security. "Why haven't you arrested him?!"

"Ms. Morgan, please calm down," the guard said.

"Calm down? This is calm!" Chaunci exploded. "If I wasn't calm, his ass would be set on fire by now! Charred! Now lock his ass up!"

"I can't do that," the lead guard insisted.

"Oh, pardon me. I forgot you were only armed with a flashlight and building keys." She turned back toward Julie. "Call the police. They shoot first and ask questions later."

"They won't be able to do anything either," the guard added. "The person standing next to you is Mr. Preston, the new owner of Morgan Enterprises. And no one can remove him from his own establishment."

Chaunci paced and then stopped abruptly. She walked over to the camera, looked into it, and said, "Am I being punk'd?"

The cameraman didn't respond.

"ANSWER ME!" she yelled.

"Chaunci"—Grant stood in front of her—"if you would allow me a moment to speak to you in my office—"

"You don't have a damn office!" she said through clenched teeth.

"I just want to go back to Iowa," Julie cried.

"Shut the fuck up!" Chaunci screamed at her. "I don't want to hear another word from your whiny ass!"

Grant reached for Chaunci's hand and held it softly. "Just give me a few moments alone with you."

Chaunci snatched her hand and pointed her fingers like a makeshift gun and pushed them into his face. "Touch me again and I will drop kick the shit out of your big ass!"

"This conversation is finished." Grant looked over at Julie. "If you want to continue to work here I need you to collect yourself. And after you collect yourself, I need you to pull the financial reports from the last two years so that I can fully understand why we're in the red and what needs to be done to return us back to the black." He slid off his suit jacket, tucked it under his right arm, and glided back to his new office.

Everyone, including Chaunci, stood silently stunned.

"Julie," Grant's voice came through the intercom, which sat on her desk, "after you pull the reports, I need you to grab me a cup of Starbucks Colombian roasted and a buttered baguette."

Click.

"Julie," Chaunci said. "You. Better. Not. Pull. Or. Order. Him. Shit." She stormed into what was once her office and instantly felt her breath being siphoned away. Her office, as she knew it, was no more. Instead, it had been cleaned out and replaced with a heavy, dark mahogany bureau, a black leather executive roller chair, a matching sofa, a Tiffany desk lamp, and two bookcases loaded with financial diaries, binders, a framed Oxford business degree; and a signed picture of Babe Ruth.

Chaunci stepped into the office and slammed the door in the cameraman's face. He opened it and slid into the room. Chaunci took a deep breath, but before she could say anything, Grant said, "If you came in here to continue your tantrum, then you will have to leave. However, if you came to speak about our current situation, then please, have a seat."

Cuss. His. Ass. Out.

No. Try a different approach.

Chaunci arched her brow and as calmly as she could, asked, "Who are you? Why are you here? And why does security think you own the place? When *we both* know that you *don't.*"

"I've told you that I'm Grant Preston. The Third. Grant Alexander Preston. The Third. To be exact. And as of last Friday, I own fifty-one percent of the company formerly known as Morgan Enterprises."

Formerly? "Excuse me." *What did he say?* "Repeat that."

"As of last Friday, I own fifty-one percent."

"I thought that's what you said."

"Listen, why don't we take a minute to regroup. Obviously this is upsetting for you. So, I tell you what. You should go home, relax for a few hours, and let me take you to dinner tonight. I'll call the owner of Le Bardin, reserve the entire restaurant for the two of us—which means you leave your fiancé at home—and we can discuss the changes around here."

She resisted the urge to slap his face. "Not even . . . if you were . . . the last white motherfucker on earth." Chaunci stood up, tucked her clutch beneath her right arm, and stormed out.

CHAPTER 13

VERA

Don't. Fuck. With. Me! oozed from the glare Vera shot Taj's receptionist as she stormed through the waiting area, past the billing clerks' desks, and into Taj's office, where he sat, eyes combing his computer screen.

"HOW DARE YOU?!" She slammed the office's glass door, causing the blinds to shake and the frosted glass to shiver.

Taj didn't flinch as he lifted his eyes over the screen and looked at Vera, unimpressed. Judging by his smirk, she knew her arrival was no surprise. Taj rose from his chair and sat on the edge of his desk.

Vera wanted nothing more than to slap the shit out of him. She settled on invading his personal space and pointing a finger in his face. "You don't put no fuckin' restraints on me! First, you want half of my money; then you have me locked the fuck up; and *now* you don't want me within ten thousand feet of yo' ass! Who the fuck do you think you are?! I will come and go as I please, and if yo' ass happens to be in the vicinity, then you leave, because I will not be going anywhere! I'm not letting you or that ridiculous-ass piece of paper control me!"

"Oh, really?"

"You heard what the hell I just said! And I will not be dropping our daughter off at a police station so you can retrieve her for visits! You may as well hang up that dumb shit. If you want to see our child, then you come to my house and pick her up. Otherwise, you will be shit out of luck! You are acting like a damn fool!"

"*I'm* acting like a damn fool?" He looked surprised and pointed to his chest. "But you're in my office, around my staff and my patients, acting ridiculous."

"I'm not acting ridiculous . . . yet. But don't make me take it there. Because I will."

"And you'll be handcuffed and carted out of here."

"So now you want to send me back to jail and humiliate me even more! I don't know what I did to you!"

"You don't recall breaking in to my penthouse and vandalizing it?"

"I didn't vandalize it. You wanted to half our shit, so I started with yours!" She paced from one end of the room to the other. *This motherfucker is trippin'.* She rushed back over to him and again pointed into his face. "Where the hell do you get off asking for half of my shit?! You have your own goddamn money!"

"Didn't you file for divorce?" he asked, matter-of-factly.

"Yes, but—"

"No buts. You filed for divorce and I want half. And I'm not budging off that. Period. You want to throw the towel in. You want to be done with our marriage, then it's going to cost you."

"I'm not giving you half of a damn thing! You can kiss my ass!"

Taj chuckled. "If only you knew how much I miss doing that."

"What is this? A game to you?"

"It's not a game to me." He stood up and the only thing that could slither between them was air, and even that was a struggle.

Taj continued, "This is my life. You're my life. And you know that. That's why you keep pushing your limits. Your problem is, I pushed you back and you didn't expect that." He placed his hands on her waist and pulled her deeper into his chest.

Vera did all she could not to get lost in his touch. "Get. Off. Me!" She attempted to push his hands off her waist, but he didn't budge.

"Stop it." Taj locked into her gaze. "Just stop."

"Taj."

"Just admit that you're scared." He stroked her hair and she bit her bottom lip.

"I'm not scared!"

"Vera."

"I'm pissed."

"The truth. Say it."

Don't say a word. "I can't." She dropped her head.

"Why?"

Because this is not the time. She looked back into his eyes. *And yes, I miss you. My body aches for you. My nipples haven't been the same without your sucks and soft bites. My belly misses the sweeping of your dreads sliding over my skin. My legs miss you parting them, kissing my inner thighs before making your wet way over my creamy mountain. I miss you kissing my ass. Literally. And my pussy misses you reaching your peak and leaving warm and liquid traces of your love.*

I miss the hell out of you. I miss your cologne, your smile, your laughter. I miss you sitting between my legs and me twisting your dreads. I miss telling you anything and everything. . . .

"Talk to me." He lifted her chin. "I'm listening. I'm here and I'm not going anywhere."

"It's just that . . ."

"What?"

All of these years I thought you were perfect. And I spent so much time trying not to fuck up . . . and for you to confess that when we broke up, you slept with someone else and out of that came a son—I just don't know what to do with that! And every time I think about it, it snatches my breath. I feel stifled. Emotionally asthmatic.

"Talk to me." He kissed her softly.

Don't cry.

"Tell me." He kissed her again.

"I'm scared." She kissed him back.

"Of what?" He held her by the waist. "We can work through this."

"What do you want from me, Taj?"

"I want you. All of you. I want you to be honest with me and with yourself. Just tell me how you really feel. I know you're hurt because of my son."

She took a step back and his hands fell from her waist. "We had a son!"

"He died." He pulled her back to him.

"So you think Aidan is a replacement?!"

"I never said that. He can never replace our son."

"Then why are you pushing him on me?! I don't hate him. I just—just can't deal with it! I feel like I'm drowning when I'm around him!"

"He didn't do anything to you, Vera. He's just as much my child as Skyy is, and I know this is difficult for you." He wiped her tears. "It's hard for me too. But he's my son and I have to be a part of his life. I can't leave my son because you can't accept him."

"I don't want you to leave him. I would never ask you to do that!"

"Then let's fix this, baby." He kissed her softly. "Let's work on it. Let's put our family back on track." He kissed her again.

Vera shook her head. She hated that she couldn't stop the tears from falling. *Stop fuckin' crying! Weak bitches cry before a man. You know that. Aunt Cookie has told you that a thousand times. Strong women cry at home, alone.* She wiped her eyes and looked at Taj. "This can't be fixed."

Taj shook his head in disappointment.

"I'm not weak," she insisted.

"Crying doesn't make you weak."

"And I'm not stupid!"

"And it doesn't make you stupid either."

"I don't hate your son!"

"I know you don't."

"I just don't want to be his stepmother!"

"So what are you saying?"

"I'm done. Fuck yesterday. And fuck that blended-ass dream you're trying to sell me! You fucked some bitch and got her pregnant! Hell yeah, I'm divorcing you!"

Taj shook his head in disbelief, and Vera could tell by the look in his eyes that she'd stabbed another wound into him. He stepped away from her. "You need to take a long and hard look at yourself. Nothing is ever your fault. You always find a way to blame it on someone else. I'm tired. I love you, but I'm tired. This is a marriage, and yes, we both made mistakes. And I miss you. I miss the hell out of you. I long for you, but I *will not* chase you. And I can't do things all over again. Your problem with Aidan is not that he's my son; it's that he's not your son. And I can't change that. And I can't bring Taj Jr. back. I can't. He was born prematurely and he died. You need to deal with that. But if you want to continue to play pretend, then you will do that alone. And if you want a divorce, then fine. But you will pay for it."

"I'm not giving you half of shit!"

"The judge will decide that." Taj opened his office door and his secretary stood with a nervous smile and a glass in her hand while three of the nurses scurried away. He looked over at Vera and pointed toward the hallway. "You need to roll up outta here because right about now you are in violation of your restraining order."

CHAPTER 14

CHAUNCI

"Where the hell have you been?" Chaunci felt a sudden yank on her left forearm, as she involuntarily spun around in the middle of the busy New York sidewalk and found herself facing her fiancé, Emory. She studied the deep lines and creases of disappointment in his caramel face and the sinking ship in his marble brown eyes.

I can't deal with this right now.

"I asked you a question." He tightened his grip. "Where the hell have you been and where the hell are you going?"

She sighed. "Listen, I know you're upset—"

"Oh, you know this!"

"Yes." She clenched her teeth, taking quick peeks at the camera. "But I need you to let go of my arm." She snatched her arm away. "And go back to your office or your apartment. I will meet you later. Now is not the time."

"You've been gone for four days, six goddamn hours, and thirty-five and a half fuckin' minutes without so much as a word to me. But you're on every goddamn blog and tabloid stepping off a plane, with a smile yay wide and a headline that says you were in South Africa having an affair with your daughter's father."

"Do you hear how ridiculous that sounds? I was nowhere near South Africa. I was in France. I needed a break. Period." She quickly peeked at the camera. "I need to go. I will call you later."

"You're not going any damn where until you talk to me!"

"I can't—"

Before Chaunci could finish her sentence, Emory took his left hand and pushed the camera by the lens so hard that he caused Isaac, the cameraman, to stumble backward off the curb and slam back first into the passenger side of a cab waiting at the light.

"*Vous pute!*" The taxi driver yelled in his Haitian accent. "*Bonii Vous!*"

"I'm so sorry," Chaunci said to the driver as she extended a helping hand to Isaac. "Are you okay? Let me help you. I'm so sorry. I am." Once Isaac appeared to be okay, she whipped back around to Emory. "Are you trying to get me fuckin' sued?! I have enough goddamn financial problems without you assaulting him!"

"I don't give a damn about him! I'm sick of those fuckin' cameras and this goddamn television show! We're supposed to be getting married in three months! You didn't even have the decency to tell me you were leaving the goddamn country and that you'd be gone for four days! I didn't know if you were dead, injured, or what the hell was going on! And now I come up here to your office to talk to you and you're rushing out of the building going God knows where again! What is really going on?!"

"I told you I would talk to you later! I have to go!"

He snatched her forearm again. "You're not going anywhere until you tell me what's going on here! Who is he?"

She snatched away. "What?" She blinked as if she were doing her best to remain on earth.

"Who the hell is he?!"

Chaunci laughed in disbelief. "You think this is about me

cheating on you! You have completely lost it! This is about me being sick and tired of being smothered by every goddamn body! This is about me needing to take care of my business! My business that I bust my goddamn ass for and now it's been stolen from me! I can't believe that you would think that I was really off cheating on you!"

I can't deal with this.

She continued, "You know what, I don't have time to deal with your narrow-ass thinking. I'm not some child. I have business that I need to attend to. And I will not have you further embarrass and humiliate me in the middle of the goddamn street because you're over here having a pissing contest with an invisible dick!"

"Chaunci—"

She didn't respond. She walked over to her silver Phantom and instead of waiting for her driver to open the door for her, she snatched the back door by the handle, got in, and slammed her hand on the lock, leaving Emory in the middle of the concrete and Isaac leaning against the cab.

"We've been looking all over the world for you for four days now!" Lawrence, Chaunci's attorney, said the moment his secretary escorted her into his conference room, where he sat at an oblong table with Samuel, Chaunci's financial advisor.

"Where have you been?" Samuel wiped invisible sweat from his brow.

Lawrence interjected, "Who leaves town and doesn't tell their lawyer or their financial advisor where they're going? Your lawyer or your financial advisor . . . ? Are you kidding me?!"

"Do I look like I came here for you two to interrogate me?" Chaunci said sternly. "I'm here to question yo' asses! And I want to know why *the fuck* I'm paying you two a salary every month and I walk into my office today and some motherfucker's got his two-thousand-dollar designer loafers parked beneath my desk telling me that he owns fifty-one percent of my company?! How did you let this happen?!" She pounded her fist on his desk.

"How did *we* let this happen?!" Samuel exploded. "Oh no, this one's on you. We tried our best to find you and couldn't! And we both told you when you released that last two percent of your company, retaining only forty-nine percent ownership, that you were gambling, which is why *I* watched that stock like a hawk every second of the day!"

"Well, apparently time skipped out on your ass—"

"No, you did."

"The plan was to release it for only a short while, enough to make payroll for the next two months, turn over a profit, and buy it back!"

"And that could've worked had I not wasted time looking for you. Grant Preston started buying your stock, little by little, and then he became more aggressive. By Friday morning, he owned forty-eight percent and by the time I realized that you were off on the moon, and I went to snatch back the remaining two percent, it was gone and Mr. Grant Preston the third was the new hostile CEO of Morgan Enterprises."

"Where the hell did he come from?" Chaunci massaged her temples. She could feel a migraine stabbing her at the back of the neck.

"He's come from a long line of old money. WASP," Lawrence added. "His father, Grant Preston the second, is *the* Grant Preston of G. A. Preston Banking Incorporated. The Grant who has ruined your life is a thirty-year-old Oxford business graduate. The only son out of six children. He's very persistent and is known for going after what he wants. He also has a very impressive résumé of taking over failing companies, putting them back on top, and selling them for a profit. It's made him an extremely wealthy man, independent of his family's bottomless fortune. Think Mitt Romney. But much younger, much easier to look at, and a Democrat."

"He cannot have my company! I want him out! Gone! Set

up a meeting with him and make him an offer so that I can buy him out."

"I tried it. And given the state of your affairs and the amount of debt you're in, believe me, you can't afford it."

"Then you need to find me some money, Samuel!"

"It won't make a difference. He made it clear that he wasn't budging."

"What the hell am I supposed to do?"

"Play nice with your new boss or sell him your portion of the company."

CHAPTER 15

JAISE

"Herbert," Jaise said to her blond-haired, brown-eyed butler. "Tell the wait staff to take the desserts into the dining room and arrange them on the buffet. I should be done with the rosemary potatoes, chicken tempura, and caviar by then."

"Yes, ma'am. And when you're done, shall I dress the table for lunch?"

"That will do. Thank you. And use the Gucci china, please. It didn't get much use this morning."

"Yes, ma'am," Herbert said, backing out of the room.

Jaise looked into the camera, then down at her butcher block cutting board. She began separating a bulb of garlic and speaking to the associate producer. "So, Renee, you asked me why I invited Journee over here." She looked back into the camera as she chopped a clove. "Well, for starters, she is the wife of Mr. *Number Three* on the *Forbes* list." She let her statement dangle in the air and tilted her head for emphasis. "And secondly, I was *not* going to waste my food. No, ma'am. I don't believe in that." She sprinkled garlic into her steaming pot of okra and asparagus. "I had entirely too much food left to toss it in the trash because Vera's inconsiderate *ass* was served with a restraining order. And she has taken to bed and is refusing all calls."

Jaise sucked her teeth as she removed her potatoes from the oven. "A restraining order? How low budget is that?! I love Vera like a sister. But obviously you can take the rich bitch out of the hood, but you can't take the hood . . . You know the rest. I tell Vera all the time to let that hood rat shit go. Just let it go. Choose a different behavior. You have access to the finer things; why are you running around here like your name is Al-Taniesha, La-La, Tah-Tah, or Peaches? That's my best girlfriend though, honey. Don't get it twisted. But the good Lord knows we have some work to do.

"Now, back to Journee." Jaise opened a jar of caviar and began topping the potatoes with spoonfuls. "I figured that since I had that most unfortunate incident the night of the network's party and wasn't able to meet Journee, I would invite her over here." She reached for her cigarette case, slid a thin brown cigarette into the left corner of her mouth, and lit it.

"Tell the camera what you expect when Journee arrives," Renee requested.

"I don't know what to expect. Especially since I've made a few phone calls and have heard some things about Ms. Journee." She blew out the smoke and removed her chicken tempura from the deep fryer.

"What did you hear?"

Jaise squinted. "Why would you ask me something like that, Renee? I know Bridget told you that I don't believe in gossip." She turned down the fire under her vegetables. "Gossip makes the Chanel body crème crawl off my skin. And yes, I heard that Zachary Dupree plucked Journee off some dick-sucking street corner, or was it a stripper's stage? Hell, same thing. Gave her money, diamonds, that private New York islet they live on. And what has she done for him in return? Nothing. Oh wait, she's done something. She's spent nearly all of his money. Because he used to be number one on the *Forbes* list, but after he married her, he dropped two slots. For that alone, Journee should be sent to the special part of hell reserved for hos who've been turned into ungrateful housewives.

"And no, I would never sell my lady treats for money, but I definitely smoke too many cigarettes and I'm certain that somewhere, in some third-world country, that's a sin. Which is exactly why I will not sit up here with you, on national TV nonetheless, and be messy. I don't do that. And please don't ask me to compromise my values."

"Mrs. Asante." Herbert stepped into the kitchen. "Mrs. Dupree has arrived. I seated her in the front parlor."

"Wonderful." Jaise smiled and tossed her cigarette into the brick fireplace. "Just in time." She turned off her stove. "The food is ready for you to bring out to the dining room table."

"Yes, ma'am."

Jaise untied her apron and laid it on the counter in her butler's pantry. She brushed invisible wrinkles from her sleeveless pink blouse and navy pencil skirt, stepped out of her mink slippers and into her navy heels. She took a quick peek in her powder room's mirror, straightened her two-strand pearl necklace, and hurried into her grand parlor.

Jaise beamed with pride as she walked in and observed Journee admiring her hand-painted Annie Lee and Leroy Campbell paintings, her camel-colored chenille sofa with nail heads outlining the arms, the matching love seat, the black baby grand piano, and the floor-to-ceiling windows that lined an entire wall.

Yes, bitch, you're not the only one living fabulously. "Hey, girl-friend." Jaise walked over to Journee. "Thank you so much for coming."

Journee, wearing a white and cap sleeve Chanel dress and six-inch signature Louis Vuittons, walked over to Jaise and air kissed her on both cheeks. "Thank you so much for inviting me. You have a beautiful home. This brownstone is marvelous."

"Girl, this old thing." Jaise waived her hand. "It is beautiful, though. It used to be an old jazz club and hotel. As a matter of fact, that is the exact piano they used to play."

"Really? That's so fascinating."

"Yes, dear. The likes of Sarah Vaughan, Billie Holiday, and Bessie Smith have performed here."

"That must be so inspirational. You sing too, don't you?"

Jaise hesitated. Thoughts of the last time she sang for Bilal flooded her mind. "Not in a long time." A moment of awkward silence filled the air. "Let's not get stuck on that. Allow me to give you a tour."

Jaise led Journee through the two adjacent parlors, one used as a formal living room and the other used as a library, which showcased signed and first edition two-hundred-year-old slave narratives. She showed Journee around her five-star kitchen, her butler's pantry, and family room. They worked their way up the back stairs, which were located in the kitchen. Their first stop was the second floor, where there were three bedrooms and an office, each with its own en suite.

They moved on to the third floor, which housed the massive master suite, set up like a one-bedroom apartment, including a small kitchen, a full spa bath, a theater room, a rooftop terrace, and a hundred-year-old canopy bed that once belonged to Dorothy Dandridge.

"What a lovely place you have here," Journee said, as they walked down the front stairs to the first floor's foyer.

"You're too kind." Jaise smiled as they entered the dining room and took a seat at the table.

"Your antiques are breathtaking."

"Thank you," Jaise said, as the butler fixed their plates and they began to eat. "I appreciate that. I've wanted to get you over here so we could chat and get to know one another. So"—Jaise sipped her glass of white wine—"do tell. What do you think of the other girls? You've met everyone, right?"

"I haven't met Vera." Journey sipped her wine.

"You will love Vera. She's a little programish. A little pro-jectish. A little rough around the edges. But I love her." Jaise stuck her fork in a piece of potato. "Now what did you think of Milan?"

"Well—"

"Don't befriend her. She's a bottom scraper."

"What?"

"A dick devourer. A vigilante for another woman's man. Keep her away from Zachary, honey, or she'll have that old and limp dick stiff and stuffed in her mouth. She damn near Mack-trucked Kendu with her vulva, trying to get him away from Evan."

Journee chuckled. "Well, it's not as if Kendu is a saint. So Milan surely didn't get a prize."

"Did you know Milan before the show?"

"No. Only Kendu."

A smile ran across Jaise's face as she slowly chewed her rosemary and caviar potato. She swallowed. "Really?"

"Yes, really." Journee picked up a forkful of okra. "Take it from me, Milan and Kendu's marriage is not as it seems. Can you say forest?"

"Forest, girl," Jaise said in amazement. "Now how do you know that? Because every time I've ever seen Kendu, he acts as if he can't get enough of her ass."

Journee removed her white linen napkin from her lap and dabbed the corners of her mouth. "Let's just say, quite a few years ago, Kendu and I had a few late nights and early morn-ings."

"Girl, stop!" Jaise's eyes shifted in excitement. "Say what now? Late nights and early mornings? Oh my!" She laughed in disbelief.

Jaise's mouth fell open as she waved her hand to Jesus. "Journee, you are giving me so much life right now!" She fanned her face. "Working me over!" Jaise placed her hand over her heart. "And all this time this bitch has been walking around here like she is married to the president. Wow." Jaise gulped the rest of her wine in one shot. "Now what do you think of Chaunci?"

"I think Chaunci is a slum bitch."

I'm about to fall out of my chair. "A what?" *I so love this girl!*

"A slum ho. A liar."

"I take it you don't care for her?"

"Not at all. She's nothing more than a thirsty bird."

"Wow. Now that's really trashy."

"Definitely trashy."

"So it's safe to assume that you knew her before the show?"

"We have a history."

"A history? Don't tell me you two were lady lovers?"

Journee arched a brow. "We were what?"

"Lady lovers. Lesbos, I mean lesbians. I could so see Chaunci as a mad dike. She is definitely suppressing something."

"A woman is certainly a special sexual treat. But Chaunci and I have never been lovers. Believe me."

A special treat? How gross. Now I know that I'll have to throw away that plate and glass she's using when she leaves. "I hope I didn't offend you," Jaise said. "I was just asking." She took a few bites of her chicken tempura, sipped her wine, and then looked back over to Journee. "Do you mind if I ask you something about yourself?"

"What's that?"

"How'd you meet Zachary?"

"On stage."

Did she just admit that she was a ho? "Stage?" Jaise did her best to sound baffled. "What were you? An actress?"

"Not at all. I stripped, and it was a wonderful entry level position. Got me a lot of places, gathered me a lot of things, and made my most valuable asset priceless. Google me. You'll see that not only was I a headlining stripper, I was the type of chick that when I walked into the club, every bitch in the place evaluated who the fuck I was."

Oh, this bitch is extra. "A stripper. And you're proud of it?"

Journee looked slightly put off. "Why wouldn't I be proud? It's how I made my money and still make money. I actually own two gentlemen's clubs. One in Atlanta and the other in Miami, and they do quite well."

Have mercy, now this bitch is a pimp? Damn. "Gentlemen's clubs? With strippers?"

"Of course."

"Oh my."

"You have a problem with strippers?"

"To each his own, honey. I just think it's a little unladylike. Unsanitary. And disgraceful. For my life, anyway. I just wasn't raised like that."

"Well, I was raised with the belief that every woman has the ability to be rich." Journee sipped more wine. "Unfortunately, most won't allow their pussies to lead them to it."

This bitch and her mama are both nasty.

Journee gathered her hair and flipped it over her right shoulder. "Now me, I was born with the balls to do it. My mother always said that pussy offered equal opportunity employment. I could've easily lay on my ass all day, gathered fucked up credit, cellulite, back fat, bills, and babies, but I choose to use what God gave me and made it happen."

I can't believe this disgraceful ho, bringing God into her mess. She is definitely going to bust hell so wide open that the earth will feel the fire splashing. Jaise shrugged. "Like I said, to each his own. I guess." *This bitch is low down. Straight gutter. I'll be needing a minister and some holy oil up in here when she leaves.*

"It's legal. And there are a lot worse things one could be doing. Maybe you'd see it differently if you came to one of the clubs."

"A strip club?"

"Yes, girl! I'd love for you, and hell even the rest of the

girls, to come to one of the clubs and hang out. We'd have a great time. We always have celebrities in the house." Journee snapped her fingers. "Perhaps we should all do a girls' trip."

"A girls' trip?"

"Yeah, we can hit my Miami spot. I guarantee we'll have a ball."

Bitch, you will never turn me out. Have me suckin' pussy and gyrating my ass on stage. Never. "That sounds like fun."

"So you'll go?"

Tramp, please, you will never have an orgy with me. "I'll have to get back to you on that. A ho spot, I mean a strip club, *a gentlemen's club*, isn't exactly on my bucket list." *And it never will be, bitch.* "But I'm all for trying new things."

Journee shrugged. "Whatever. The choice is yours." She ate a piece of chicken. "Jaise, this food is absolutely delectable. Who's your chef?"

"Chef?" Jaise said, "I made this."

"You did what?" Journee paused midbite and looked at Jaise, surprised. "You made this?" She swallowed. "All of this?" She pointed to the food around the room, her eyes skipping from the dessert table overflowing with pastries to the dining table filled with enough food to feed an army.

"Yes," Jaise said. "Why do you seem so surprised?"

Journee curled the right corner of her top lip. "You *really* don't have a chef?"

Why the hell is she curling her lip? Jaise leaned forward. "No. I don't."

Journee placed her white linen napkin over her mouth and did her best to hide her snicker. She failed. "Is money a little tight? I know you're separated. Can you no longer afford one?"

Is this bitch crazy? "First of all, I don't *need* a chef. I got this. See, that's the problem with these slores today. They're too busy clapping their ass cheeks, sliding upside down on a pole, and marrying the first scrotum who throws a dollar bill their way, instead of learning how to be ladies and take care of themselves."

"Excuse me?"

"I'm simply making a point. That the true way to a man's heart is not twerking an overworked vaginal canal. It's food. But then you wouldn't know that being as though your man is so old he has to be fed Ensure through an IV drip." *Take that, bitch!* "Now, I need you to excuse me for a moment."

Jaise huffed as she rose from the table with the camera following closely behind her. She walked into the kitchen, slid the double pocket doors closed, paced, and then turned to face the camera. "Let me tell y'all something; when it comes to my food, my cigarettes, my child, and my man, I don't play. I will snatch a blind bitch if that heifer sees fit to come at any of those four things! I just don't believe this."

She resumed her pacing. "And this skeezer sits at my dinner table, with her slutty ass, channeling all kind of STD's into the air, I'm sure—I may have to get an exterminator in here when she leaves—and she has the nerve to laugh because I cook my own food? Bitch, you and your mama are both whores. You probably don't even know who your daddy is. And you want to put me down because I like to cook? Who does that? I'll tell you who. A strippin'-ass ho! That's who! Why should I have a chef when I can burn with the best of 'em?"

Jaise fanned her face. "Dear God, I have a lot going on and the last thing that heifer needs to do is try me." Jaise took a deep breath. "*Woosaah*, let me relax, go back in there, and be the bigger person."

Jaise slid the pocket doors open and as she entered the hallway, approaching the dining room, she heard Journee say, "You are really handsome. I mean you were fine on TV, but seeing you in person is a whole other level of finery."

What the . . . !? Jaise stepped into her dining room and there stood Jabril smiling at Journee. Standing six feet, bare

chested, rippled eight-pack gleaming, white Calvin Klein box-
ing shorts barely fitted on his hips, and his left hand stuck in his
waistband, giving quick snippets of his hard dick.

"Jabril!" Jaise peered at him. "Go back downstairs to your
room."

Journee smiled. "Oh, your room is in the basement? Your
mother didn't show me that part of the house."

Jabril blushed. "I could show you."

"No. The fuck. You can't," Jaise said, tight lipped, never
taking her eyes off Journee. "Now I said get back to your
room, Jabril."

Jabril shook his head and looked toward Journee. "Maybe
another time. Another place."

Journee smiled, but didn't answer. Once he left the room,
Jaise walked into Journee's personal space, pointed her finger,
and scolded, "You skanky-ass, strippin'-ass slut! I should slap
your damn face! You don't come in my house and throw your
ass at my son! Your low level ass has insulted me and now
you're trying to sink your infected fangs into my baby!"

Journee blinked, hard, obviously caught off guard. She picked
up the empty wine bottle, hit it on the edge of the table, and
cracked it in half. Pricks of glass scattered across the room. She
held up the broken and jagged bottle edge. "Bitch, you just put
your life in danger! You don't run up on me like that! I don't
know what the fuck you smoked in that kitchen, but don't you
ever step to me crazy! Fuck around and get your throat sliced!
Wake up in your grave with me standing over it and spittin' on
that motherfucker!"

Jaise took a step back. "You have lost your mind! Let me
explain something to you—"

"You can't explain a motherfuckin' thing to me, bitch. You
don't even have your mind together. I'm not Vera, I'm not
Milan, and I'm definitely not Chaunci! And as far as your son,
he's nothing more than a baby with a big, hard dick. Standing

up here and his damn breath reeks of your tittie! With his broke ass!"

"You—"

"And instead of being worried about who your son is fuckin', you'd better be worried about who's fuckin' yo' husband. 'Cause obviously the way to his heart wasn't through your fuckin' meals. Otherwise, he'd be here for your feast."

"I can't believe I invited you—"

"That's right; *you* invited *me*! I didn't call you seeking your friendship. I don't want your damn son. I have a husband. A very rich one. Don't play me."

"You need to leave!" Jaise snatched the front door open.

"Bitch, please! I've been tossed out of better places! You up in this old-ass motherfucker tryin' to be the black Paula Deen. Bitch, you'd better get into it! This ain't the Food Network. Ain't nobody checkin' for you, boo! You supposed to be flossin' and you up in this antiquated motherfucker cracking eggs and frying chicken and shit! *Silly-ass* beyotch!" Journee swerved her neck as she stormed out the door and Jaise slammed it behind her.

Jaise spun around toward Renee. "I can't believe you just stood there while that ghetto whore just tried to kill me! You and your film crew need to get the fuck out too! I *will not* film with you or Journee's ass *ever again*! As a matter of fact, let me get Bridget on the phone. I want both of you off the show!"

CHAPTER 16

JOURNEE

"Can you tell the camera what just happened?"

Journee dropped the jagged half of the bottle she'd held on Jaise's brick portal as she clicked her heels down the stairs and onto the sidewalk. The bottle exploded and scattered into shards and broken bits of green glass.

She slid on her round-eyed Chanel sunglasses, stormed to the nearest corner, and looked up the street, toward the direction she expected her driver to come.

What did he just ask me?

She turned toward the camera, which was zoomed in on her, and frowned. "What type of question was that?" she asked Bryan, the cameraman. "You saw what just happened. The bitch was almost on her way to the coroner's office." She lit her cigar, eased it between her KissKiss-Gold-and-Diamonds-covered lips, gracing the cool cream tip with a hard, much needed pull.

She blew a serpent of smoke into the air. "Trust me. She's lucky. The old me would've murdered her ass and let the police investigation find out what the fuck her problem was."

Journee flipped her hair over her shoulders. "She'd better be thankful I've changed. 'Cause in my stripping days, I would've flanked her down to the white meat. Running up on me is never a good move. You can talk all day, but once you get in my face and threaten to put your hands on me . . . oh, baby, you have officially walked your ass into the *Twilight Zone*."

A black Lincoln town car pulled up and parked in front of them. Journee nodded, as her driver exited the car, walked around and opened the back door for her. "Did you enjoy your late lunch, Mrs. Dupree?"

"Don't even ask." Journee eased into the backseat and sank into the smooth leather. Once Journee reached the pier, she stepped into her gleaming white and regal boat, and headed home to Millionaires' Row.

Thirty minutes later, Journee happily accepted the extended hand of her boat chauffeur, who helped her out of the boat and onto the dock.

She sauntered up the wooden planks, headed up the walkway.

"Afternoon, Mrs. Dupree," Mary, the house manager, said as she held the front door open.

"Afternoon, Mary. I need a shot of Hennessy right away." Journee stepped out of her heels and walked barefoot into her living room.

Immediately she halted under the curved archway, stopping short of a slight stumble.

She released a quiet gasp.

Relax.

Regroup.

And whatever you do, do not take out your thirty-two and shoot his ass.

CHAPTER 17

MILAN

A month ago . . . at an ESPN charity event.

"Kendu.,"

"Yes, baby."

"Who is that?"

Kendu turned his head from one side of the crowded ballroom to the next. "Who are you talking about?"

"The blonde lurking in the corner who's been watching you all damn night."

Kendu stared at the woman and then turned back to Milan. "I don't know who she is. Maybe she's a fan of yours."

"Of mine?" she said. "My fans don't stalk me. But she has clearly been following your every move—"

"Are you serious right now? Really. Truly. Serious? You know how many people are in here. She could be looking at the dude standing behind me. Why does it have to be me? And I don't appreciate you accusing me all the time."

"I didn't accuse you of anything."

"No, not yet."

"Why are you overreacting?"

"I'm not overreacting, Milan. I just know you, and I don't want to hear about some random blonde all damn night. I'm trying to have

a good time with my wife and take my career to the next level. Now, unless she can help me do that, I don't give a fuck who she is."

Two weeks ago . . . in Central Park.
"Shelly," Milan said to her nanny, "do you see that white woman over there?"
"The one bouncing the baby on her lap?"
"Yes. She's been following us through the park."
"Mrs. Malik." Shelly smiled, the look in her eyes clearly dismissing Milan's suspicions. "I don't think she's following us. She just might be a fan. You are famous."

Today . . .
There she is again.
Milan drew in a deep breath as she spotted Bridget and the camera crew parking.
Damn.
Relax.
You can handle this.
Milan's hips swayed as she crossed the street and stood before the woman, whose red, blotchy hands were wrapped around the handles of an umbrella stroller. Milan's eyes dropped to the cooing baby, and without blinking, she looked up at the woman and smiled. "Why are you following me?"

"I'm not following you," the woman said matter-of-factly. "And actually, I was thinking of asking you why you've been following me."

What, bitch? Milan peeked over at Bridget and the camera pointed her way. "Listen." She turned back to the woman. "I'm not following you. And you know that. Now, it seems that you might be a fan, which is fine. If you want to take a picture with me or want me to give you an autograph, I have no problem doing that, but I need *you* to stop following *me*."

"I'm *not* following you. And I am *definitely* no fan of yours."

"Then what the fuck—" *Breathe.* "Look. Just leave me alone, and the next time I see you outside my home, I'll be calling the police."

"This is a public street."

Milan said, her South Bronx accent in full effect, "But when I beat yo' ass on this public street for stalking me, that will be a very private affair." She peeked at Bridget and wished she could wipe the smirk off her face.

Milan proceeded to cross the street—stopping midway when she heard the woman call Kendu's name. "What did you say?" Milan spun round and furrowed her brow, as a car screeched and swerved around her.

"Stupid ass!" the driver roared out his window, flipping her the bird. Milan ignored him as she yelled at the woman, "Repeat that!"

"I *said* I need to speak to you about Kendu."

"That's what I thought you said." Milan stormed back across the street and stood a few steps closer to the woman than she'd been before. "What about Kendu?"

The woman tightened her grip on the stroller. "I've been waiting for him to tell you about us."

"Us?" Milan blinked. Squinted. Lowered her eyes to the baby. *Brown skin. Curly hair. Kendu's Egyptian-shaped eyes.*

Immediately Milan's breathing felt stifled. She looked up at the woman and without thinking twice, she yanked this bitch by her hair, forcing her to let go of the stroller, and then followed up with a snatch to the throat. "I will fuckin' kill you *and* Kendu!" Immediately security stepped in and pulled the two women apart.

"You stepped in too damn soon!" Bridget said. "I hate that the network forces security to travel with us!"

"Are you fuckin' insane?!" Milan screamed at security as she clawed in the air, watching the woman grab the stroller and run away. "Get the fuck off me!" she yelled at security. "I'll see you again, bitch!" she screamed as the woman continued to run down the street. "I'll see you again and whenever I do, I'm going to kick your motherfuckin' ass!" She pushed the security guard in the chest. "Get off me! I don't believe this shit! You don't grab me when I'm trying to snatch that bitch!"

"Exactly!" Bridget agreed. "Carl, you come with me. The rest of you go after her! Find out who she is and have that information on my desk in an hour!"

"I tell you what," Milan said to no one in particular as she charged into the house. "I. Know. This. Much. Fuck a three-day wait, I'm going to LA today! Rightthefucknow!" She rushed into her master suite, continued into her dressing room, picked up her Louis Vuitton suitcase, and slammed it on her bed. "And I'll try not to kill this motherfucker. But one of us has got to go. And it ain't gon' be me!"

Bridget smiled. "So we're going to LA? Let me inform the network."

Milan turned to Bridget. "Don't fuck with me right now, especially since I'm about two seconds off your ass any damn way! And if you don't step the fuck back, I promise you it ain't gon' be pretty."

"My, my . . ." Bridget clutched invisible pearls. "Aren't we touchy."

"I know I shouldn't jump to conclusions." Milan spoke outwardly to herself as she held back tears. "But this motherfucker's an athlete." She walked back into her dressing room and blindly snatched three pairs of jeans and three Prada blouses from their cedar hangers. She tossed them into her suitcase.

"And above all *I. Know. His. Ass.*" She walked into her shoe closet, grabbed two pairs of heels, stormed toward the door—and a vision of the white woman and her brown baby danced before her. She turned around, put her heels down, grabbed the Vaseline off her dresser, and made a beeline for the sneaker rack, reaching for a pair of Air Max.

She wiped away the tears she could no longer put on hold.

"I knew when this bastard came waltzing in and interrupting my interview that he was up to some bullshit."

She wiped more tears. Closed her suitcase.

"But we will get to the bottom of it. Today. And please"— she lifted her eyes toward the heavens—"please, when I confront this son of a bitch and ask him to tell me the truth. Please, oh please, don't let this motherfucker lie and try to play me . . . because then, I'll have to kill him!"

She grabbed her suitcase, walked out of her room, down the stairs, and into her pristine garage, where her driver sat on a metal folding chair, his feet on the hood of her Bentley, leafing through a *Hustler* magazine. "Get your damn feet off my car!"

"I'm so sorry, Mrs. Malik." He jumped up and stood at attention, dropping the magazine to the concrete floor and kicking it out of sight.

"I don't have time for your triflin'-ass sorries! Just get your freaky ass behind the wheel and take me to the airport. Right fuckin' now!"

"Yes, ma'am." The driver took Milan's suitcase from her hand, opened the car door, and before Milan could have a seat, Bridget and Carl rushed in.

"What are you waiting on?!" Bridget yelled out the window to the driver. "Let's go! We have a flight to catch!"

CHAPTER 18

JOURNEE

"Well, well, well, isn't this a pleasant surprise. Granddaddy, you're out of your room." Journee beamed as she walked over to where Zachary sat in his wheelchair and gently brushed his lips with a kiss. "It's so good to see you in the gallery."

He squeezed her hand and smiled. "I . . . missed . . . you . . . this . . . afternoon," he said slowly, as if he were running out of breath.

"How sexy is that? My granddaddy missed me. I missed you too, my love." She stroked his cheek as she looked at the man standing next to him, soaking in his smooth, caramel skin, copper eyes, broad shoulders, and muscle-bound body. "And whom do we have here?" She held out her hand. "I'm Journee. Granddaddy's wife. And you are?"

He accepted her gesture. "Xavier."

"Xavier?" Journee squinted. "Is this *the* Xavier you're always talking about, Granddaddy?"

He nodded as his lips turned up and into a smile. "Yes, my son."

Journee's eyes grew bright with surprise. "You're family! Your father has spoken so much about you over the years. Hoping and praying that he'd see you again."

"Well, the parole board certainty made that happen."

Parole? "How wonderful you must feel. Well, we're glad to have you here." She opened her arms and pulled him into her embrace. "It's so great to finally meet you!" She squeezed him tighter. Pressing her nails into his back, she whispered, "What the fuck are you doing here?" She released him from her embrace. "Will you be staying for dinner at least before you leave? Our chef is a marvelous cook."

He'd better say no.

"Of course I'll be staying for dinner."

Motherfucker.

"Journee," Zachary said, "I invited him . . . to stay with us . . . for a while."

You did what? "Oh, really?" She softly clapped her hands and braided her fingers together.

"Yes. He has . . . nowhere to go. I . . . haven't seen him . . . since he was fifteen and his mother took him away. And like you said . . . he's family and I really want to . . . spend as much time as I have left . . . with him."

Don't worry, you two will be together forever, in hell. "Anything to make my Granddaddy happy." Journee looked over to Xavier and smiled. "Welcome home, son." She opened her arms, pulled him back into her embrace, and whispered, "I want you out of here tonight." She took a step back. "I'll go and tell the chef to whip up something extra special!"

An hour later, the family enjoyed a feast of buttery lobster tails, linguini and prawns covered in garlic and Alfredo sauce, freshly baked bread, crisp spinach salad topped with crumbled blue cheese, and a bottle of uncorked 1907 Shipwrecked champagne.

"I'd like to make a toast." Xavier lightly tapped his butter knife on the side of his flute. "To my father and his beautiful bride. Thank you for welcoming me into your home. Given everything that I've been through, I really appreciate you two.

I hope you know that I'm here in your lives to stay. And, Journee, I'm sure out of everything you've ever imagined, you never thought you'd have a son who was older than you."

Was that supposed to be a joke? Journee smirked as she tapped Zachary on the knee. "Granddaddy."

"Huh? What?" He yanked his neck up and smacked his dry lips. "Yeah, yeah. Son, you were . . . going to make . . . a toast?"

"He already did," Journee said.

"Beautiful, son." Zachary yawned and raised his glass a wobbly inch off the table. "I want to make a toast. . . . Here's to . . ." He tilted his head to the side, and while they waited to see what he would say, Zachary released a light snore from between his lips.

Xavier looked confused while Journee removed the glass from Zachary's hand and scolded a snickering maid via a hard glance.

"I do believe it's time," she said to a sleeping Zachary, "for you to call it a night."

"Does he usually fall asleep like that?" Xavier asked. "It's only eight o'clock."

"No. Your daddy's usually asleep by seven."

"Damn. And what is that smell all of a sudden?" He frowned and looked around.

"Well, it looks like," Journee said matter-of-factly, "your dear ole daddy needs his diaper changed. Why don't you handle that, son? Because I've had enough for the evening and I'm going to bed."

Journee sauntered out of the dining room and into the elevator. She stepped out on the third floor and walked over to the west wing, where her bedroom suite was located.

She made her way into her bedroom, leaned against the door, and took three deep breaths.

What the fuck?! What the fuck?! What the fuck?!

Okay . . .

Regroup . . .

Think this through.

Pay him off. And if he's the same grimy motherfucker he's always been, he'll take the money and you'll never see him again.

That's it.

She took another deep breath and stepped into her en suite. Her spalike bathroom was lined with clear blue tiles, a black soapstone floor, and a massive river rock shower.

I can't believe that bastard is back to haunt me.

Stop worrying . . .

Besides, Zachary has already made me the sole beneficiary in his will.

A smile ran across Journee's face as she held her head back, and the rainspout washed warm streams of water all over her body, slicking her jet black hair to her head and running over her hard, chocolate nipples. She felt her mind easing into a memory of Xavier licking and nibbling on her nipples before he would . . .

Stop it!

She held her head up, wiped the excess water from her face with the back of her hands, turned the shower off, and stepped out. She walked into her bedroom and a slither of fright ran through her.

"Don't be scared, baby," Xavier said as he lay in the center of her bed, completely naked, his hard and thick ten-inch-dick standing at military attention. He followed her eyes as they gazed over the tip. He stroked it.

Her mouth watered.

Damn, that's a pretty dick.

Don't fall for it.

She dabbed the corners of her mouth with an index finger.

"Did you really think that I would leave just like that?" He gripped his sack and Journee bit her bottom lip. Visions of his beautiful member sailing its way into her sticky sea and pounding through it flooded her mind. Her pussy pumped and her clit swelled.

Stop it!

"What are you doing?" She sat on the leopard chaise adjacent to her bed. She slowly crossed her legs and reached for her cigar that sat in the ashtray on her end table. She lit it. "What are you doing here?" She took a pull and immediately blew out the smoke.

"It's obvious I want to fuck you."

"You know what the hell I mean! Why are you here—and don't give me any bullshit about you wanting to get closer to your damn daddy."

"Touchy. Touchy. You wouldn't happen to be taking advantage of my dear ole damn daddy, would you? You seem so in love with Granddaddy." He laughed.

"Just answer the question."

"Well, I'm here for lots of reasons. For one, the last time I saw you, you were running down the street after you'd stolen my money. You and some other bitch."

"I didn't steal your money."

"Who did?"

"That other bitch."

"Oh, your costar?"

Journee arched a brow. "How do you know about that?"

"I've been in prison, not lost at sea. I also know that while I was living on Cell Block D and eatin' prison fuckin' slop for ten damn years, you two thieving bitches grew a set of golden goddamn balls and decided to become reality stars. I couldn't believe it. I'm sitting in my cell and all of a sudden you're on the evening news being announced as not only the new star of the *Millionaire Wives Club,* but as the wife of Zachary Dupree. My damn daddy."

"So what do you want? Money? How much—ten?—twenty million? If so, we fuck, and before the sun goes up, you find another place to stay. And before the week is up, I'll get the money to you."

He stroked his dick. "If you think that any number in the millions and some pussy will get rid of me that easily, you're dreaming. I'm entitled to all of it. But I won't be selfish. We'll start with the pussy and then you can sign your clubs over to me by the end of the week."

"My clubs?"

"You heard me. And when Pop's stankin' ass kicks the bucket, we'll settle up on the rest. Which will be half of everything."

Journee took one last pull of her cigar and blew smoke into the air. She mashed the head into the ashtray, walked over to the bed, and straddled him. Easing down on his long and never-ending dick, she moaned as the thickness more than filled her and the length reached parts of her she'd though for sure had died. She gathered herself and looked him in the eyes. "I'm fucking you because I want to, but the only thing you will get half of is this damn nut. I don't split my money with anybody."

He gripped her behind and pressed his fingertips into her cheeks. "Hmm," he moaned. "This fat pussy is tight. Damn, Granddaddy ain't fucking you at all, huh, baby?"

She bucked her hips, swinging her breasts and bouncing them in his face, brushing against his lips.

He squeezed her behind before placing his hands around her waist and lifting her slightly off his dick. "Look at that shit." They both looked down at the remnants of her enjoyment. He flipped her over, tossed her legs over his left shoulder and said, "If you don't agree to half, then I'll just have to tell dear ole Dad about us."

"Tell him." She wrestled her way back on top. "Because then I'll be sure to mention that me marrying him was your idea to begin with. And then I'll have to give all the details of all the nights you told me just what to do and what to say to get his attention." She slid a breast into his mouth and he sucked and bounced her nipple on and off his tongue.

Giving her breast one last lick, he said, "You wouldn't do that because you know that then neither one of us would get a thing."

"It's a chance I'd be willing to take."

"Are you sure?" He turned her over and pulled her ass into his shaft, pounding her with deep thrusts, rendering her speechless. Her mouth hung open and all that would escape were moans and groans and "Dear God" babbles. He knew he'd hit her spot. And he was the only one who could hit it . . . like this. "I asked you a question," he said, feeling her back curling beneath his chest.

The truth was, she wasn't sure. Actually, she was sure. Sure she didn't want to lose the money she'd worked so hard for, and yeah, maybe . . . maybe Xavier appearing here was an unwanted surprise, but then again, maybe she could promise to give him half and in the end find a way to kill his ass.

"Whatever you want, baby." She shivered.

"Half." His back arched.

"Yes!" she screamed, coating his lifeline with icing.

"That's my girl." He gifted her with a string of pearls. "That's my girl."

CHAPTER 19

VERA

*"T*here's *nothing like vinyl, baby."*

Vera could hear Taj's voice as she carefully placed the needle on the record player. John Coltrane's "In a Sentimental Mood" filled the surround sound as she lay back on the white quilted leather chaise in her bedroom, her mind's eye traveling back in time to gray summer skies and train rides uptown to a snug jazz and poetry club, where the backdrop was small bistro tables, a makeshift stage, and a cello.

Vera would always swear to Taj that one day she would muster up the nerve to get on stage and spit out the one poem she'd ever written in her life. . . .

> *There's no more emotional war*
> *between my mind*
> *and my thighs. . . .*
> *Finally,*
> *They can all come together.*

And while she laughed, Taj would say, "That's beautiful, baby."

Her mind continued to drift. She could clearly see them at the reggae spot they used to hit in downtown Brooklyn where they would dance the night away.

Then there were the nights at home. In this very room. Where they would share secrets and make love until the moonlight met the sunlight and promise each other forever. Never thinking that their forever had an expiration date marked "yesterday."

Vera opened her eyes and wiped away the hot tears that ran down her cheeks. "I'm not doing this shit." She walked onto her rooftop terrace.

A rainbow of dancing lights twinkled from the New York City skyline as tears flowed harder than they ever had before.

"Vera." Poured from behind her.

She quickly wiped her face, gathered a smile, and turned around.

Her mother, Rowanda, a paper bag brown, five foot even petite woman, with salt and pepper hair styled into a short and cropped bob, stood there. Rowanda squinted as she looked into Vera's dark eyes. "What's wrong?"

"Nothing. I just needed some air." She brushed past her mother and rushed back into her bedroom. "Did the music wake you?"

Rowanda hesitated. "Vera, how long are you going to do this?"

"Do what?" Vera snatched the needle off the record player, causing a screeching sound to slice through the air. She looked up at her mother, who'd come to stand across from her by turntable. "What are you talking about?"

"How long are you going to act like nothing's wrong? Like you don't care."

"Just leave it alone." She shot her mother a hard glare. "Now, let's talk about something else." She walked into the kitchen and opened the refrigerator. "Would you like a glass of wine?"

"No. I wanna talk about what's going on with you. I've been here for a week and every night you're crying yourself to sleep. If you miss your husband, call him."

"Didn't I tell you nothing was wrong? And did I ask you for any advice?" Vera slammed the refrigerator shut and roughly sat the wine bottle on the lava countertop.

"You didn't have to ask me. I know you."

"You don't know shit about me!"

"You better watch your mouth!"

"I'm grown."

"But I'm still your damn mother!"

Vera paused and, as she slowly drank Rowanda in, an unwanted twenty–five-year-old memory danced before her.

Rowanda stood, rail thin, wearing sagging jeans and a worn and baggy blue t-shirt, the collar stretched out of shape, hanging off the right shoulder and highlighting the protruding collarbone. Rowanda snorted and licked the white crust around her dry lips. She looked down at a nine-year-old Vera, who lay asleep on a bare mattress and snatched her up. "Here she go," she said to a woman who stood behind her.

"What is you doin', Rowanda?" Vera stumbled to the floor, half asleep.

"See this lady," Rowanda said, "This is a social worker. She came to take you. You gotta go."

Vera fell silent as she looked around the room. "Rowanda, I don't wanna go with her."

"You got to."

"Why?" Tears filled her eyes. "I told you I was sorry about telling the teacher you get high or that I be home by myself all the time. I said I was sorry! Gimme another chance. I'ma be good! I promise. And I won't fight no more and I'll try real hard not to cuss."

"Be quiet Vera," Rowanda said. "You ain't that bad. Matter a fact, you ain't done nothin'. Now get up! This has to do with me and not you."

"Look, though." Vera pushed out of Rowanda's arms, ran past the social worker and over to small dresser where she yanked a rusted cof-

fee can that she kept pennies in. "Here take these!" She turned to her mother and, as she took a step, she tripped over her own feet, causing the pennies to rain all over the wood floor. Tears fell from Vera's eyes as she scurried around the room, picking up the pennies.

"Here, Rowanda, take this money and buy us some food. I won't tell nobody else that you smoked up all your money. I won't say nothing. I know I be too fresh, I know I'm bad, but I'm sorry. You forgive me? Now, please, can I stay?"

"You gotta go."

"Why?"

" 'Cause I'ma damn fiend, girl."

"So? Ain't everybody 'cept the social worker and the teacher a fiend?"

"No, they is not. And look, I ain't got shit and I can't give you shit! And they is not gon' let me keep you."

"I ain't goin'."

The social worker placed a hand on Vera's shoulder.

"Get offa me!"

Rowanda snatched Vera off the floor and carried her outside to the social worker's car. "You gettin' yo' ass outta here! You not gon' stay here like this! Told you I ain't got shit and you tryna hold on. Open the damn door!" She screamed at the social worker, who nervously snatched it open.

"Mommy, please! Rowanda, please. I'ma be good!"

Rowanda peeled Vera off her, quickly placed her in the back seat, and slammed the door.

"Why is you doing this?!" Vera cried as she thrashed around in the back seat desperately trying to get out.

" 'Cause I'm your damn mother!" she spat as she stood there, watching the social worker hop into the driver's seat and ride off into the distance.

Vera did her best to blink away her memory. She swallowed and tried to see her mother for who she was today. It was a struggle. "Leave the shit alone," she spat. "Now either you want some damn wine," Vera snatched two glasses from the cabinet. "Or you don't." She filled only one. "But all this mother-daughter confessions session shit you're trying to have with me is not about to happen. Now I'm warning you, drink up or take your ass back to bed!"

"I'm warning you to watch your damn mouth and don't speak to me like that!"

"Speak to you like what?" Vera frowned. "Let's not pretend here. The only reason you even show up here every year—this damn time—is to make yourself feel better and to bask in my success. What the fuck do you want? Fame? Fortune? A standing ovation? Yeah, that's it." Vera clapped her hands. "Job well done, Rowanda. You did a wonderful job of gettin' high, helping me into foster care, and giving me a boatload of goddamn trust issues. Wonder-fucking-full!"

"I did my best!"

"Then you need to up your damn standards!"

"I'm trying to tell you—"

"I don't need you trying to tell me shit! When I needed you, you gave me away!"

"I made sure that Cookie was able to raise you!"

"I wasn't her child! Like you said, you're my *damn* mother! You should've raised me! Instead, all you did was get high and whore your ass in the street! And now that you're clean—off of my dime—and you live out in the suburbs of Chicago with your husband, mega pastor Doctor Reverend, you think you can come and tell me about my husband? Never. Because you and I both know that the only damn man you've ever consistently been with is a glass dick!"

Whap!!!!

Rowanda slapped Vera so hard that her ears rang and her neck twisted to the left. She fell into the counter, knocking the wine bottle and the glasses over. Vera lifted her eyes and peered at her mother as she pressed a palm against her burning cheek.

Rowanda pointed a finger in Vera's face. "Don't you *ever*

speak to me like that again! Or I will knock your damn head off! And yes, I'm your damn mother and no, I didn't raise you! And yes, I was a damn junkie and a whore! But I made sure that you lived with someone who could love you and give you more than I could. I couldn't have you going from dope house to dope house! That's not a life for a little girl! Why can't you understand that?!"

Silence.

"I've been sober for six damn years and every year we do this same damn dance! You want me to come and when I get here you constantly bring up my past. You don't take me around your friends—you keep me here and I stay here hoping and praying that if I please you and do what you want me to do, that you'll accept me. But enough of that shit."

Silence.

Rowanda continued, "Don't you think I know what I've done and who I am?! Trust me. I have a lot of shit that I deal with every day! Half of it you can't even begin to imagine! And if I had to do it all over again yes, I would have gotten off drugs and raised my own babies! But I couldn't do that then! And I need you to understand that!"

Tears poured down Vera's cheeks as she pressed her back against the counter and slid to the floor. "I'm sorry." She cried. "I never meant to hurt you or take it out on you. I'm just . . . just so confused and hurt. And I want to move on, but it's soooo hard. It's so hard. I want to accept you as my mother and the woman you are today, but I don't know how."

"Just give me a chance to be your mother and you be my daughter. Be my baby girl for once." She kneeled before Vera and pulled her head into her chest."

"I feel like I'm losing everything."

"But you don't have to, baby. I'm here. I love you and I ain't goin' nowhere."

"But Taj—"

"He loves you too. All you have to do is go and get him."

"I can't."

"Why?"

Vera stared off into the distance, then brought her eyes back to meet Rowanda's. "I just can't." She rose from the floor and brushed invisible dust from her robe. She wiped tears from her cheeks. "I guess we've had one helluva night."

"Vera—"

"Rowanda, please. I don't wanna talk about it. The only thing I can promise right now is that I'm going to do my best to get things right between us. That's it."

"And Taj?"

"I'm divorcing him."

CHAPTER 20

MILAN

The Next Day . . .

*K*eep *it classy.*

Milan tapped the tip of her manicured index finger on the marble counter. "Run that past me again. He's not what?" She looked at the hotel clerk.

"Ma'am, just as I told you last night when you arrived and am telling you again, this morning, for the third time"—the clerk clenched her teeth—"there's no one here by the name of Kendu Malik."

"Try Knott Harris, Kaareem Davis, or Carl Worthington." Milan rattled off the aliases Kendu had been known to use when he traveled and wanted to avoid the ballyhoo of the press and the fans.

The clerk, a middle-aged black woman with mahogany skin and blond hair, pursed her lips and struggled to keep her attitude intact. She pushed her wire frames up the bridge of her broad nose and scanned the computer screen. "No one's here by any of those names. *Either.*"

"I need to speak to the manager. Now."

"I *am* the manager."

"Then get me the goddamn CEO, because I don't like your attitude, Shaquita. Apparently you don't know who I am."

"My *name* is Helen. It doesn't matter who you are, *ma'am,* because your husband still isn't going to be here."

Oh no this bitch didn't! "I will have your job! Don't you ever speak to me like that, because hopping over this counter and beating your Poise-wearing ass will be just the stress reliever I need!"

"Ma'am—"

"And don't call me another motherfuckin' 'ma'am,' Sophia! You're standing here trying to tell me that you haven't seen a six-three, two-hundred-fifty-pound, double-dipped in molasses football legend and number one ESPN commentator, that everybody in American seems to know, except your lopsided, wig-wearing ass! What the fuck, do you have cataracts?!"

The clerk arched one brow and then the other. "If you and those cameras do not step away from the counter and leave, I will call security and have you removed!"

"Call 'em. I'm not scared of security! Fuck security!"

"Milan," came from behind her.

The rubber soles of Milan's sneakers squeaked as she spun around. There stood Kendu. The invisible drop kick that he'd imprinted deep in her chest, before he left, rose to the surface. Pressure filled her neck and her eyes grew wide. She quietly watched him cross the threshold and walk into the lobby, dressed in a navy blue Versace suit, a crisp white shirt with the top two buttons open, and a briefcase in his left hand.

He looked at the cameras and then back to Milan. Twice.

There was a rising buzz among the guests in the lobby, some who eased through with a simple, "What's going on?" but never staying long enough for an answer. And others who stopped and became a part of the action by snickering, whipping out their cell phones, snapping pictures, and recording. "You came a day early," Kendu said, looking perplexed. "Let's go upstairs." He walked toward Milan.

Despite the building crowd, all Milan could focus on was

Kendu. She curled her lips and said sarcastically, "Go upstairs?! Where? To the rooftop? 'Cause according to Mable over there"—she pointed to the hotel clerk—"you don't have a room up in this here bitch! And *I'm* here a day early, mother-fucker? No. *I'm* right on time. Yo' ass is here a day mother-fuckin' late. Now where were you? And don't lie, because I've been calling you, and calling you, and calling you, for two god-damn days and you haven't answered any of my calls!"

"I lost my phone when I was at the convention. Now can we—"

"Stop lying! Because I went to that whack-ass convention center yesterday and guess what? There was no convention! I've been to your favorite restaurants and nobody has seen you! I've been all over this damn city, not to mention that I've been at this motherfuckin' counter, twice since last night, and guess what? You ain't been here either! Now where were you?"

"Milan—"

"Just spit it out!" She pointed in his face. "What ho are you fucking down here, 'cause your stringy-haired crazy white bitch is in New York strolling your black baby around and stalking our goddamn house!"

"What?!"

"Cut the stupid act! Now where the fuck were you?"

"Listen—"

Milan balled a fist and released a finger with every word, starting with her pinky. "Your statement needs to start with your exact location, then go to who's the bitch down here, and end with you explaining why I got some blond-haired, wet-dog-smelling whore showing up at my front fuckin' door, with some baby, saying to me that she was hoping that you had told me about the two of you! Now I need some answers! And don't lie, 'cause tricks are for kids and clearly I am not in a good fuckin' mood. So don't give me any bullshit!"

"Milan—"

"There you go again about to lie!" She pounded a right fist into her left palm. "Why don't you just tell the damn truth? 'Cause in a minute it's gon' be some slow singing and flower bringing! Now who are you *fuckkinnnnn'*?! Why couldn't I get you on the *phooooone*?! Why did you lie about the *conventioooon*? Why was there some crazy-ass white bitch at my front *dooooor*?! Who is that goddamn *babeeee*? Why does it look just like your *asssss*?! And why did Miss Celie over there say you didn't have a room in this *motherfuckerrrrr*?" Milan turned toward the clerk. Back to Kendu. "Or are you fuckin' that bitch? Is that it? What kind of Tiger Woods shit are you into? So you down here dusting off rude-ass old bitches now! You just a dick slangin' motherfucker! You ain't shit! I have asked you at least fifty goddamn times for explanation after explanation and you haven't said one damn word. Not one. Now. I'm asking you nicely—please stop fucking with me because in a minute it's going to be a deadly misunderstanding."

"Milan—"

"You know what; you know what." She took two steps back from Kendu, lunged four steps forward, and shoved him in his chest. "I have to get the fuck out of here. 'Cause I can't listen to another one of your lies. I'm tired of your shit. I've been bitching about you since I was eight years old and it's time to make a motherfuckin' change. So I'm going to just leave you here with that old bitch who's obviously suckin' your dick! Because if I stay here a moment longer, they'll be drawing white chalk around your ass!"

"Milan—" Kendu reached for her hand and she snatched it away, stormed through the crowd of shocked picture-snapping and video-recording people in the lobby, and rushed into the limo that awaited her, with Bridget and Carl on her heels.

Tears knocked at the back of her eyes. *You'd better not cry.*

"Take me to the airport," Milan ordered the driver. "I need to get home."

"Milan," Bridget called, doing her best to hold back her smile. "Tell the camera how you feel right now."

Silence. Instead of responding or busting Bridget in the mouth, which Milan desperately wanted to do, she turned toward the window and did her best to swallow the iron fist that had wedged its way into her throat and pushed tears through her eyes.

CHAPTER 21

CHAUNCI

I *don't believe this. . . .*

Chaunci sat on her sofa in pure darkness. Lights off. Blinds closed.

Everything has been taken.

My dreams.

My plans.

My company.

My secrets . . .

She held her face in her hands. *I promised myself that I would go to hell before I'd ever step back into seven-inch glass slippers and pussy pop on a handstand, but I think I might need to reconsider things. After all, this is hell.*

Knock . . . knock . . .

Startled, Chaunci looked from side to side in the darkness.

Knock . . . knock . . . "Chaunci!"

"That cannot be." Chaunci hopped off the sofa and turned the light on.

Knock . . . knock . . . "Chaunci, are you there?"

"Milan!" Chaunci opened the door in disbelief. "What are you doing here at midnight?"

"I need a drink," Milan slurred, holding a large brown paper bag in her hand. "And I need to tell you some shit." She stumbled a bit as she walked in.

Chaunci closed the door behind Milan and she said, "Where are you coming from?"

"LA. With the exception of the stop I made at the liquor store." Milan sat her bag on the marble coffee table.

"Why were you in the liquor store? You have a personal assistant. Why couldn't she go to the winery for you?"

"Bitch, fuck that bitch. And the rest of them personal assistant bitches. All they do is gather all your business," she slurred, "and write a book about you. And I don't need that bitch writing a book about me and telling anydamnbody how I liked to go to the damn liquor sto'." Milan flopped down on the sofa. "And besides, I'm from the Bronx and I can go into the goddamn liquor sto' and get my own shit if I want to!"

Chaunci looked astonished. "You are drunk as hell. And you need some coffee."

Milan wagged an index finger. "Why would you say something like that? All I had was four shots of Cîroc on the plane. I have enough rumors being spread about me. Don't add to 'em. I am not . . . not . . . not . . . ummm . . . drunk. I just have a li'l preparty buzz on."

Chaunci frowned. "Preparty? There's no party over here."

"I brought the party with me." Milan pulled two bottles of Merlot out of the bag, along with a corkscrew and two extremely long and bendable straws. She looked up at Chaunci. "Would you sit your ass down? You're making me nervous. And where have you been for four damn days? Do you know the whole world has been looking for you?"

"Yes," Chaunci snapped. "I know that because everydamnbody keeps telling me that. Shit, I'm entitled to go somewhere without everyone knowing my every move. Damn. And for your information, I was in France."

"France? Heifer, you were supposed to be with me at that miserable network party, meeting your new costar, Journee Dupree."

Oh, please. "So you met her. You like her?" Chaunci uncorked the two bottles of Merlot and handed Milan a straw.

Milan leaned back on the arm of the sofa. "Remember in high school how it was that one particular girl you always promised that you would beat her ass on the last day of school?"

"Yeah."

"Well, Journee would be that bitch for me."

Me too.

Milan continued, "I can't stand her."

Me either.

"And I want to punch her so hard in the throat," Milan carried on, "that she would feel like I just put her in a choke hold."

"Damn." Chaunci fell out laughing.

"Let me tell you, I tried to be nice to that bitch and she tried to play me. That whore has the ghetto in her turned on extra high. And do you know who she's married to?"

Of course I do. "Who?"

"Two-hundred-year-old Zachary Dupree. Now how the hell is she riding that brittle-ass dick?"

"I don't think she is."

"That's probably what the hell her problem is. She needs some dick. That's a whole other category of pitiful women." Milan pointed into the air and shook an index finger with every word. "Those. Who. Need. To. Be. Fucked."

Chaunci chuckled as she slid her straw into her bottle. "Now you didn't come over here to talk about Journee, so wassup?"

"First, let me make a toast." Milan held her bottle in the air and Chaunci followed suit. "To men. Fuck. Each. And. Every. One. Of. Them. All of 'em!"

"Why?"

" 'Cause they ain't shit. They ain't worth shit. And the richer they are, the bigger pieces of shit they are!"

They clinked their bottles.

"Now would you like to tell me what that was about?" Chaunci sipped.

"Kendu's a cheatin' motherfucker," Milan said casually. "That's what that was about."

It took everything in Chaunci not to spit out her drink. "What?"

"You heard me."

"What happened?"

"Well, starting a little over a month ago, I began seeing this white chick everywhere I went. The park, The Met Gala, et cetera, et cetera. But of course Kendu claimed he didn't know who she was."

"Did you?"

"Hell no. So to make a long and fucked up story short and fucked up, I caught this chick standing across the street from my house yesterday morning, so I confronted her."

"You did?" Chaunci's eyes grew wide.

"Hell yes." Milan cocked her neck for emphasis. "And I tried to beat that ass too."

"Milan—"

"And how about she had a black baby with her." Tears welled in Milan's eyes.

"A baby . . . ? Well . . . maybe she was the nanny."

"She wasn't the damn nanny. And after, she asked me if Kendu had told me about them—"

"Them?!"

"Yes, them! I knew then that she was the mama and my husband was the damn daddy!" Milan took a swig and tears streamed down her cheeks. She flung the tears away with the back of a hand.

Chaunci's mouth dropped open. "Are you serious?"

"As serious as the drop kick I wanted to lay in his damn

chest when I ran up on him in LA." She flung more tears away. "I've had it! It's over. We're done. And that damn surprise birthday party I've been planning for him . . ."

"What about it?"

"I'm changing the motherfucker to a divorce party."

"Milan, I think you might be overreacting a bit. Did you ask him to explain?"

"Explain? I flew out to LA and tried to give this mother-fucker a chance to explain."

"And?"

"He told lie after lie after lie. And then when his lies weren't working, he asked me to come back to his hotel room."

"Did you go?"

"Hell no! He didn't have a room up in that bitch! He was lying about that too! I am finished with him!"

"I think you should've at least heard him out."

Milan looked at Chaunci in shock. "Did you forget that you're my friend?! You're on my side! And you know you don't like his ass! You never have and you never will. You're the one who told me not to marry him in the first place!"

"I'm not taking his side. I just know you. The sober you. And this is your marriage."

"Fuck that marriage."

"Milan—"

"Look at me!" Milan demanded, and Chaunci observed Milan's hazel eyes drooping, the lids half-mast, and her bottom lip glazed with slicked saliva. Milan continued, "Does this look like the face of woman who doesn't mean what she says? No more of that forgiving shit." She belched. "I'm serious. Me and Kendu are done." She sipped and found herself sucking air through her straw. She turned the bottle upside down, causing the straw to slip to the floor and a single drop of Merlot to splash on the table.

She looked over at the coffee table, where Chaunci's bottle sat. "You're not going to drink that. I'll finish it for you." Milan picked up the bottle, and after a few sips, said, "Now, what's going on with you? Did you tell me where you were for four days? Did I tell you that the whole world was looking for you?"

"Yes, you told me that. And, yes, I told you that I was in France."

"Oh, okay. So what'd you do in France? And why are you looking like somebody stole your damn bike?"

Chaunci chuckled. "You are officially crazy as hell. My company," she shrugged, fighting back tears, "was taken from me."

Milan held her head up straight as if she were trying to get her thoughts together. "Say that again."

"My company was taken from me. Stolen."

"What do you mean?" Milan squinted. "Somebody stole the whole damn building? Oh my God. Only a crackhead would do some shit like that. And I betchu that ass was a man too. Don't worry; someone had to see 'im. Did you contact security?"

Chaunci wiped her eyes. "Milan, please. Not the whole damn building. The company."

"So somebody stole the whole twenty-seventh floor? Now that's fucked up."

Chaunci sighed. "You know what, it's a long story. One you'll understand when you're sober. Just know that I can't eat, can't sleep, and for the first time in many years, I feel lost." Tears streamed down her cheeks.

"Don't cry." Milan pulled Chaunci into her bosom. "Don't. It'll be okay. 'Cause only a motherfuckin' crackhead man would steal a goddamn floor out of a building and think his ass'll get away with it. I promise you we'll find him! 'Cause it ain't too many places in this tight-ass borough that he can hide that shit."

CHAPTER 22

JAISE

The wee morning breeze was cool as it blew into Jaise's face and she stared into the new day's darkness.

What the hell am I going to do?

She huffed. Turned from the window and leaned her back against her farmer's sink.

There's nothing left to cook.

Her eyes scanned her kitchen table, which overflowed with the hot and piping feast she'd just completed minutes ago:

Chicken smothered in homemade gravy.

Yellow rice.

Steamed cabbage.

Cheddar cheese grits.

Scrambled eggs.

Maple bacon.

Biscuits.

Boiled apples.

Banana bread.

Cigarettes.

She walked over to the table and reached for her cigarette case, which sat on the edge of the table. She fumbled as she tried to open it.

Why does this always happen?

Jaise tapped the case's clasp on the edge of the table and it popped open with ease. "Nothing?!" A lump filled her throat as she stared at her reflection in the mirrored case.

You don't need any cigarettes any damn way. And you need to stop cooking and eating everything in sight. You've resorted to wearing leggings, wrap dresses, and stretch pencil skirts in a piss-poor effort to avoid seeing the ten pounds you've gained. You are just a fat, miserable ass—!

Stop it!

Jaise closed the case and fixed herself a full plate of food. She sat down on her antique church pew and crossed her legs. The ten pounds she'd gained must've all gone to her thighs; resting her left thigh over her right one was a struggle. She eased her leg down and settled for crossing her ankles.

Jaise sopped a biscuit in the gravy on her plate and took a bite.

All you do is eat, cook, smoke, and sleep, and none of it makes any damn sense. All you're doing is running away. Well, your size-sixteen hips, double D breasts, and those love handles you try and hide will not let you run that fast, and one day, you're going to sprint your chubby ass into a mirrored brick wall right smack into the miserable bitch you really are.

Stop it!

Jaise looked down at her plate and realized that she'd eaten everything on it. She replenished it. Sat back down and sopped her biscuit.

You've always wanted a good man . . . and you had one. One who loved you. And he didn't call you fat, miserable, slap the shit out of you and tell you you deserved it. He loved you just the way you were. You were enough for him and he was exactly who you'd prayed for. But you didn't want a good man. The motherfucker who kicked your ass got more respect than the one who truly loved you.

Stop it!

She reached for another biscuit.

Stop what? Telling yourself the truth? You don't have anything else to cook and no cigarettes left to smoke. There's nothing left to do but listen to your damn thoughts, 'cause nobody knows you like I know you. And I know you may have prayed for a good man, but you have never felt like you deserved him. Because your grown ass is still the same fat-ass little girl who your daddy told you would always be second best. And you believed him. So when a great man came along, you put everything and everyone before him because you couldn't believe that you were actually his top priority. And you couldn't believe that because underneath all of your testimonies of love and light you are a low-down, greedy-ass, emotional liar who will never feel good enough!

Stop it!

It's not true.

It is true and you know it!

She reached for a biscuit. They were all gone. She opted for two pieces of chicken, thought it over for a minute, and reached for a third piece.

Why don't you have your man at home?

"Instead of worrying about who's fucking your son, you'd better worry about who's fucking your husband!" Journee's voice invaded her head.

Shut up!

Somebody's fucking him!

"Bilal wouldn't do that to me," Jaise said to no one in particular.

You don't know that. You don't know what he would do. The only thing you knew about your husband was that he would leave you. And he did.

Tears ran from Jaise's eyes and under her chin. She chewed slowly at first, but soon quickened the pace. The iron fist in her throat made it hard to swallow, but she attempted. She failed, and gagged. She reached for a napkin and spit out what was in her mouth. She wanted desperately to stop the tears, but she couldn't. Her chest hurt, her back hurt, her eyes burned, and her cheeks felt deflated. Everything was a blur. She even thought she could see Jabril sneaking a girl out the front door, but she wasn't sure. And she didn't give a damn. She just wanted her thoughts to stop kicking her in the head and shooting the pain down her spine.

She wanted to eat her miseries away in peace. But she couldn't. And here she sat, a bumbling fool, holding her third plate full of food, yet feeling like she was starving to death.

Call him.

I can't.

Why?

I don't deserve him. . . .

You're stupid. So you're just going to give your man away!

No.

Then call him.

What if he doesn't answer?

What if he does?

Call him.

Jaise walked over to the vintage pay phone on her kitchen wall. She reached for the quarter she kept on top of it and dropped it in the upper slot. Instead of dialing, she listened to the dial tone and a few minutes later, a loud busy signal invaded the line and the quarter dropped into the bottom slot.

She reached for the quarter and held it in her hand.

Call him.

She dropped the quarter in the slot and dialed the number quickly. He answered on the third ring. "Hello?"

"Bilal."

"Jaise?" She could hear a slight panic in his voice. "Are you okay? What are you doing up this time of the morning?"

"I just called to see what you were doing."

He hesitated. "I'm in my car. Just getting off work and headed home."

Hearing him say he was "headed home" felt like someone had pounded her in the lungs and knocked the breath out of her. *Say it.* "I want you to come home," she said quickly, before her tongue changed its mind.

Silence.

"I love you and I need you. I do. I'm lost. I'm confused. I want to make love to you. I need you. You're my best friend. My everything. And there's nothing left for me to cook and all my cigarettes are gone. And I'm so, so sorry. I just—" Her words turned into inaudible sobs.

"Baby," he called.

"And I'm so sorry. Please forgive me. Please give us another chance," she cried.

"Jaise, calm down and listen to me."

She shuddered and wiped tears. "I'm listening."

"This time it has to be all or nothing."

She wiped tears from her eyes. "It is. It's all and everything."

"No half ass. We're in this marriage and we're committed to it. You and I. That's it."

"That's it."

"And I understand that you love your son, but he has to leave. We can't live in the same house. He needs to make it on his own."

She sighed. "I know."

"I know you want what's best for Jabril, and I do too, but you're going to have to practice tough love so that he can learn how to be a man."

"I hear you, Bilal."

"I want my wife. The woman I fell in love with. I want it to be us."

"Yes, yes, yes. Just say you'll come home."

Bilal released a deep sigh. "Open the door, baby. I'm already here."

CHAPTER 23

MILAN

Summer 1991.

Playground 52.

South Bronx.

R & B singer Aaliyah was hot. Hip-hop artist Ice Cube was even hotter, and his hit "The Wrong Nigga to Fuck Wit" floated like a musical cloud through the air. And while eight-year-old Milan turned double Dutch, ten-year-old Kendu break-danced.

"That is so played out." Milan smirked as she looked at her friend Sharifa. "Who is that bama?"

Sharifa cheesed. Hard. "That's Kendu. My home skillet. My boo."

Milan stopped turning, causing the girl who jumped to step on the rope and be called out by the other girls who stood waiting. She completely faced Sharifa and said, "That's who? And he's your what?"

"My home skillet. My boo."

"Why you lying? Your mama won't even let you talk to a boy. So you know that is not your boo. You probably don't even know him." Milan twisted her lips.

"So what if I don't know him yet. He's lives down the hall from me with Ms. Lucy. You know—she keeps foster kids and he came last week. Special delivery for me."

"Whatever. Foster kids are scrubs anyway, and you need to tell him to stop dancing like that. 'Cause it's played out."

"Milan, would you come on!" yelled the girl holding the opposite end of the rope. "They wanna jump."

"You'd better slow down!" Milan cocked her neck and yelled back, "I'm coming." She looked back at Sharifa. "You always like them dirty boys." She began to turn.

"Wassup?" came from behind them.

Milan dropped the rope and she and Sharifa turned around. Kendu and his friend stood there. "Wassup?" Kendu repeated.

"Hey, Kendu." Sharifa grinned. "I live down the hall from you."

"Word." He nodded, looking Milan up and down. "Who you?"

Milan fought back a blush. "Somebody and that's all you need to know."

"You real cute, Somebody."

"I know this."

"I got a dollar; we can get some ice cream and kick it for a minute."

Milan looked toward Sharifa, who stood with her mouth hanging open. She handed her the ropes. "Turn. I'll be back." Milan walked toward the ice cream truck with Kendu. "You'd better have a dollar too."

"I got you. I promise."

5 a.m.

I should've kept turning and let Sharifa have the ice cream.

Tears filled Milan's eyes as her memory faded and she ran her hands over Kendu's cold and empty side of the bed.

Maybe I should've stayed at Chaunci's a little longer.

I don't believe this.

Believe it.

She glanced at the sitting area in her master suite and her eyes landed on the red leather sectional. Her mind drifted into a memory of sitting there and watching Kendu on *Scoreboard*, his ESPN morning show, feeling privileged to be his wife.

She smiled and her eyes danced to the fireplace mantel where their wedding picture hung. A jagged pain sliced down the center of her chest and tears eased down her cheeks.

Stop crying.

She stirred and turned toward the French patio doors.

You've been crying for way too long.

This wasn't meant to be a fucked up fairy tale.

Well, it is.

I love him so much.

He doesn't appreciate it.

I don't know what to do.

Yes, you do.

Should I leave?

Hell no.

Milan wrestled in the sheets as she turned back toward the double door entrance and saw Kendu, standing there, just arriving from California with his suitcase in hand and his tired eyes locked into hers.

She quickly wiped away the tears that continued to escape down her cheeks. *Breathe.*

"We need to talk." He sat his suitcase on the floor.

"Why?" she answered. "I don't have shit to say to you."

"Then you need to listen. Now, I love you and I'm sorry that I lied to you about what I was really doing in LA—"

"Oh, so now you want to confess the truth?"

He ignored her comment and continued, "There was no convention—"

"I would've never guessed."

"And I actually spent the night in West Hollywood—"

"Hollywood?" She felt an invisible fist shoot through her chest. "So you got a famous bitch in addition to the side slore who was at my door? I should slice your fuckin' throat."

"I went out there because I was given an opportunity to

start my own sports network. I wanted to actually purchase it and surprise you with it before I told you. That's why I lied to you. But that other shit about some chick and some baby, I don't know what you're talking about."

"You expect me to believe that?"

"Here's what I expect: for you not to ever lose your damn mind again, run up on me, and show your ass like that in public!"

"Excuse you?"

"I don't know what is wrong with you! But you'd better get it together."

"You can't be serious." Milan hopped out of bed, feeling like she was in Oz. Did he think he was going to waltz in here and she was going to care that she embarrassed him? This motherfucker was crazy. Had to be. "You have lost your mind! Do you really think you're going to apologize and then put this shit on me? You're the one fuckin' bitches, making babies, lying about where you've been. You ain't shit!"

"What baby?! I don't have another damn baby and the only one I'm fuckin' is you!"

"Oh, puhlease! So the whore who was at the Met Gala, the *same* bitch who followed me and the nanny through the park, and the *same* bitch who showed up at our doorstep is what? A figment of my imagination? Spare me. I know and you know that you're a cheatin' motherfucker—"

"I never cheated on you. I *cheated with* you!"

"Whatever. That has nothing to do with that bitch coming to my door telling me how she thought you would've told me about the two of you—" .

"What?!"

More tears filled Milan's eyes and streamed down her cheeks. She quickly flung them away. "That damn baby looked just like you!" She pointed into his face.

Kendu shook his head and said more to himself than to Milan, "I'm going to find this bitch and when I do, she's dead."

"How would you know where to find her if you don't

know who I'm talking about? You need to work on telling better lies!"

"What's the bitch's name?" he pressed.

"What? You know her damn name! Don't play dumb!"

"I promise you, if I knew her name and I knew who she was, I would be leaving here right now, going to find her and fucking her up!"

"Whatever!"

"What the fuck is her name!" He clenched his jaw.

"You tell me; you're the one sleeping with the bitch!"

"Do you even know her name?!"

"I don't have to know her name to know you're her baby's daddy!"

"I have two babies: Aiyanna and KJ."

"That baby looked exactly like you!"

"Did she tell you that was my motherfuckin' baby?!" The veins in his neck stood out and his eyes bulged. "Answer me!"

"She didn't have to say that! I know what the fuck you look like and I know what that damn baby looked like. White chicks are not just floating down the street with black babies unless there's a black daddy attached to their asses! I'm sick of your shit! I've been putting up with it since I was eight and I've had enough!"

"Then maybe you need a damn change! Because I'm tired too. You're accusing me of something I didn't even do behind some bitch I don't even know!"

"You know who she is!"

"I just told you that I didn't!" Kendu walked up so close to Milan that she was forced to take steps backward, stopping when her head hit the wall. "You just let some random chick and her baby come up to you, call my name, and instead of you cussing her out and telling her to get the fuck away from here, you take a plane to come see me and ruin what the fuck we got?!"

"I handled her! And that's right. I got my ass on the plane because I had to handle you!"

"Let me tell you something, Milan. I love you. I would die for you. But I will divorce your ass."

"What?" Milan gasped. She expected to curse him, dig her way to his core and force him to feel the ache she'd been rocking in her chest since she laid eyes on that trick and that baby, but him threatening to divorce her was never on the agenda. If anything, that was her damn line. Yet, here they stood, locked in an intense stare that felt more like a test of their hearts than of their wills.

Milan sucked in a deep and painful breath, not knowing how she would force it to come out—would she bellow it out of her mouth or would she hold it and pass out? Her marriage flashed before her eyes. More tears slipped out. She wanted to believe him. She needed to believe. But her mind held on to the possibility that none of this was true. Her heart pounded.

She searched for words.

Nothing.

He wiped the stream of tears that covered her cheeks and for a moment they stood in toxic peace.

"I love you," Kendu whispered, breaking the silence. "But I have to know that you trust me. I have to know that my wife will not believe anyone else over me—"

"Knott." She called him by the childhood nickname she'd given him.

"I have to know that, Milan. Otherwise we don't have anything."

"But the cheating—"

"Have I ever cheated on you, Milan? Ever?"

Silence.

He continued, "And, yeah, I had a wife before you, but I was always in love with you—"

"Do you think I liked always being on the fuckin' side?" She pushed him on the shoulder.

"I didn't force that on you! You agreed to it. You played your damn position and that's what the hell you need to do now. Play your damn position as my wife and stop acting like some insecure side jawn."

"Fuck you!"

Kendu looked Milan over and said, "Fuck me? Is that how you really feel? So we're done here? This is it?"

Fix it. Suppose he's telling the truth.

Suppose he isn't.

"Knott, I just—"

"Milan, I don't want anybody else but you. You gotta know that. I love you. You and my kids are my world. I need you to believe that."

Trust him.

I can't.

Fix it.

"Knott, I just . . . I just . . . felt like I was losing everything."

"I would never do anything to intentionally hurt you." Kendu pressed his forehead into hers, softly kissing her on the lips. "I've never loved anyone the way that I love you."

She kissed him back, slipping her tongue into his heated mouth.

"I'm sorry, Milan. I won't lie to you again." He lifted her up and laid her on the bed. "But you gotta know I would never cheat on you."

I don't know that.

But I want to know that.

Stop thinking.

Milan watched the moonlight slip between the eyes of the electronic miniblinds as Kendu undressed. His beautiful body, highlighted by protruding muscles, deliciously suckable pecks, and a dick so pretty that she grew a new appreciation and admiration every time she saw it. She ran her hands over her nipples and squeezed.

Kendu lifted her gown over her head, pushed her breasts together, and latched on to her chocolate nipples. He gave them one last kiss and pinch before he made his way down to the center of her belly, arriving at her shaved middle, slowly parting it, easing his tongue into it, and tasting her pussy—made butterscotch one tongue stroke at a time.

Milan felt her volcanic mountain preparing to erupt. She opened her eyes and swore she was in heaven. She had to be. Because the ecstasy that cocooned her body and caused her to thrust uncontrollably against Kendu's mouth couldn't have come from any other place.

"I want you to rub it on my face." Kendu lay on the bed and Milan sat on his face. He dipped his fingers and tongue back into her wetness. Sucking her erotic lips into his mouth, squeezing her clit, and licking the sides of it. Her thighs shook, her pussy pumped, and sweet milk escaped from between her pink lips into his mouth and oozed onto his chin.

"Every time that I'm with you, that I feel you, that I taste you, I know that I'm home," Kendu said, as he pulled Milan's ass onto his shaft. She arched her back and held her head down and he spoke with every thrust and pound of his never-ending inches. "And don't you ever let anybody"—he yanked her hair—"ever fuck that up."

CHAPTER 24

CHAUNCI

Two Days Later . . .

In the year they'd been a couple, no moment between them had ever been this quiet.

Their times together were always chock-full of endless conversations. Laughter. Talks of their respective daughters. Reminiscing about the sweetness of yesterday and anticipating the promise of tomorrow. Their lovemaking had been filled with the sounds of yanking hair, ass clapping, shaft slapping, and pounding, until their bodies cried out in shivering screams of "I love you," and panting whispers of "Jesus. . . ."

Now they sat in silence beneath the morning sun, in the center of a grassy Manhattan fork in the road known as Bryant Park, at a small bistro table, with the camera hovering over them. Chaunci looked to her left and Emory looked to his right, both watching the dance of New York City traffic.

"I can't do this," Emory said, and then turned to face Chaunci, who slowly turned her head toward him. She looked down and then locked into his stare. "It's too much," he said.

"What's too much?"

"This." He stretched his arms out to each side and then brought them together with a clap of the hands. "We're always on display. Always. We're sitting in the middle of a public park, for Christ's sake, and for what? Because this is where your producer told you to be? Will we ever get a private moment to discuss how fucked up our relationship has become? Or is this it? Our problems are made-for-TV drama. I'm so sick of this shit!"

"What do you want me to do?"

"I want you to quit!"

"I can't do that!"

"Well, then I can't do this!" He pounded his fist into the table. "You can't ever do anything I ask you to. Who disappears for four days straight without a word to her man? Had I done that, you'd be finished with me. But you, you have yet to explain where you were! And on top of that, the last time I saw you, you left me standing in the middle of the street!"

"You were making a scene. Like you are now. And you need to lower your voice and talk to me like I'm sitting in your face and not a block from you."

"Where were you, Chaunci?"

"I told you! I was in France. My God, will you let it go?! How long are you going to focus on me being gone? I'm back now; can we deal with that?!"

"You are selfish as hell."

"I resent that."

"Join the club."

"Emory, listen. I'm sorry that I left without saying anything to you, but I had to. I felt overwhelmed and crowded. And I just . . . I just needed to get away."

"So, I'm crowding and overwhelming? That's what you're saying to me?"

"That's not what I'm saying—"

"Then what are you saying? Because the way I'm feeling right now, there'll be no wedding."

"What?" Chaunci said. "So you're calling the wedding off? Are you serious?"

"As serious as you were when you left me for four days without so much as a damned text message."

Chaunci pushed an index finger into her left temple. "Didn't I just apologize for that?! Would you get the hell over it? Damn! Do you understand that I've lost my company! That Grant Preston has stolen it from me!" Tears welled in her eyes. "I worked my ass off to go from a struggling writer, to one magazine, to ten different magazines, to being a publishing machine. Morgan Enterprises was my dream! And he just comes along and takes it from me, and is now sitting in my office running my company. And you're supposed to be my future husband and instead of you asking me how I feel, you'd rather argue about bullshit!"

"So now my feelings are bullshit?"

"I never said that."

"That's exactly what you said. And as far as your company, of course I know about it, but not because you told me—I read it in the paper. All you've done lately is shut me out! You don't talk to me. You don't confide in me anymore. Your goddamn lawyer knows more about you than I do. Hell, are you fuckin' him?"

"Don't be ridiculous!"

"I'm not being ridiculous. Here I was calling hospitals, calling your assistant, a thousand times a day, and nothing. And where were you? In France. Working on not being overwhelmed!"

"How many times do I have to apologize? Damn it! Okay, I left town. I didn't call you. I'm sorry. But. Please. Let. It. Go."

"It's not about you leaving town; it's about you being inconsiderate of me! If you're going through something you should've talked to me!"

"Every time I tried to talk to you, you would say shit like, 'That's business. Put your big girl panties on and deal with it.' I don't want to hear that shit!"

"No, you don't want to hear the truth. You think my business doesn't have its ups and downs?"

"A hundred-thousand-dollar cleaning business funded by a bank does not compare to a multimillion-dollar publishing empire financed by shareholders. I am not giving presentations while holding a dustpan and a broom in my boardroom."

Emory hesitated and Chaunci knew by the look in his eyes that she'd shot an invisible round of bullets into him.

She sighed. "I'm sorry. I shouldn't have said that. But, Emory, listen . . . I'm scared." She let the tears glistening in her eyes fall. "I'm scared as hell. And I'm taking it out on the wrong people. I feel like I don't know what to do. I know that what I did to you wasn't right, but I can't undo it. I can only ask you to please forgive me because I love you and I need you."

Silence. Emory looked to be in deep thought as his eyes bounced around the park and his fingers danced an accordion on the table. He looked at Chaunci and stared through her.

"Would you say something?"

"I don't know what to say."

"Say you forgive me. Say you love me. Say you'll be here for me. I need you more now than I ever have."

He stared back into the space. "You have to stop pushing me away." He brought his eyes to meet hers. "You know that I'm here for you." He wiped her tears. "But as much as you need me, I need you to talk to me. You don't have to keep everything so bottled up."

"I love you." She stood up and walked over to him.

He stood up and pulled her into his embrace. "I love you, too."

CHAPTER 25

BRIDGET

After being here for close to two hours waiting for a cast that had yet to arrive or even call, I was exasperated. I looked around the empty dining room before turning to my camera crew, who were all set up and ready to record the cast's swanky, private lunch at Per Se, the most fabulous French establishment in all of New York City, and said, "These whores. Wear. Me. Out!" I took a deep breath and slowly released it through my nose. "But I refuse to let these bimbos make me sweat. I will keep cool. Remain calm and—" I spun on my heels and turned toward the door, observing Vera and Jaise chatting feverishly as they sashayed in.

"WHERE THE HELL HAVE YOU BEEN?!"

Vera and Jaise both stopped in their tracks. Looked at each other and then over to me. "Bridget, let me just add you to my list of who I'll be getting straight today," Vera said, then placed her clutch on the oblong, white-linen-covered table. "Don't you ever in your damn life speak to me like that again. And I mean *ever* again. When I walk into the room you are to greet me with a 'good morning,' a 'good afternoon,' or a head nod."

"My, my." I grinned impishly. "Who pissed in your stiletto?" I clutched invisible pearls.

"Well, damn." Journee sauntered in, her pale peach, chiffon minidress flowing with the sway of her stride. "Looks like I arrived on time."

Jaise rolled her eyes and mumbled to Vera, "Grab your purse; the ghetto tramp just walked in."

"Journee, dear," I greeted her. "I don't believe you've met Vera. You do know Jaise, don't you?"

Journee cut her eyes at Jaise while turning to Vera and smiling. "It's a pleasure to finally meet you."

"You as well," Vera said. "I've heard a lot about you."

"Well, whatever you heard"—Journee shot a look at Jaise—"it's not true. I'm much worse."

Vera snickered and Jaise looked her over from head to toe. "Umm, excuse me," Jaise said. "We don't entertain wild beast."

I turned and gave Carl the signal to zoom in.

Journee placed her purse on the table. "See, Jaise, I was going to be gracious and give you a pass."

Sure you were.

"But you insist on fucking with me."

Because that's what she does. She fucks with everybody and then sings "Kumbaya."

Journee carried on. "Now don't make me step out of my Jimmy Choos—"

"You know what," Vera interjected, "I don't think you need to do that. Because if you do, I'll have to get involved and I am not in the mood. I didn't wear the right shoes. This is a limited edition Chanel dress. We just met. And you seem to be the kind of chick I would like."

"I respect you and Jaise being friends," Journee said, "but if you get into it, I'll just have to open two cans of whoop ass instead of one. Now you seem like I might like you too, but your girlfriend is a whole other story."

"Look," Vera said, "I know Jaise can get out of pocket."

"Excuse you." Jaise batted her mink lashes.

"And bourgeois," Vera carried on.

"You call it bourgeois. I call it manners and speaking correctly, not butchering the English language with truckloads of 'ain'ts,' 'motherfuckers,' and 'bitches.' "

Vera took her right thumb and index finger and made the signal for Jaise to zip it. "Didn't we discuss you being quiet sometimes and listening to what other people had to say?" She mumbled, "I got this." Vera turned back to Journee and pointed at Jaise. "Now that bitch is mouthy, but that's my damn girl, and unless we're going to get this party started by kicking each other's asses, then I think we should all take a step back, have a seat, and start over."

"Excuse you, Oprah," I said to Vera, as they silently agreed and took their seats. "But this is reality TV and if Gayle needs to get her ass kicked, don't you dare stop it. Now, let's just move on because I feel my blood boiling and I will not let you three get under my skin. Besides, I need to show you all something before Milan walks in." I pulled an article out of my briefcase and handed each of them a copy. "Read that."

They each read the two-page article intensely.

"Oh no, this bitch-ass whore didn't!" Jaise said, slapping the article on the table. "Milan has lost her damn mind. This interviewer should've kicked her ass! I ain't never seen no shit like this! Oh, this cannot go to print!" She snapped her fingers. "Someone get the editor in chief on the phone."

"Wow, Jaise. For someone who doesn't believe in butchering the English language, you certainly just slaughtered it." I laughed. "And besides, they're running this baby next month. Just be thankful we got an advance copy of it."

Jaise carried on. "How can this bitch say *I* don't know how to keep a man and class *me* as an angry black woman?! I am far from angry! And for her information my husband is home with me. How's that for angry! How dare Milan say that I'm angry! Have you seen her viral YouTube video where she cussed King Cheatin' Ass out for whoring around?!" She looked at Journee. "You hit that damn nail on the head!"

"I sure did. And don't even get me started on how I woke up to a series of text messages from him this morning."

Vera's mouth flew open. "Are you serious?"

Jaise turned to Vera. "I meant to tell you that hozilla said that . . . I mean our new good girlfriend, Journee, told me that she and Kendu did a little bust-bust back in the day and that she whipped it on him so bad he continues to call and text her years later."

"That's not exactly what I said," Journee chimed in.

"It's the same point." Jaise shook her head. "And me angry? How dare that bitch say that about me when every hashtag on Twitter is 'Whitetape yo' ass!' And this tramp wants to insult me?"

"She cussed out every black woman in the world," Vera said. "Not just you, Jaise. She talked about me and Journee too! This is a mess!"

"And I told Milan to keep my damn name out of her mouth," Journee added.

"Somebody's looking for me?" Milan stepped into the room.

Thank you, Jesus, for perfect timing.

"Hey, girls!" Milan air-kissed them all before taking a seat at the table and picking up the menu.

"Milan."

"Yes, Jaise."

"I'm trying to think of a way to say this."

Milan placed the menu on the table. "Say what?"

"That it's come to our attention that you've been—"

"Why the hell were you talking shit about us in your *Sister2Sister* interview?!" Vera pounded on the table, shaking the silverware.

Milan looked completely caught off guard. "Because it was my interview," she retorted as she looked over at the waitress who walked toward the table.

"Good evening, I'm Tara. And I'll be your server. May I start you off with a bottle of Romanée–Conti?"

"Yes, Tara," Milan said. "That would be great."

Vera slid her earrings off and placed them on the table. "I don't think I heard you correctly, Milan. Now what did you say?"

"I said it was my interview. Now you either accept what I said or you don't. But those are my views. Period."

"*Guuuuurrrrrl,* I will elbow slap the shit out of you!"

"Oh my, look at what a weekend in jail teaches you," Jaise remarked.

Journee smirked. "Chile, Vera, that's too much work. I got a thirty-two that will end this real quick."

Milan blinked and wagged an index finger. "You three bitches are trippin'. All of this because I told the truth? This just further proves that you three are a squad of angry bitches who add to the population of fucked up people, and if you think I'm going to sit here and let you all gang up on me, you are sadly mistaken. Now either we speak civilly and eat or I'll leave." She pushed her chair back.

"There's no reason for you to leave, Milan," Jaise said. "You need to suck it up and apologize. Then we can all have some wine." She pointed to the server, who set the wine on the table and filled their glasses.

"Milan," Vera called, "don't let Jaise steer you wrong. I advise you to tuck your clutch back beneath your arm. Because if you keep sitting there, you will have a problem called knocked the fuck out."

"Vera!" Jaise said sternly. "Listen, Milan, all we're simply saying is that you cannot say whatever you feel like saying about people. You really need to find yourself a filter because your mouth is disgusting. And you're a young lady and that is really not attractive." She sipped her wine.

"Is this what you invited me here for, Bridget?" Milan asked. "So they could gang up on me? Really? You already know I don't do messy hos!"

"Journee"—Vera looked to her left—"do you have any Vaseline?"

"No. But as long as there's a wine bottle on the table and a loaded thirty-two in my bag, we got this."

"Ladies, please," Jaise stressed. "All they're saying, Milan, is that instead of being concerned about what the three of us are doing and calling us angry, you should hone in on your husband. Who keeps calling Journee and inviting her for sex? She's not about that ho-ass life anymore, but apparently your husband is!"

Milan quickly glanced at the camera and then back to the other women. "Y'all bitches stay trying me. You all created that lie because you're mad about the interview I did. Stick to the facts."

"The facts?" Vera said. "The facts are here in black and white. You talk too damn much. The facts are also in that damn YouTube video of you spinning out of control because your husband is out fucking some trick!"

"And for the record, Milan," Journee said, "no one needs to lie on your husband. Trust me, we've both seen that tiny black mole that sits on the left side of his head and you know what head I'm talking about!"

"Fuck you!" Milan stood up and Journee and Vera both hopped out of their seats.

Vera looked at Journee. "I thought I was the only one who didn't do well when slick-talkin' bitches start standing up."

"Hell no!" Journee said, giving Vera a high five.

"My, my, look at these hood heifers here . . . bonding." Jaise twisted her lips.

Milan rolled her eyes. "See, this is why Chaunci said she wasn't coming here today, and this is why my husband told me that I needed to stay home. Because you birds are nothing but drama, and since I don't do drama, violence, or negative energy, I'm going to excuse myself."

"Guilty hos love to run." Journee popped her lips.

Milan stormed out the door and down the hall as Jaise sipped more wine. "Now that was not right, what y'all just did."

"Jaise." Vera sat down and picked up the menu. "Order you something to eat and shut the fuck up."

CHAPTER 26

JAISE

The next morning

They'd made love every chance they got—little sleep and even less to eat—and Jaise couldn't believe that Bilal didn't seem to notice the ten pounds she'd gained since they'd been separated.

She thought for sure when he insisted that they make love with the lights on, so that he could see and enjoy every minute of her, that he would notice the extra jiggle in her belly or meat between her thighs. But he didn't. Instead, he made love to her the way he always had. Slow. Deliberate. Passionate.

"I love you so much," Jaise said to Bilal as she watched him sleeping. She kissed his lips softly. Moved to his chin. His neck. His chest.

"Don't stop there," he said, eyes still closed.

"You are so nasty." Jaise let her tongue trail down his belly to his erotic sweetness where she took him into her mouth inch by inch. Licking. Sucking. Bouncing the head on and off her tongue as he softly gripped her hair and moaned, "Damn, baby."

Thanks for the compliment. Her tongue glazed his scrotum before she deep throated him until she felt him shiver and creamy salt filled the space between her welcoming jaws.

An hour later, Jaise lay with her head upon Bilal's chest. Stroking his chest hairs, she said, "I'm so happy you're home. I feel so complete."

"I'm happy to be here too, baby." He ran his fingers through her hair. "And I want it to stay that way, which is why you can't get off track."

"Off track?"

"With what we agreed to."

Here he goes with this shit.

"Agreed to what?"

"Jabril has to leave."

Jaise sat up straight and looked Bilal in the eyes.

He sat up beside her. "I know it's hard."

Hell yeah, it's hard. That's my damn baby and I don't think he's ready to be on his own. "He's my son. I can't just toss him out in the street."

"Look, it may sound cold, but you will need to give Jabril two weeks. And that's it. Or I will leave."

What? "What?"

"You have coddled him long enough and it's time for him to get his act together. Or else you will forever be raising a grown-ass little boy. I know you were seventeen when you had him and you did the best you could, but if you don't make a change now, he will always be in and out of your house. You'll always be paying his child support—"

"He'll have his trust in five years."

"Jaise, you and I both know you're not balling like Bill Gates. You're talking a trust worth what? Two, three million?"

"Five."

"And he will blow through every dime of it because he doesn't have any skills and doesn't know how to make it on his own. You won't always be here to catch him, Jaise. Teach him how to be a man *now* by making him do it on his own. So that when he gets his trust, he will appreciate it and keep it."

"Bilal—"

"Look, ultimately the choice is yours, but know this: If I leave again, I'm done. That's it."

Jaise knew by the look in Bilal's eyes and the tone in his voice that he was serious. And if he left again, he would never come back. She couldn't risk that.

Besides, he was right. The only way Jabril would ever change his life would be if she made him stand on his own.

"Hopefully, he'll be here today so that I can talk to him. He hasn't been home in a few days and he doesn't even know you're back—"

Bilal shook his head. "He's been gone for a few days? Jaise, he doesn't have any respect for you or your house rules. He thinks he can come and go whenever he chooses to. It doesn't work like that and you need to let him know that too—"

"I heard you," she said with a little more aggravation than she intended to. "I get it. And I will handle it."

"When?"

"Right after this." She straddled him.

Jaise stood at the stove cooking apple pancakes, maple bacon, and fried eggs. Jabril's favorite meal.

"Ma, that smells *sooooo* good!" Jabril said, slamming the back door and kissing her on the cheek.

"Boy, where have you been?"

He smiled and took a seat at the table. "I was over at this li'l chick's spot for a minute." He grinned.

Jaise frowned. "Little chick's spot? There you go again with these food-stamp hos! I just don't understand why you are sooo addicted to ratchet. It's like these bitches have sunshine tucked away in the lining of their pussies or something."

"Ma!" Jabril smirked as Jaise sat his plate in front of him.

"Don't 'Ma' me, Jabril. I just don't know where I went wrong. Instead of dicking down some street whore, you should've been looking for a job."

"Here we go with this again." He rolled his eyes and stuffed a few pieces of pancake in his mouth.

"Don't you think you need a job?" Jaise said.

"I'm looking for one!" he said with a full mouth.

"Looking where, Jabril? In some ratty asshole? Your dick doesn't need any more employment!"

"I just said I was looking for one! Dang! Why you sweatin' me so hard?!"

"Because I'm tired of taking care of your ass! You are a man! Not a child! And I've been babying you too damn long! When are you going to grow up? I could halfway understand it if you at least had a job and took care of your kids. Maybe went back to college or something, but you don't even want to do that!"

"If you would give me my trust, you wouldn't have to worry about taking care of me!"

"I'll be damned if I give you your trust so you can trick off on some project hood ho! Hell no! Never. And the longer it takes you to get your ass together, the more I'll push back that damn age for you to receive it! Now you have two weeks to get you a job so that you can pay your rent."

"Rent?" He looked confused. "You're charging me to live here now? Oh, that's how you doin' me?"

"No, baby, I would never do that. You'll be paying rent at your own place. The one you're going to get in two weeks when you leave here."

"What?"

Jaise sat down next to him. "Brilly-boo, you know that Mommy loves you dearly."

He eyed her suspiciously. "Yeah. And you just said I wasn't a kid, so stop calling me Brilly-boo and just say what you gotta say."

"Look, I'm just trying to tell you in the best way that I can that you have to move."

"Move? And where am I s'pose to go?"

"I don't know. All I know is that it's been six months, when it was only supposed to be a few weeks. You haven't found a job yet—"

"The economy—"

"Don't give me shit about the economy. Walmart is hiring every goddamn day!"

"Like they pay enough to live!"

"You will have to figure that out. Because as of this moment, I will not be paying your child support anymore and I'm not going to be taking care of you. It's time for you to make it on your own."

"Yo', I don't believe this."

"Jabril, I'm tired. Nothing I say matters. You come and go as you please. And don't think I didn't see you sneaking some skank out of here the other morning, because I did. And I'm tired of it. I want more for you than this. I want you to have a great job, be able to survive on your own, take care of your own children—"

"And you think I'm supposed to be able to do this in two weeks?! Really, Ma? Really?"

"Are those apple pancakes, baby? I can smell them all the way upstairs," Bilal said as he stepped into the kitchen in his gray pinstriped boxers and bare chest. Immediately he locked into Jabril's stare and then into Jaise's. He looked back to Jabril. "I didn't know you were home, Jabril. Or I would've come down here with some clothes on." He mustered up a smile. "It's been a long time. Good to see you."

Jabril ignored him and looked up at Jaise. "So this niggah's home now and suddenly I gotta go. You choosing this niggah over me?" He stood up. "This niggah is more important than your own son!"

"I never said that!"

"You didn't have to!"

"Jabril, you're grown!"

"I've been grown, but now that he's back, it's a problem with my grown ass staying here! I should've known you would do some shit like this! You don't give a damn about me—"

"Yo', you don't speak to your mother like that!"

"Fuck you!"

"Jabril!" Jaise screamed.

"Man, fuck both of y'all!" Jabril muttered.

WHAP! Jaise backhanded Jabril so hard that his face flung to the left and seemed to get stuck there. Fire filled his eyes as he looked at Jaise. "You ain't never cared nothing about me! Everything's about this niggah! He don't give a damn about you! You want me out of here so he can lay up here and fuck you in peace. Then, cool, I'm gone!" He charged toward the basement.

"Jabril!" Jaise followed behind him with Bilal on her heels. "Just calm down!"

"Calm down?" Bilal scowled. "Don't you dare let him speak to you like that! That's your damn mother, Jabril! Don't you ever speak to my wife like that!"

"Like I said, fuck your foul ass, Bilal! You want me to be like you! Got all up in my mother's head and got her kicking me out just so you can get your dick sucked in peace! You ain't—" Jabril started to gag as Bilal rushed him against the wall and pressed his elbow into his throat.

Jaise jumped.

Bilal commanded, "Don't you fuckin' move, Jaise." He turned back to Jabril, who was struggling to breathe. "You could never be like me. You're too busy wanting to be a street niggah and it's not an ounce of street in your punk ass. 'Cause if you knew any damn thing, you'd have you a fuckin' job and handle your damn business so your mama wouldn't have to throw your ass out!" He pressed harder.

"Bilal! Let him go!"

"Sit down." Bilal eyed her. "Jabril, you'd better get yo' punk ass together before you find yourself running up on the wrong motherfucker, 'cause if I was half the niggah that I used to be, you'd have one to the head already."

"Bilal!"

"Now your mother said two fuckin' weeks, but if you look at me wrong or say one goddamn thing crazy to her, I will throw your ass out immediately!" He released his hold.

Jabril grabbed his neck and struggled to catch his breath. A few seconds later, he tossed some of his things in a backpack.

"Jabril," Jaise said. "Just calm down. Let's talk this out!" She grabbed his arm and he snatched away.

"Let him go!" Bilal said sternly as Jabril took off for the stairs.

"Bilal, please, this is not how it was supposed to be! Jabril, just listen to me."

"I don't want to hear shit you have to say! I'm outta here!"

"Jabril!" Jaise cried. She turned to Bilal and as she went to speak, her words died in her mouth and tears poured from her eyes.

Bilal pulled her into his chest and wrapped his arms around her. "Listen to me. You have to let him go. It will make him a better man and one day he will thank you. I promise you, baby. I know it's tough, but it's love."

CHAPTER 27

CHAUNCI

Chaunci lay in her king-size bed next to a sleeping Emory, holding her engagement ring in the palm of her left hand and drifting into the memory of Emory dropping to one knee. . . .

Six months ago, he'd popped open a burgundy velvet box revealing a cluster of white diamonds designed to look like a single solitaire. She hated it. It screamed cheap, and struggling, and trying entirely too hard to be something you were not.

She'd told him a million times that she wanted to pick out the engagement ring with him, especially since she had to wear it; and she wanted a Tiffany ten-carat, emerald-cut, chocolate-diamond solitaire.

Yet, what he did and what he presented her with was the exact opposite. And the media dragged it, titling the ring "the ugliest thing they'd ever seen."

But not once did Chaunci complain. She smiled and encouraged Emory to ignore the media because it was in their fabric to be nasty. Besides, she knew it was all he could afford. After all, he was a blue collar Joe, who proudly ran his family's cleaning business. The same business his grandfather had run, and his father. The same business, he told Chaunci, that he wanted their future son to one day take over. But that would be over her dead body.

Chaunci bounced the ring in her palm. It felt extremely heavy—the clunky makeup of it and the weight of one day being Emory's wife. . . . Emory the son-in-law every mother wanted. A stand-up kind of guy who treated his mother well, admired his father, made an honest living, and was an honorable man with old-fashioned values. A man who played fair. Loved hard. And didn't care whether he was wealthy or not; he just wanted enough money to pay his bills, take care of his family, and put a little away for retirement.

A rare jewel of a man whom Chaunci knew she needed to have. Hell, she'd been engaged once before and this was her third relationship in two years. She needed to get herself together, because as her mother always said, "You're not getting any younger. And every woman needed more than one baby."

But this wasn't about babies.

This was about being turned on to the core. About desiring to have a man who dreamed big and fought hard to have those dreams manifested. She didn't need a man who played fair all the damn time. Shit, there was something sexy about a man who wore a hand-sewn Italian suit, two-thousand-dollar Gucci loafers, and would slice your damn throat if you got in the way of what he wanted.

She liked those kinds of boys.

Corporate thugs who rolled dice and wagered all or nothing. That turned her on.

Money. Arrogance. Assertiveness. And ferociousness made her cum.

Not the missionary position. Not dinner and a movie. And definitely not a clustered up bunch of thirteen flawed diamonds worth no more than three or four hundred dollars. Jesus.

But.

What she needed and what she wanted were two different things, and for once she needed to play it safe.

Chaunci slid her ring back on her finger, and as she turned over to plant a morning kiss on Emory's lips, the doorbell rang.

Emory stretched and cracked open his eyes. "You expecting company this early?"

"No. And I'm not due to record today. Someone's probably at the wrong door." Chaunci tossed the covers off and reached for her terry cloth robe. She slid it on and walked into the living room. She looked at her security camera and couldn't believe her eyes. "What in the hell?"

She opened the door.

"Consider this a rare favor because this will be my first and last time coming to get you out of bed."

"Excuse me?"

"You're supposed to be a businesswoman. A brand. But you've been curled up in the covers instead of handling the financial ruins of your company. Completely unacceptable. Most definitely a wage worker's mentality."

This motherfucker is crazy. Chaunci's eyes quickly raked over Grant, not once, but three times. He stood there in his light tan, hand-sewn Italian suit and Fendi loafers, looking at her as if she had two heads.

"Why are you here? And how do you know where I live? You stole my business and now you're stalking me?"

"Stalking you? Please, what a low level crime. As you can see, anywhere I want to be I step up and make my appearance known. I don't have time to lurk and strike. I make immediate moves. Now, it's been a week and you haven't been in the office at all. You haven't called to say you were working from home. That you were sick. Or even that you were taking some time off. Perhaps this is how you got into the hole you're in, and I have to tell you that this has to be the most unprofessional *shit* I've ever seen."

Chaunci stood at her apartment door completely bemused. "It's eight o'clock in the morning and the last thing I need is you at my door."

"That's exactly what you need, because apparently whoever is in your bed doesn't know how to push you out of it."

"Chaunci," Emory called, "who was that?" He walked into the living room and spotted Grant at the door. He walked over and Grant held out his hand. "Grant Preston."

Emory accepted Grant's gesture and then looked over at Chaunci. "Is this the same man who stole your company?"

"Should I take that as a good morning?" Grant asked, seemingly amused.

Emory and Chaunci ignored him. "Yes. This is the hostile takeover in the flesh."

"What the hell are you doing here?!" Emory pointed into Grant's face. "You don't show up here and especially at this time of the morning!"

Grant smiled and it was obvious that he was doing everything in his power not to laugh. He looked at Chaunci and squinted. "Who is this guy—your accountant? No wonder your financial judgment has been a mess!"

Emory took a step into Grant's personal space. "Let me tell you something—"

Chaunci wedged in between them. "Emory, calm down. Please."

"He'd better take that damn smirk off his face before I wipe the floor with his ass."

"And we both know you're more than qualified to wipe a floor."

Emory pushed Chaunci to the side. She slid back in front of him. "Calm down."

"Look, you need to go," she said to Grant.

"Listen, if I was ever privileged to wake up next to such beauty, I'd want to defend my honor as well. However, while we're still in the business realm I need you to put on some clothes and get to the office today. Otherwise that one percent advantage I have over you allows me to fire you."

"And I'll sue your ass!"

"Then I guess we'll dance in court. But make sure you can afford to do that, because I have enough money that I will have you tangled up for years. So my advice to you is to gather your pride, slide on a power suit and stilettos, and bring your ass into the office this morning. By nine a.m."

I should slap his damn face. "Are you done?" she asked.

"No, the question is: Are you done? Have a good day, Emory." He turned on his heels and left them standing there, Emory with a clenched fist and Chaunci feeling a mix between pissed and intrigued.

"Ms. Morgan." Julie ran around the counter and greeted Chaunci. "I thought I'd never see you again. I'm so glad you're back!" She whispered, "None of us can stand Mr. Preston. Do this, Julie; copy that Julie. Julie, Julie, Julie! And then he wants you in the building at your desk at nine o'clock. Even on a Saturday. Demanding that the entire staff does mandatory overtime! He's turned this place into a third world sweat shop. He will not allow any of the other employees to come to my desk and tell me how their night was. And lunch! He's slaughtered it! Exactly an hour. Not one minute longer, and if you are late from lunch, he's such a bastard. He demands to know what type of time you're going to use. He wants no fraternizing, no personal calls on the office phone. And every time I turn around, he has more work for me to do. I have zero time to meditate. He's such an asshole!"

"Excuse me, Julie." Grant stepped outside his office door. "The next time you want to talk about how much of an asshole I am, you might want to be sure that your direct connect to my office isn't turned on."

Julie's face turned beet red as Grant looked over at Chaunci and said, "I need to see you." He turned around and walked into his office.

"Well, that will have to be after she sees me," drifted over Chaunci's shoulders.

She quickly turned around and immediately her knees felt like brittle branches. She could've sworn she saw a ghost.

"Ms. Morgan," Julie said. "Are you okay?"

"Yes," Chaunci hesitated. "I'm fine."

"Are you sure?"

"Yes."

"Okay, well, Mr. Dupree here has been to the office every day this week to see you. He says it's extremely important."

Xavier smiled and Chaunci gave him a nervous grin. She turned back to Julie and then looked up one side of the hallway and then the other. She no longer had an office, and at this moment she couldn't remember where her boardroom was.

"Ms. Morgan," Julie said, "I fixed you up a new office. Mr. Preston was such a bastard for what he did to you!"

"Julie!" Grant yelled through the intercom.

"Oh dear, he's like the Wizard. He's everywhere." She pointed. "Ms. Morgan, your new office is over there."

Chaunci followed the direction of Julie's finger and spotted her name on the door.

"Thank you, Jules." Chaunci nodded. "Mr. Dupree, will you follow me?"

"Sure will," Xavier said, and as he walked behind Chaunci, his eyes soaked in everything in his path.

"After you," Chaunci said, closing the door behind him.

Xavier walked in, sat down in the black leather wing chair, and propped his feet on the edge of Chaunci's desk.

She knocked them off. "What the fuck do you want?"

"Whoa, whoa, whoa. Why the hell do you have an attitude? I tell you, you and Journee are two of the most ungrateful motherfuckers I've ever seen. You two bitches have gone from strippin' hoes to living the life of Riley while my ass fought every day not to get shanked and wifed up in mess hall. And you have the nerve to be pissed with me? I'm sitting in prison for a crime we all committed and you two hos are on television, running companies, strip clubs, and are making lots and lots of money, while ten years of my life has been taken from me."

"What. Do. You. Want?"

"Well, a little 'hey, how are you?' would be nice."

"I don't give a damn how you are! All I care about is knowing what the hell you want."

"Not much."

"What's not much?"

He stroked his chin and his eyes scanned her office. "Well, seeing this nice ole office you got here, I'd say about ten million will do."

Chaunci lost her breath. "Ten million." She struggled to breathe. "You want ten million dollars to disappear?"

"Oh, you want me to disappear? Now that will cost you a little more. To never see my ass again, I'll be needing at least twenty million. Cash, of course."

Chaunci's heart stopped. Her life flashed before her. She could've sworn that the room had started to spin. She cleared her throat.

"I don't have twenty million to give you."

"Well, you'd better figure it out. Didn't I read somewhere that you went to college and got a damn degree? Use that motherfucker. Sell some pussy; get your ass back on the pole. Hell, you were good at that. You could always rob a bank, again. Do whatever you gotta do, but I want my money and soon!" He stood up. "Have a good day, Ms. Morgan." He walked out of her office and Chaunci knew for sure that she was due to have a nervous breakdown at any moment.

Get it together . . .

She picked up her phone and made a call. "I need you to meet me in half an hour at the Deck in midtown." *Click.*

She walked out of her office and spotted Grant giving Julie a pile of records to copy. "I need to see you," he repeated.

Silence.

Chaunci turned her back and looked over to Julie. "Send all my calls to Mr. Preston. I'm taking the rest of the afternoon off."

CHAPTER 28

JOURNEE

Journee slid her bumble bee Chanel's down the bridge of her nose and placed them on the table next to her glass of white wine. She looked over at Chaunci, who marched to the table, flopped down in the booth, and said, "What the fuck is Xavier doing out of prison!"

"Ask the parole board."

"You told me he had life!"

"I'm not the judge and jury! Shit. I wasn't there when he was sentenced. I thought he had life. I guess I was mistaken, because he's walking the damn streets, living in my damn house, and haunting me!"

"So you knew he was out?"

"Obviously."

"And you didn't think to tell me?"

"Bitch, I don't speak to you. Remember?"

"Look, your ex-boyfriend showed up at my office demanding twenty million dollars in cash! I don't have twenty million to give him!"

"Hell, he wants even more from me! He wants half of Zachary's fortune—"

"That is his father!"

"That's not my damn problem!"

"I don't believe this." Chaunci shook her head. "What the hell are we going to do?"

"We have to pay him."

"I don't have the money to pay him!"

"Then we'll have to kill him!"

"Oh, God!"

"Either that or we go to prison because this mother-fucker's set us up and sold the feds some craziness! You know his ass is mad and ruthless."

"We can't kill him." Chaunci shook her head.

"Then what are we going to do?"

"Pay his ass." Chaunci stood up. "I need to go."

"Where?"

"To get some damn money." She stormed out, practically knocking the waitress over on her way to the door.

Journee sat and sipped the rest of her wine. She fiddled with her cell phone before dialing a number. "Hey, I need you to arrange something for me."

CHAPTER 29

CHAUNCI

"You wanted to see me." Chaunci walked into Grant's office, placing her purse on the edge of his desk.

"I should fire you; you know that." He leaned back in his black leather chair.

"Please do, so that I can sue your ass. I could use the money. Now what do you want?"

"I'm not sure how to answer that. Should I start with the business and end with the personal?"

"Personal? And what would that be?"

"That I want you. I thought that would be obvious."

"Never. Now you may have bought this company, but my ass didn't come with it. Now. What. Is. It?"

"So let's start with business. We need to pull *Nubian Diva* from the stands."

"What?"

"We need to make it an online magazine only."

"Hell no."

"It's not making any money in print. All of the money is made from the sponsors on the electronic version."

"No."

"The cost to print the magazine far exceeds the profit. I

don't see any other way to turn this around. Also, *Morgan Financial* needs to become a quarterly magazine as opposed to a monthly one. And those book deals you were negotiating—off the table."

"What?"

"Oh, and we need to fire Julie."

Chaunci tapped the soles of her shoes on the carpet. "I tell you what—do whatever you want to do; obviously I don't have any power anymore." She sat back in her chair.

"I'm trying to include you."

"You're trying to include me in your hostile takeover of my company? Hilarious."

"Listen—"

"No, you listen. Just buy me out. I'll sell you my forty-nine percent and the entire company will be all yours."

"And why would I want to buy you out?"

"Because we will never be able to work together. I can guarantee you that I will be the nastiest bitch you've ever seen. So just buy my shares and let me walk away free and clear."

"You got it." Grant pulled twenty dollars from his wallet and slapped it on his desk. "There you go."

Chaunci was stunned. "Are you crazy? Twenty dollars? What are you trying to do, insult my intelligence?"

"You're trying to insult mine. You tore this damn company up making piss poor decisions. Perhaps instead of being on a reality show, you should've been present in your reality and dealing with your company. Now you want me to buy you out. So here you go." He stabbed an index finger into the money. "Take the twenty dollars and leave."

"It's taking everything in me not to haul off and slap the shit out of you."

"Aggressive. I like that." He smiled. "So does that mean you'd want your hair pulled when I hit it from the back?"

"Fuck you!"

"That's what I'm trying to do. That's the point of it all.

Now if you seriously want me to buy you out, then you and I could go away for a night, have the time of our lives, and who knows, by the end of the night, let's see what we can arrange."

"So you think I'm a whore? That's what you think this is?"

"A whore?" He frowned. "A whore is a lowlife with low standards and absolutely no money."

Chaunci walked over to Grant and sat on his lap. She stroked his face and kissed him lightly on the lips. "You are fine as hell. I'll give you that. And this package that I'm sitting on seems to defy the white boy myth, that's for sure. But you will never ever hit this from the back or otherwise." She stood up. "Good day, Mr. Preston." She walked out of his office and quickly doubled back. "And, no, you cannot fire Julie!"

CHAPTER 30

BRIDGET

A Month Later

"The exclusive club Noir Amour was filled wall to wall with A-list celebrities, athletes, a multitude of reporters, bloggers, and of course, *Millionaire Wives Club* cameras were there to capture the night.

"Ladies." I walked over to Jaise, Vera, and Rowanda. "I have to say, I'm surprised you two came. Say something to the camera for me please. Let's start with you Rowanda." Carl zoomed in. Rowanda smiled and it was beyond obvious that she was not ready for prime time. "I'm just happy to be here." She nervously shifted her eyes. "This is a beautiful club and I think we're going to have a fabulous time tonight."

"And you, Vera?" I said.

Vera popped her lips and looked directly into the camera. "I only came because I'm contracted to be here." Vera cocked her neck to the right for emphasis.

"Well"—Jaise batted her lashes—"I'm here because I always try to be the bigger person."

Vera looked at Jaise in shock. "Bitch, swerve. You know you can't stand her."

"I can't stand her. And I absolutely think she's South Bronx ratchet. Hoodboogger. But we had to make an effort. You know Milan doesn't really have any friends."

"And after that nasty interview she did cursing out every black woman in America, she will never have any friends."

Jaise paused. "And where the hell is Chaunci? Did she or did she not sign the same contract that we did? And if so, why is she never around? And where is Journee? What kind of games are you playing this season, Bridget?"

"Don't worry about them." Vera waved her hand. "We have fulfilled our contractual obligation and now we gon' eat, drink some of this liquor, and go home with a buzz."

"Shhh . . . everyone, here they come!" The host spoke softly into the microphone. "Someone hit the lights."

"Surprise!" The crowd yelled as Kendu took a quick step out of the door and then reentered, obviously caught off guard but happily surprised.

"Happy birthday, baby. Tonight is all about you," Milan said as she hugged Kendu tightly before holding his hand and walking him to the center of the dance floor.

The host handed Milan the microphone. She turned and looked at Kendu. "I would like to wish you, my best friend, my lover, my husband, my everything, a wonderful birthday! I know you don't like surprises and you've never wanted a party, but I feel you deserved one! You're the best, baby, and there's nothing I wouldn't do for you. And absolutely nothing I would trade you for."

"I love you, too," Kendu said as he took the microphone from Milan's hand. "This is . . . this is such a surprise. She got me. I thought we were coming here for an intimate dinner." He laughed. "I just wanna take this moment to thank my wife. The love of my life. She's been there when I didn't have nobody and was moving from foster home to foster home. Most of you know I was a foster child until the age of ten. Which is why I never thought my birthday was a big deal. Until now. Which is why I'ma end this with saying, let's turn up!"

"I have to go." Rowanda looked at Vera, her eyes gleaming with tears.

"You have to go? What do you mean you have to go? What's wrong?" Vera looked confused. "Tell me."

"Nothing. I just need to get out of here. I can't breathe."

CHAPTER 31

CHAUNCI

"I know what you're thinking," Emory said, looking at Chaunci's reflection as she sat at her vanity mirror and brushed foundation onto her face.

Don't try and read my mind.

He continued, "I don't have anything against your friends. You already know Kendu is my boy, but I just don't want to be bothered with those cameras. I just can't with reality TV."

"You told me that already."

"I've had enough of those cameras in my face and in my life."

"You've said that too."

"I've had enough of people stopping me on the street. I'm tired of media saying and printing shit about me—none of it true—and on top of that, the publicity does nothing for my business."

"I get it, Emory. You don't have to keep explaining."

"I just want you to understand."

Chaunci lifted her eyes from her foundation compact and looked at Emory's reflection. "I never expected you to come. So you don't have to keep explaining yourself. The surprise for me would've been you agreeing to be on screen."

"Thank you for being so understanding."

Chaunci turned and faced him. "Of course I understand." She kissed him. "And I'll call you when I get back in. You're going back home to your place, right?"

"Yeah, at least for tonight. I haven't been there in weeks." He tapped her on the behind. "Make sure everyone sees that ring and knows that you have a man."

Chaunci chuckled. "I will make sure everyone sees the ring."

"I love you."

"I love you, too. Now," She pointed to the massive gift in the corner of her dressing room. "Can you help me carry that downstairs to my car?"

"Of course." Emory picked up the wrapped box and cradled it in his arms. "Damn, baby, what's in the box?"

I have lost my mind. Chaunci unwrapped the gift and took out her overnight bag, tossing the happy birthday wrapping paper onto her backseat. She took one last peek at herself in the mirror before stepping out of her car and onto the private tarmac.

Just relax.

It's business.

"A share for your thoughts," Grant said as he walked out of the hanger and kissed Chaunci softly on the cheek.

Chaunci pursed her lips. "Funny."

Grant smiled as he reached for her bag and escorted her to his private jet.

Chaunci took her seat on a chocolate leather sofa. "Why couldn't we stay the night somewhere in the tri-state?"

Grant frowned. "The tri-state? I'm trying to impress you."

"Oh, you're trying to create ambiance?"

"Exactly. Can you allow me to do that? I'm on a mission here."

"And what mission is that?"

"To make you mine."

"So you think you should have me and my company. So you're hostile in everything that you do."

"Let me make this clear. At any given moment, you are free to leave. Just let me know and I'll tell the pilot to turn the plane around and take you home. Choice is yours."

Chaunci hated that his cockiness was a complete turn-on. "When I'm ready to leave, I'll be sure to let you know."

"Sounds like a plan to me." He handed her a glass of wine.

I have truly lost my mind. I've lied to my fiancé. I've lost my company to this man. And I'm sitting here with a wet pussy hoping that his slick tongue knows how to eat it and his dick is as big and aggressive as his actions.

"So . . ." Grant sat down next to Chaunci. "You want to do small talk first or would you like to start by telling me why you really want me to buy your share of the company?"

"You know why. We can't work together."

"You're a horrible liar."

"So then why don't you tell me why I want to sell you my part of the company?"

"Well, I know that it has nothing to do with you not being able to work with me. Because for the past month, we've managed."

"You wouldn't stop flirting with me. Everywhere I looked, you were in my way."

"I was trying to be in your way."

"You've succeeded. But you still haven't told me why I want to sell you my part of the company."

"Xavier Dupree, that's why."

Immediately, sweat bubbled on Chaunci's forehead. "What?"

"Come on, Chaunci. I know you need the money to pay him off."

"Who told you that?!"

"A man comes to see you every day for a week and he

might think that no one knows who he is, but I know exactly who he is—oil tycoon Zachary Dupree's troubled son. He was just paroled recently after committing a bank robbery ten years ago. He was the only one the police caught. One died and the other two—two women—both got away. I've seen the tapes and one of the women was about your height. Your size—"

"How did you see the tapes?"

"It was my father's bank."

Shit. "All you need to know is that I need to give him some money so he can get the fuck away from me. Period."

"And that's why you want to sell me your share of our company."

Our company . . . "Exactly."

"I'll take care of it."

His ease made Chaunci shift in her seat. "Why? Why would you want to do anything for me?"

"The real question is why can't you accept anything. I don't know about anyone else in your life, but I play for keeps. And two people I don't need getting in my way: your fiancé and some two-bit junkie-ass ticking time bomb."

"You just take care of the time bomb."

"And you take care of the fiancé."

No matter what, I'm not fucking him.

That was what Chaunci thought the moment she stepped off the plane at a small hangar on Pine Island, off the coast of Florida. Grant held her by the hand as they walked down the dock and stepped onto his snow-white yacht.

The yacht was breathtaking. Three decks overlooked the moonlit water. A double staircase seemed to rise out of the gleaming hardwood floor in the foyer, leading to the second floor where there was a massive master suite, a game room, movie theater, and a great room, all with panoramic views of the Atlantic ocean. "This place is beautiful," Chaunci said in amazement. "Absolutely breathtaking."

"Thank you." Grant held her around the waist. "It's a place I come to when I need to think."

"A sanctuary." She snuggled her back and behind deeper into his body.

"I guess you could call it that."

Grant held Chaunci's hand and led her to the upper deck to a white linen-covered table with orchids in the center. A chef stood behind a portable platinum dinner cart.

Grant held out Chaunci's chair and she took her seat.

"Before the night gets started, can you do something for me?" he asked.

"What's that?"

"Forget about everything in New York. Be present in this moment. Just for tonight, all that exists is you and me."

Chaunci hesitated. She looked into the distance and as the ship set sail, she looked down at her engagement ring.

Grant slipped it off. "Nothing else exists." He slipped the ring into his pocket.

"Only for this moment."

"That's all I need."

"This evening," the chef said, "I have prepared a dish of curry duck with a sauce made from okra and peppers."

"That sounds wonderful!" Chaunci smiled.

The chef served them their dinner and left. Before either of them could finish their meals, they'd talked about practically everything under the sun.

"You mean to tell me that you are really a Knicks fan?" Chaunci laughed. "Grant, you're far too intelligent for that."

"I'm a die-hard Knicks fan. Spike Lee has nothing on me. They are the best team in the league." He picked up a forkful of duck and ate it.

"What league? Geriatrics? They're all old, injured, and the last time they had any hope of a ring"—she popped her fingers—"was never."

"False. Remember twenty-twelve? Knicks versus Heat."
He sipped his wine.

"And why the hell are you so invested in the Knicks?"

"I own them."

"Figures," she retorted.

"What do you mean 'figures'? So are you one of these traders who switched up and became a diehard for Brooklyn?"

"No. I'm a Lakers girl." Chaunci ate a forkful of vegetables.

"Lakers? How did a New York girl become a cheerleader for the Lakers?"

"First of all, I'm originally from North Carolina."

"What part?"

"A small town called Murfreesboro."

"Ahh, east Carolina. A country girl." He smiled.

"You could say that."

"You get back there often?"

"No. But my family is still there. Now, let's talk about you and why you really insisted on having a date with me."

"I told you I was trying to impress you."

"Why?"

"The truth?"

"Always."

"Because the first time I saw you on TV, I had to have you. My assistant was sneaking and watching your show and I walked in. I thought you were the prettiest woman I'd ever seen. I had to know who you were."

"Oh, I get it now. You're an egotistical maniac whose rich boy way of courting is to play dirty by coming after my company and making me pay you some attention."

"What if I said you were right? Would it change the way you're feeling right now?"

Chaunci stared off into the distance and then brought her eyes to meet his. "No."

By the time they had finished dinner, they'd held a million

different conversations. All made both of them laugh, smile, and lose track of time.

"This was a beautiful date." Chaunci laid her head on Grant's chest as they sat on the deck, reclining on a sofa overlooking the water.

"It's just getting started."

"Is that so?" Chaunci stroked his rugged beard and ran a hand across his lips.

He kissed her fingertips and Chaunci looked intensely into his green eyes and kissed him, deeply. Passionately. She felt his hands easing up her thighs and she let them travel and wander into her pulsating middle, seducing her wetness to run its course.

He lifted her dress over her head and stared down at her body. "Damn, you're beautiful."

Chaunci unbuckled his pants, revealing his beautiful eleven inches. His dick was one of the prettiest she'd ever seen. The veins pulsating on the side of its mushroom-shaped head made her salivate.

Grant leaned in and kissed her, his sensual sucks going from her bottom lip to her chin, to her chocolate nipples, which he licked and kissed, pulled and popped between his lips. And as he sucked her right breast, he fingered her left one.

Chaunci's thighs nervously twitched as he moved down her stomach, kissing every inch of her skin, moving his mouth to envelope her clit. He French-kissed her slit, snaking his tongue in and out of it. Licking and lapping until all Chaunci could do was pant until he entered her.

He slid his hard and pulsating member into her wetness. Chaunci drew in a deep breath and then she hummed a sensual moan to accompany the sweet music of his scrotum slapping against her pussy lips.

He pounded. She pushed back. And their hips danced until she rolled on top of him with the ocean breeze blowing against her back.

CHAPTER 32

BRIDGET

I had to admit this A-list crowd was having a ball. They were posing for pictures and showing my cameras lots of love. There were even a few stars who asked me how they could be cast next season.

"Bridget," Milan slurred. "It's my husband's birthday and I'm having a ball!" She did a quick spin and just as she started to moonwalk, she moonwalked right into Emory.

Where the hell is Chaunci? I'm going to have to fire this trick. She is really pushing it!

"Hey, hey, hey, Emorrrrrreeee," Milan slurred. "I didn't even know you were behind me. Where's my girl?"

"What do you mean?" Emory arched a brow. "She's here."

"No, she's not." Milan did a spin. "I've been waiting for her to walk in, but she hasn't gotten here yet. She'll be here soon. Go have a drink. It's open bar."

Emory stared into space and looked back at Milan. "Are you sure she's not here?"

"I don't think so, but hell, maybe she is."

"When was the last time you spoke to her?"

"Emory"—Milan held up an index finger—"give me a

minute." She walked away from him and followed behind Kendu, who'd just stepped into the corner of the room with a familiar blonde.

"Let's go, Carl!" I shouted as Milan stormed over to Kendu, who looked to be enthralled in a conversation with the same woman Milan had attacked on the street.

"This bitch?!" Milan screamed. "I thought you didn't know her, Kendu!"

"Milan," Kendu said. "Listen, she just came up to me and asked if she could speak to me about my charity and I said yes."

"Speak to you about a charity!" the woman cried. "Kendu, why are you lying?! Please just tell the truth! I'm tired of being hidden and I'm tired of being alone!"

"I'll beat your ass!" Milan lunged, and immediately security stepped in.

"Goddamn you!" I screamed. "I just can't deal with you all traveling with me! You are completely ruining my fuckin' vibe! I haven't had a knock-down-drag-out all season!"

"Let me go!" Milan yelled, clawing over one of the security guard's shoulders. "How could you do this to me, Kendu?! This damn party wasn't a surprise to you! You invited this bitch here! How could you!"

"Milan, you need to calm down! I don't know her!" He gawked at the blonde. "Tell the goddamn truth before I choke the shit out of you! Tell her."

Tears streamed down the woman's face and her voice cracked. "Kendu, I can't lie anymore. I can't. I'm tired of you denying me and I'm tired of you denying our son!"

Kendu screamed, "I will—"

One of the security officers stepped in front of Kendu as the blonde ran off and Milan took off behind her. Some of the guests continued to party, but most were looking to see what was going on. By the time Milan made it onto the sidewalk, the woman had disappeared. "Where the hell did she go!?"

Milan screamed, as tears raced down her face. "I don't believe it. This motherfucker is a liar, a cheat! He ain't shit! As much as I stood by his side!"

"Milan," I called. "Can you please look into the camera and repeat everything you just said?"

She didn't respond. However, Jaise looked directly into the camera and said, "Mph, once a cheat, always a damn cheat."

"Really, Jaise." Bilal frowned.

"I'm just making a statement, Bilal. After all, when he was married to Evan he did the same exact bullshit!"

CHAPTER 33

JAISE

"Bilal, I thought you had the night off."

"I do."

"So, why is one of your officers standing on our stoop?" Jaise said as their driver held the door open for them and they stepped onto the sidewalk.

Bilal looked up at the officer and said, "That's Darnell. Something must've jumped off at the station."

"Well, I'll meet you upstairs because I can't wait another moment to get out of these Spanx."

"Hi, dear," Jaise said as she approached the stoop. "Would you like to come inside and speak with Bilal?"

"No, ma'am," the officer said. "I'll wait here for him."

"Darnell," Jaise heard Bilal say as she walked into the house, "what are you doing here?"

Jaise walked upstairs to her master floor and before she stepped into her dressing room she pulled her cell phone from her purse. While at the party Jabril had called her at least twenty times, but at Bilal's insistence, she didn't answer. Every time the phone rang he would say, "He needs to know you're serious."

Jaise quickly dialed Jabril's number and tapped a foot nervously. "Boy, would you come on here and answer this phone."

Jabril's phone rang four times before his voice mail picked up, and Jaise mumbled, "Damn it, boy. I know your ass is somewhere raw doggin' it with some fast-ass ho!"

Jabril's voice mail began its spiel: "This is Jabril. You already know what to do. But if this is a chick and you're calling because I didn't call you back, get a hint and hang the fuck up."

Beeeeeeep!

"Jabril," Jaise began her message, "this is Mommy and that message is ridiculous. Now I can't talk long and I'm not going to keep calling you back. I hope you still have your ATM card because I'm going to put five thousand dollars in your account tomorrow morning. I love you, son, and I miss you."

"Jaise."

She dropped the phone. "Oh, Bilal." She jumped, spotting him in the doorway. "You scared the hell out of me. I was . . . umm . . . just checking my voice messages." She walked toward the door. "I have a taste for some apple pancakes tonight. How about breakfast food for dinner?"

"Jaise—"

"I know you hate eggs at night. But I just have this urge to whip up a pancake feast."

"Jaise! Damn, I just need you to be quiet and listen to me for a moment."

"Oh, that was rude. I don't know what your officer told you, but I didn't piss in your Cheerios."

"I need you to sit down."

She looked into his eyes and they were bloodshot. A chill ran through her. She'd never seen Bilal cry. Ever.

"What's wrong?"

"Sit down."

"I don't want to sit down."

"I think you should."

"I said no. I'm not sitting down. The last time I was told to sit down my daddy had dropped dead in his mistress's bed. So I'm not sittin' down."

Bilal stared at her in silence, his eyes completely wet with falling tears.

Jaise's heart raced and she felt like a bomb was building in her chest and set for an explosion. "Would you just tell me! Did something happen to Vera or one of my sisters?"

He shook his head. "Jaise, baby . . ." His voice trembled. "I'm so, so sorry. I never thought—"

"Never thought what?"

"Jabril."

Her breathing stopped and her heart was on its way to follow suit. "What about Jabril?" She felt her body shutting down.

"Baby, he was out in Brownsville and he was shot."

Jaise felt like a bullet had soared through her chest. Everything burned. Her eyes. Her arms. Her thighs. Her feet. Her stomach. She could barely breathe, but somehow she managed to swallow. "What was he doing in Brownsville? Of all the goddamn holes in the earth, he picks the most dangerous part of Brooklyn, and I know he was chasing some damn ho!" She wiped her eyes and grabbed her purse.

"Darnell, the officer, said he was selling drugs."

"Selling drugs? My son? Oh my God. It's like he seeks to outdo himself every damn time!" She wiped more tears. "Let's just get to the hospital."

"Jaise." Bilal reached for her hand.

"Bilal! I have to go! My son needs me. He's been shot and I don't want to hear shit about him needing to be a man. Right now he needs his mother!"

"Jaise!"

"I don't want to hear it! I have to get to the hospital!"

"I need you to listen to me!"

"No, you don't!"

"Baby, Jabril . . ."

"No." She backed away from him.

"Was killed."

Black . . .

All she could see was black, and then suddenly a gray fog settled in and she could see her body on the floor, knees pressed into the carpet, and she could hear a wail sounding as if it had come from the pit of her womb. She could see tears slicing through her cheeks and snot oozing like glaze over her lips and running into the saliva that dangled from the corners of her lips.

She could see Jabril shrinking into the little boy she never wanted to grow up. The one who used to beg to sleep in her bed with her. The one who always thought he was Superman and could fly through the sky—which was why he walked across the kitchen table, jumped off, and landed on his elbow, breaking his arm in four places.

She could see him dressed in a black tuxedo on his way to his fifth-grade prom. His face chubby and his stomach pudgy.

"Mommy, girls don't like me."

"Jabril, why would you say that? You are quite handsome!"

"But I'm fat."

"You're perfect just the way you are. One day, I promise, you won't be able to keep the girls off you."

She could see Jabril at sixteen. Skinny. Tall. And thinking he was the coolest sixteen-year-old in all of New York. "Ma, I think I can sing."

"I know you can. I told you, you got it from me."

"I want to try out for this talent show."

"Try out and you're sure to win!"

And he did.

She could see him at twenty packing his clothes and screaming, "You don't love me! Fuck you!"

"I do love you! Mommy loves you more than life itself!"

She could see him running out the door. "Come back, Jabril! Come back!" And no matter how loud she screamed, he wouldn't come back and he wouldn't get up.

Jaise wasn't sure how she'd gotten to the hospital, if she'd magically appeared or someone had driven her there. All she knew was through the gray fog she could see Jabril's lifeless body on the gurney and she could hear glass-shattering screams as every part of her wept. She could see her face pressed against his as she called God and cursed him. "Your word said I could move mountains! That if I believed in Your son! That I had not because I asked not! That all I needed to do was knock and the door shall be opened! Your word said it and I'm here standing on Your word and in need! Please bring my baby back to me! Please! Please! Give him back. I want him!"

She could hear the doctors, nurses, and Bilal begging her to calm down. But she couldn't calm down. All she could do was bellow in agony.

She could see herself holding Jabril's lifeless body. She could feel her blood pressure reaching its peak, her womb about to burst, her head due to explode, and she could see herself passing out and silently asking God to not ever let her wake up.

CHAPTER 34

JOURNEE

Two Days Later

G*od is good!* Dressed in her erotic Catholic school uniform, Journee stood over Zachary and watched his lifeless body in bed. She pressed two fingers into his neck—and nothing.

Dear God, You may not come when I want you to, but You are always on time!

She eased out of Zachary's room and headed back to her wing of the estate.

"You give that ole dirty bastard his pussy for the morning?"

"He's dead," Journee said in glee, as she hurriedly changed clothes.

Xavier hopped out of bed. "What you mean 'dead'? Out of this bitch? Like slow singing and flower bringing? Like will reading and half of my money about to grease my damn palms? That kind of dead? Or you playing?"

"Dead. Like bye-bye motherfucker."

"You call the nurse?"

"No."

"Journee, you're fucking up. You need to ride this doting wife shit out to the end."

"Look, I got this and I know what I'm doing. I've had this day planned out for years. I'm going to go downstairs for my morning tea and wait for the nurse to come and get me."

"You do that. And while you're sipping your tea make sure you map out how soon you're going to give me my money, and I mean it. You and Chaunci think I'm playing with your asses, but I'm not. Now I'll admit, the pussy has been sweet, but it ain't like that."

"You have to be patient. The amount of money you're asking for is not that damn easy to get my hands on! Now I don't have time to argue with you. I have to get to the kitchen."

Journee changed into a fitted navy skirt and beige blouse. She pulled her hair back into a bun and draped pearls around her neck.

Should I break down and cry when the nurse comes in? No. I did that the last time. I'll be strong. No tears. That may seem odd though.

She walked into the kitchen. "Good morning, you two." She greeted the house manager and the chef as she sat at the table.

I'll sit silently and let a single tear slide down my cheek.

Journee watched the kitchen door, waiting for the nurse to bolt in at any moment.

The chef handed her a cup of tea. Journee sipped and waited. A half hour went by and no nurse.

An hour passed.

Nothing.

Where the hell is she?

She shot the chef a Barbie doll smile as she got up from her seat and headed to Zachary's room.

"Where the . . . hell . . . have . . . you . . . been?!" Zachary peered, as Journee stepped into the doorway. "You're late! Now . . . let's . . . go . . . back . . . upstairs!"

Journee felt a wave of heat come over her body as she saw Zachary sitting there in his chair.

Maybe I'm seeing things.

"Journee, do you hear me?!"

It's really him. She dropped like a stone, her head making a thumping sound as she hit the carpet.

CHAPTER 35

VERA

"Mommy!"

"Ms. Vera!"

Skyy and Aidan, Taj's son, greeted Vera with bear hugs around her waist as she opened the door.

"Mommy! Mommy! Me and my brother—"

"My brother and I," Vera corrected Skyy.

"My brother and I saw you on TV!"

"You did?" Vera forced herself to smile.

"Yes, Ms. Vera." Aidan giggled.

Why is he here? I just want him away from my door. He's a child. I know. But every time I look at him, I see my husband making love to his mother.

This shit is sick.

I need to shake it. . . . He hasn't done anything to me.

But I feel like he has. Just saying hello to him is a struggle.

Act like an adult for once.

Damn.

"Ms. Vera," Aidan carried on, "I was sooooo excited when I saw you on TV. I had no idea you were a star!"

"Don't worry, Mommy, I checked 'em on that," Skyy interjected. "I let him know that you were a star, you were rich, and that when you stepped into a room, you give all the chicks fever. Oh, and you know what Aidan asked me, Mommy?"

"What's that?"

"Why you and Daddy don't live together if you're married." Skyy placed a hand on her hip and twisted her lips like a miniature Aunt Cookie. "I told him, 'Li'l boy, you're being a little too nosy. You ain't, I mean you haven't, lived but thirty bleep-bleep-bleepin' minutes—' "

"All right, Skyy," Taj warned.

"Daddy, I wasn't being grown. Was I, Aidan?" She turned toward her brother.

Aidan hesitated, and Skyy said, "Boy, don't make me elbow slap you. 'Cause I will cut you so deep down past your bone marrow that the only thing left of you will be your shadow!"

"Skyy!" Vera tapped her lightly on the mouth. "Apologize right now!"

"Mommy!"

"Or would you like to be marched into the bathroom so you can do a little painful tap dance from my hand slapping those thighs?"

"Sorry, Aidan." She dropped her head, her two ponytails swinging forward over her shoulder.

"And it won't—" Vera stressed.

"And it won't happen again."

"Now you need to stop being so fresh."

"Mommy, I was just trying to tell Aidan that Daddy didn't live here because you tossed all of his clothes over the balcony. And when you two stop being mad at each other, then you'll stop crying at night and Daddy will come home. And, Mommy, did you know that someone broke into Daddy's place and tore it up? Killed the fish and everything!"

Vera didn't respond. Instead she glanced at Taj and then back down to the children.

"Mommy, can I show Aidan how we redecorated my room?" Skyy pulled Aidan's hand and brushed past Vera and into the house before Vera could say "hell no." She turned back to Taj, who stood on the opposite side of the threshold. "So what are you going to do? Sit in the hallway, wait in the lobby, or come back in an hour or two?"

"None of the above; I'll be coming in." He placed his hands on her waist, moved her to the side, and walked in.

"Aren't you violating your restraining order? And why didn't you call for me to come to the police station? Isn't that the arrangement, Dr. Bennett?"

Taj placed his hands on Vera's waist and pulled her into him. "Is this what you really want to do? You want to argue? Did you drop her off at the police station or did you call me like you had some sense and ask me if Skyy could please stay with me for a couple of days while you stayed with Jaise?"

Silence.

"Exactly. Now cut that shit out and act like you remember how to hold a decent conversation with your husband." He kissed her lightly on the lips and tapped her on the behind. "How's Jaise?"

"Not good." Vera felt a rush of tears inching up on her. "The funeral was yesterday. And every time I think about Jabril lying in that casket, it breaks my heart." Unable to hold back her tears any longer, Vera wept into Taj's chest as he wrapped his arms around her.

"It's painful, baby. I know it is. And you and Jaise are so close."

"And he wasn't that bad of a kid."

"I know. But some of his choices were, baby."

"Maybe you're right." She wiped her eyes and softly stepped out of his embrace. "Are you hungry?"

"No. But I'll have a glass of—"

"Perrier."

Vera poured Taj a glass of the French mineral water and dropped two ice cubes in it. "You can keep the glass." She placed it in front of him as he sat at the kitchen island. "There were only two in that set and being that you're going for half of everything . . ."

"You just can't help yourself." Taj shook his head. "Why can't you just give in to the feeling of enjoying my company? Are you that scared to admit that you made a mistake when you filed for divorce?"

"I'm not—"

Bzzzz . . . Bzzzz . . . Taj's phone vibrated on his hip. "Who is this?" He squinted at the phone. "One minute, Vera. Let me get this. "Hello?" He paused. "Uncle Boy, why are you calling me from a blocked number and why are you whispering?"

"That's a damned good question," Vera said.

"No, I can't meet with you right now," Taj said into the phone. "I'm with my wife at the moment." He paused again. "Producer? What producer— I'm not talking loud, Uncle Boy. . . . Maury Povich? Why do Maury Povich's producers keep calling you?"

"What is he talking about?!" Vera demanded. "I know his ass doesn't have a baby!"

"Uncle Boy, that's ridiculous. I will not be using my lab to run some bootleg blood test for you. And a forty-five-year-old woman is not a baby. Her mother can threaten you all day, but she cannot get any child support from you, so your Social Security is safe. Now who you need to worry about is Aunt Cookie. I won't tell Vera. A'ight, bye."

Taj looked up at Vera. "My uncle is crazy." He laughed.

"He's *my* uncle."

"Damn. We're not even family anymore either? So you want me completely out of your life, huh?"

"I didn't say that."

"So what are you saying?"

"I'm saying that perhaps right now *we're* family, but that has an expiration date. I know you received your letter for the divorce hearing."

"An expiration date?" Taj said, and looked at Vera in disbelief. "You know what? Maybe I need to leave before this turns into another argument. Let me get my son, whom you really don't want here anyway." He stood up.

"I resent that! I don't mind him being here, and if I did, he wouldn't be here, or your ass either. Now sit down and stop starting shit that you can't finish."

"I can finish everything that I start." He stepped around the island and into Vera's personal space. "I'm not the quitter in this marriage."

"You're calling me a quitter?"

"If the shoe fits." He kissed her on the forehead.

"Look, let's talk about something else."

Taj shook his head. "If you insist. Uncle Boy told me that Rowanda was here visiting from Chicago. Where is she?"

"I don't know," Vera said matter-of-factly. "I haven't seen her for two days."

Taj looked confused. "What do you mean?"

"In the middle of the party Milan gave for her husband, she up and told me that she had to go. That she couldn't breathe."

"Why didn't you go after her?"

"She flew out the damn door before I could say a word or follow her."

"Vera, what the hell do you mean? You expect me to believe you couldn't follow her?"

"What do you mean, 'what the hell'? Look, we both know that my mother is a junkie, okay? There's no hiding and no escaping that. This is part of the reason I hate for her to come back to New York, because . . ."

"Because what?"

"Nothing."

"Say it. Tell me."

Unexpected tears streamed down Vera's cheeks. "I'm just tired of her always pulling this shit! And no matter how damn grown I am, I still feel like that same little kid on edge, waiting for her mother to bust out the crack pipe of disappointment." She wiped her eyes. "Look, ummm . . ." She turned toward the hallway. "How about you let Aidan spend the night with his sister and you come back tomorrow and pick him up?"

"He can spend the night. But I'm not leaving and coming back tomorrow. I'm staying right here and we're going to deal with this. We need to call the hospitals and the police stations."

"I did that. I even called the city morgue. They don't have her ass. You know who has her—the glass dick she's somewhere sucking on. Look. I have my own child. I can't raise my mother too. I'm tired of feeling like I have to be watching over her all the time when she's here or she'll sneak out somewhere and get high. I would like to be her damn child for a change and not her overseer! Damn!"

"It's not your fault, baby. And you're not responsible for your mother."

"I know it's not my fault. But I feel like it is." She wiped tears. "Do you know how many times I dragged my mother out of an alleyway? Nursed her back from a damn overdose? Waited by the bathroom door while she stayed in there all damn day? Do you understand that? She begged me to give her another chance and now this is the shit she pulls?"

"It could be something else, V."

"It's not, Taj. We've been together long enough for you to know that her ass is somewhere probably sucking dick for a hit."

Taj pulled Vera into his chest and he rested his chin in the center of her head. "I want you to know that you are not responsible for your mother's addiction. Your mother is an adult."

"Taj."

"Listen to me—" He held her head up. "Rowanda is *your* mother. She is the parent in this situation. She failed you. *Not* the other way around. And if she makes a decision to get high, you are not to blame. You are not to blame now and you were not to blame when you were a little girl dragging her out of the alleyways or stealing food from the corner store. And you are not to blame because you went to school when you were eight and told the teacher that your grandmother had died and you were home alone. That is not your fault."

Vera wiped her eyes. "I know you're right. I just want to truly feel that way." She looked into Taj's eyes and slid her arms around his neck. "Thank you," she said as they began to kiss passionately. Soul stirringly.

He ran his hands up her thighs and ended their kiss with a suck of her chin. "You want me to stop?" He unbuttoned her blouse and caressed her hard nipples.

"No."

"Then tell me you love me and take responsibility for what is your fault and apologize for all of the crazy shit you've done to me."

"What?" Vera frowned. "Apologize? I'm not apologizing. I'm not doing that."

"Then I'm not doing you. Because if you think I'm going to sleep with you and help you run away from what you need to be dealing with, you're wrong. This is a marriage and it's not all about you and what you need. And instead of laying up here at night and crying over me, you need to be talking to me. Now, if you want to talk about your mother, let's do that. You want to make love to me, then you'll need to hollah at me with an apology."

"Then I guess I'll be seeing you in court next week."

"I guess so, and make sure you bring your checkbook."

CHAPTER 36

JAISE

*A*shes *to ashes . . .*
  Dust to dust . . .
  Black suit . . .
  Slick mahogany coffin . . .
  White satin lining . . .
  Yea, though I walk through the valley of the shadow of death . . .
  You choosing this niggah over me? Your own son!

"Noooo!" Jaise screamed as she jumped out of her sleep in a sweat. Her eyes moved around her bedroom in a panic: from the caramel painted walls to the rod iron railings of her bed, to Bilal, who lay next to her sleeping.

Jaise felt nauseous as she tossed the sheet off and eased out of bed. She headed for the bathroom and immediately her stomach boiled and her mouth watered. She gripped the edge of the toilet and dry heaved into it.

"Are you okay, Jaise?" Bilal rubbed her back.

"Yeah. I just feel really, really fucked up." She dry heaved again. After a few seconds of trying to get herself together, she walked over to the pedestal sink and splashed water into her face.

"Maybe you need to sit down and let me fix you some tea."

"I don't want any tea. I want a cigarette and I have this urge to cook apple pancakes." She looked over at Bilal. "I feel so weird." She looked around the bathroom and saw that the butler had let the camera crew upstairs and they were filming her.

Ignoring the camera, Bilal said, "You're going through a lot right now."

She looked at him, confused. "What do you mean?"

"I mean with Jabril passing away, it's a lot on you."

Passing away . . . passing away . . . Jaise looked into Bilal's face.

Ashes to ashes . . .

Dust to dust . . .

Black suit . . .

Slick mahogany coffin . . .

White satin lining . . .

Yea, though I walk through the valley of the shadow of death . . .

You choosing this niggah over me? Your own son!

"Passing away," Jaise said as tears streamed down her face. "He wasn't sick. He wasn't some old-ass man. No one expected him to die."

"Jaise, calm down." He reached for her hand and she snatched it back. "Calm down."

"Get. Off. Me!" Jaise screamed.

"I know you're upset."

"You know I'm upset? I'm more than upset. I'm enraged and I want to kill your fuckin' ass! Passed away! My son didn't pass away. He was murdered, motherfucker, and as far as I'm concerned, you might as well have pulled the trigger!"

"What?"

"Get the fuck out!" She pushed Bilal. "Get your shit and get the fuck out! Had me put my child on the street because he wasn't man enough for you! Because he didn't meet your standards, so he had to go! All this fuckin' house! Six bedrooms, a full and finished basement! And you had me put my baby on the street! You killed him!"

"Jaise—"

She pushed past him, ran into the closet, yanked his clothes from the hangers, and tossed them out of the closet. "Get the fuck out!" She flung his shoes. Took her hand and in one swipe knocked everything off his dresser. "Out!" She opened the bedroom window and began sailing his things into the street.

"Jaise." He grabbed her, his hold paralyzing her.

"You killed my baby." Her voice ached. Her body ached. Everything felt weak. "I need you to leave. You killed my baby."

"Jaise."

"I don't want to see you ever again. This marriage is over. I chose you over my baby and now I'll never see him again."

Bilal's face was wet with tears. "Jaise."

"Let me go and leave."

He released her from his hold and gathered what he could of his things. "I love you and I loved Jabril. I just wanted what was best for him. Had I known—"

"Go!" She yelled at the top of her voice, "GET OUT!"

Bilal threw some things in a bag, picked it up, and walked out of the room. Jaise could hear his feet slamming against the steps, and once they stopped she heard the front door slam.

"My baby's dead!" she cried, and curled into a ball on the floor for what felt like forever.

CHAPTER 37

MILAN

This wasn't meant to be a fucked up fairy tale. It was meant to be as sensual as the first night Kendu grooved between her thighs and they made love until sunrise. As surreal as her heartbeat used to be when she'd whimsically doodle his name.

Never. Ever. Did she imagine, at least until this moment, that she'd dream of pointing a gun to his head and pulling the trigger.

Motherfucker.

She sipped her smooth black tea and looked around at her kitchen, from the sleek black and cherrywood cabinets with the chrome handles, to the chalkboard wall that encompassed the doorway—which led to the hallway. She glanced over at the camera zoomed in on her and then skipped her eyes over to the open space, designated as the family room. Her gaze landed on the red leather sectional and her mind was quickly lost in a memory of once sitting there and watching Kendu on *Scoreboard,* his ESPN morning show, feeling privileged to be his wife.

Milan giggled and her eyes danced over to the fireplace mantel where their wedding picture used to be until the night of his birthday party, when she'd snatched the picture off the mantel and tossed it across the room.

She couldn't believe he was having an affair.

An affair . . .

I can't live like this. I have to leave him or kill his ass.

Tears filled her eyes.

You'd better not drop a damn tear.

"Milan," Kendu's voice boomed into the kitchen from the hallway. He stepped in through the doorway, wearing gray sweats, a ribbed white tank top, and Adidas slippers. "We need to talk."

Silence.

He sat at the kitchen table. "I need you to talk to me."

More silence.

Milan quickly wiped away the tears that had escaped and returned to looking down at the concrete kitchen table she'd filled with pictures to place in her son's baby book. She reached for a photo that she and Kendu had taken a few months before the baby was born. In Vegas. Standing before a black Elvis who renewed their vows.

The corners of Milan's lips stretched toward her ears as she smiled and picked up the scissors. She traced the sharp and cutting steel around the shape of her image and then moved on to Kendu's, stopping short at the outline of his ears.

I'm so exhausted.

Tears haunted her eyes. She cut around the side of his face, over the crown of his head, down the other side, and slowly slid the scissors partially across his paper neck. She stopped and ran a finger across the slice.

I'm so sick of your shit.

She decapitated him and his head slipped to the floor, where she left it.

"Milan." He waved his hands before her face as if he were seducing her out of a trance. "You just cut my damn head off in the fuckin' picture?!" He looked disgusted. "What kind of drugs are you on? Yo', what the fuck?"

"You better get away from me."

"We need to talk."

"I don't have anything to say." She walked over to the stove and stirred her pot.

"Milan—"

"Mr. and Mrs. Malik." Rosalynn, the maid, hurried into the kitchen, breathing heavily. "Did either of you happen to see Aiyanna's rabbit?"

"No." Kendu frowned. "Why?"

"I went in there to clean the cage and it's gone! The thing is gone!" Rosalynn looked perplexed. "I looked everywhere."

"Calm down, Ros," Kendu said. "I'm sure you'll find it."

"But how does a caged rabbit disappear? You think the nanny moved it?"

"No," Milan said. "She's been out all morning, taking the baby for a stroll."

Rosalynn shook her head. "Well, I'm going to keep looking. I promised Aiyanna I would take care of her rabbit while she was in South Africa. Now I don't know what I'm going to tell her." She walked out of the room, shaking her head.

Kendu stared at Milan and she could tell by the look in his eyes that he attempted to read her mind. "I'm not having an affair," he said.

She ignored him and instead walked over to the stove and removed the lid from her pot.

"Damn, this smells good." He gave her an awkward smile. "The chef made it?"

"No."

"Who made it?"

"Me."

"Where's the chef?"

"Off."

"Do you think you can say more than one word?"

"No."

Kendu gave Milan a once-over before cupping his hand over hers. She shot him a look that ricocheted a round of invisible bullets into him.

He inched his hand back and sat up straight in the chair. "You know I love you. And I would never do anything to hurt you. Please talk to me."

Talk to you? Talk to you? You'd better get the fuck out of my face playing stupid. You know as well as I do that you are a lyin' piece of shit who only thinks with his dick. But I got something for you and that tramp-ass whore you're cheating on me with! And as soon as that private eye I hired gives me the information I need, oh, baby, I will show you and your prostitute a thing or two!

"I don't have anything to say." Milan turned the fire off under her pot and the spicy smell of fresh curry, carrots, pigeon peas, and mixed peppers greeted her nose. She inhaled the aroma. "It's done." She turned to Kendu. "Would you like some?"

"Hell, I don't know. Should I eat it?"

"Choice is yours." She fixed herself a bowl.

"A'ight, I'll take a little. Maybe while we eat, we can discuss some things."

"Sure." Milan grabbed two porcelain bowls and filled them with curried shreds of meat and chunky vegetables. She set Kendu's bowl before him.

"This looks good." He dug in. "Is this curried chicken?"

"No," Milan said as she set her bowl on the table and took her seat.

"No?" Kendu dipped his spoon back into the bowl and filled his mouth. "What is it?"

"Rabbit."

Kendu froze. "What?"

"It's rabbit," she said calmly.

Kendu sat completely still. Then, as if a slow, shocking wave washed over him and suddenly crashed and exploded in the center of his stomach, he heaved and hurled across the table, turning the sleek black cabinets speckled orange. Kendu leaped from his seat, rocked the table, and sent the bowls to the floor, shattering them and covering the wood planks with shards of porcelain and lumps of food.

"Sick ass! Are you fuckin' crazy?!" Kendu ran into the powder room. "What the fuck," traveled down the hallway as Kendu emptied his stomach into the toilet, "is wrong with you?!

"I don't believe you did some shit like that, Milan!" He continued to vomit. "You cooked the fuckin' rabbit?! I should kick yo' ass for that! What the fuck is wrong with you?!"

"Nothing." Milan cracked half a smile.

"I knew your ass was crazy!" He gagged, hurled, and hard splashing sounds rose from the toilet.

"I'm fine."

"I don't believe this shit!" he said, struggling to breathe. "Fuckin' twisted!"

Milan wiped the corners of her mouth and as she rose from her chair, she spotted the rabbit hopping toward the powder room. "I'll be back."

"Yeah, you do that. You need to take your sick ass out of here!" He gagged. "Motherfuckers get killed for less than that! How the hell could you cook my daughter's pet and then feed it to me!" Kendu heaved and as Milan walked past him, she picked up the rabbit, whom she'd hidden in a makeshift cage behind the sofa, opened the front door, and set it free.

CHAPTER 38

CHAUNCI

Monday afternoon is when Chaunci realized she'd fucked up. She stared at her engagement ring on the nightstand and into the band where Emory's name was engraved. She closed her eyes and wondered what he was doing and how he would feel if he knew she'd spent a taboo weekend with another man.

She pulled the sheets over her breasts as she looked down at a sleeping Grant. She wanted desperately to nurse his morning hard-on, but decided she needed to get her thoughts in order so that she could return to New York ready to meet her knight. Emory. The man who'd practically saved her life when she was emotionally bankrupt.

What the hell am I going to tell this man? This was only supposed to be overnight. Not all weekend.

"Tell him you've changed your mind."

Chaunci froze. "I thought you were sleeping . . . and how did you know what I was thinking?"

Grant sat up with his back pressed against the headboard. "It was a wild guess. Are you regretting this weekend?"

"No." She kissed him. "It was one of the best weekends of my life. I just can't do this again."

"Why not?"

"I'm engaged to be Emory's wife." She tossed the covers off her and headed into the bathroom.

Grant followed her. "You don't have to marry him."

"I love him."

"If you could so easily spend a weekend with me, then loving him is not even part of the equation."

"You are out of line." Chaunci turned on the shower and stepped in.

"Am I?" Grant stepped in behind her, the water gracing both of their bodies. "Or are you trying to fulfill an obligation that you are no longer required to meet?" He placed kisses from the base of her neck to her ass, where he tossed her salad, forcing her to cry out his name. Spinning her around and licking her clit, he said, "Don't worry about calling the wedding off. I'll do it."

CHAPTER 39

VERA

A Week Later

Vera sat in her office, watching red numbers flash across her iPad. She tried her best to muster a smile for the camera, but she couldn't.

She hadn't heard from her mother in a week, and instead of the days getting better, the wounds of having a drug-addicted mother and fucked up childhood memories felt like fresh slices to her skin.

Tears filled the corners of her eyes as her cell phone rang. She read the caller ID: Private.

"Hello?" She cleared her throat.

"This Vera?" a raspy and unfamiliar male voice said.

Her heart dropped into the pit of her stomach. "Who is this?"

"This Vera?"

"Yeah," she said in a panic. "Who is this?"

"Don't worry about who this is. Just know you need to come and get yo' mama. She down here in Lincoln projects courtyard lookin' sick off that shit and you know what shit I'm talkin' 'bout."

Click.

Vera held the phone to her breasts and looked into the distance. She shook her head and placed the phone back on her desk.

Doesn't matter.

Fuck Rowanda.

Vera nestled into the soft leather of her seat seeing visions of her mother—naked. Needle in her arm. Belt wrapped around her bicep. Nodding out. Slipping. Banging her head on the claw-foot tub. Dead. Arms stretched out and blood dripping like she hung on the crucifix.

What if she dies?

She's already dead to me.

That's your mother.

Fuck. Her.

No.

Fuck. Her.

You don't mean that.

Vera sat up and ran her hands over her face. This was not the plight she was supposed to have.

Fuck.

Shit never ends.

The Lincoln projects felt like the longest ride of her life. She hated that cameras refused to leave her side once she told them where she was going, but whatever.

This is reality TV.

Well, welcome to my reality.

Vera parked her BMW X6 in front of a rusted, red, and graffiti-painted sign that read, "Welcome to Lincoln Garden Projects." She sat for a moment and stared into the memories dancing through the courtyard. There was something eerily tranquil about this place—the place she once called home.

She spotted Rowanda sitting on a park bench in the center of the courtyard, next to an unraveling basketball net and concrete checkerboard table, sipping a beer as she stared into the street.

"What the fuck are you doing?" Vera said with every ounce of venom that she could.

"Why are you here?" Rowanda looked around. "This ain't no place for you."

Vera smirked. "What. The. Fuck. Is wrong with you?" Before Rowanda could answer, Vera continued, "I'm sooooo sick of saving you, and looking out for you, and mothering you, and being all this shit to you and you give me nothing but false goddamn hope and grief. I *was not* pregnant with you. You *are not* my child. You are my mother, so why the hell am I always saving you?!"

"Go home, Vera," Rowanda said quietly, as if she were talking more to herself than to Vera. "I am who I am, and I don't need you saving me. Okay? So go back to Fifth Avenue."

"What is that supposed to mean?" Vera looked her over. "Don't pull that 'go back to Fifth Avenue' bullshit on me, as if that's all I understand. I know what it is to be in hell and not be able to leave that motherfucker."

"No, you don't, Vera." Rowanda sipped her beer. "You can't even begin to understand what it is to have demons that ride your back, day in and day out. Night after night."

"So you go back and get high? That's the solution? Smoke the motherfuckers away."

"I never said that."

"Then what are you saying? Why do you keep doing this to me?!"

"This is not about you!"

"It's never about me! It's always about you and your monkey. Fuck me." Vera stabbed her finger into her chest. "Fuck my child. Fuck our hopes that finally you have got it together. Fuck it all, because suddenly you need to outrun some bullshit and I should just deal with it."

"Listen to me. Me getting high is about me. Not you. Stop taking responsibility for me and my shit."

Vera wiped tears and bit down on the inside of her cheek. "If you would stop fucking up, I wouldn't need to keep taking responsibility for your shit. Got strangers calling me to come and get you. I don't need that shit."

"I didn't tell nobody to call you. Go home."

"Well, somebody called me and I'm here now, damn it! "

"Go. Home."

"You think it's that easy?"

"It should be!"

"It's not!" Vera screamed. "Now why did you do this? And why are you looking like you're about to pass out?" Vera's eyes combed Rowanda's flushed skin and the sweat dripping down her face.

"It's nothing wrong with me!"

"It has to be something wrong with you. Or at least it better be, because after tonight, if this is the goddamn life you want"—Vera pointed around—"then I'm done with you. And I mean that."

Rowanda hesitated. "Vera, I don't need you passing judgment. Just listen."

"Judgment about what?" Vera said, aggravated. "What would make me more judgmental than I'm feeling at this moment?"

Rowanda shook her head. "Listen to me."

"I'm listening."

"I was so deep into my addiction—"

"You could never be deeper than you are at this moment."

"Would you just listen to me?"

"I'm listening."

"Not long after you went to live with Cookie, I had a baby."

"What?"

"I was so out there and getting so high that I didn't even know I was pregnant."

"You had a what?"

"I was too busy gettin' fucked up. Out there prostituting. Doing anything to get high. Trying to run from all sorts and shades of shit. So busy in search of something to take me out of this motherfucker, that I didn't even know I was carrying a baby."

"A baby?"

Tears poured from Rowanda's eyes into the creases of her neck. "And when I gave birth to him."

"Him?"

"Him." Rowanda snorted and attempted to crack half a smile. "He was a beautiful baby. He had deep chocolate around his ears and fingertips, and he was so long. . . ." she said to the distance. "And I knew he was going to be dark, strong, and handsome."

"What happened to the baby?" Vera.

"I wanted him so bad." Rowanda rocked. "I wanted me and you, and him, to run off and leave this goddamn dump. I wanted to so bad, but I was soooo deep into my addiction, that I couldn't stop getting fucking high. No matter what. I had to have that shit. Smack. Dope. Suicide. I had to have it. And even though I was in labor with him, I stayed in that abandoned, nasty-ass, get-high palace, sucking dick and snortin' that shit. And when my water broke and the baby started to bust through my goddamn pussy, er'body in that spot fled and the only one who stood by me was my friend, Queen. She practically carried me to the hospital."

"Where was the baby's father?"

Rowanda sipped her beer. "I was a junkie, Vera. He had a million fuckin' fathers."

Silence.

She continued, "After I had him, the hospital wouldn't let me take him. They said I wasn't fit. And I wasn't, but I still wanted him. So I would go to the hospital every day to feed him. They would let me hold him and kiss him. But he couldn't go home with me. And Cookie had you, so there was no way I

could call her and tell her that the junkie done had another
baby."

"So what did you do?"

"I fed him every day, until the day I went back to the hospital and the nurses said that Social Services had placed him."

"Oh, my God."

"And do you know what?"

"What?"

"I kept up with him for a while. I found out where he was
and I would go to the school yard and watch him play. Sneak
and take pictures of him."

"Did he ever see you?"

"No. I did that for years and then I went on a drug run one
week and when I went back to that school, I didn't see him
anymore."

"So you don't know what happened to him?"

"I know that he grew up, got married, had two children,
and became a football legend." She pulled a picture from her
pocket. "Look at him. I took this picture when he was five."

Vera looked at the picture. "I don't even know what to say."

"I found him, Vera," Rowanda said as silent tears ran from
her eyes and over her lips.

"Who is he?"

"Ken . . . du."

"Kendu?" Vera looked into the distance and the vision of
the way Rowanda stared at Kendu when he entered the party
played before her. She continued to look into space and
thought about how tears danced in Rowanda's eyes when
Kendu told his story.

"Oh my God, Rowanda!" Vera turned back toward her
mother and screamed as she saw Rowanda convulsing with
foam oozing from the sides of her lips.

CHAPTER 40

JOURNEE

"Are you sure he's dead this time? I'm telling you I'm not getting my hopes up," Journee mumbled to Xavier as they paced the hospital waiting area. "Every other year he pulls this 'I'm dead' shit and I fall for it."

"I think he's done," Xavier said. "The nurse said she couldn't wake him this morning and he didn't have a pulse."

"I don't trust it. He has nine goddamn lives."

Journee's heels clicked against the tile. "What's taking the doctor so long to come out here?!"

"I don't know."

"I know he isn't dead. I just know it. Trust me, they'll come rolling his decrepit ass out of here at any moment."

"Mrs. Dupree." The doctor stepped into the room. It was hard to read his face, but Journee tried. "He's alive!" she attempted to say with glee.

"I'm sorry. We tried all that we could."

"He's gone . . ." Journee moaned.

"I'm sorry." The nurse offered her sympathy.

Thank you, Jesus! "Oh no, not my Zachary!" She turned to Xavier and he held her.

"Mr. Dupree was a great man," the doctor said. "And he held on as long as he could."

Too goddamn long. "He was a wonderful man, Doctor. I loved him so much!"

"I know." Xavier's voice trembled. "I loved him too!."

CHAPTER 41

MILAN

*B*_{*rnggg.*}

*B*rnggg.

Milan looked at the number on her cell phone and a smile ran across her face. She closed her bedroom door before answering. "Hello?"

"Milan?"

"Yes."

"This is Charlie, the PI. And I have that information you need."

"So this motherfucker's fuckin' some Garden State wanna be Hollywood skeezer," Milan said to no one in particular as she drove over the George Washington Bridge headed for Jersey. "Tinsel Town ho and shit. I guess reality TV wasn't enough for this son of a bitch! He had to go and get some video, movie, red-carpet, walk-of-the-stars ho! Honey, I'm going to slice her fuckin' throat."

No you're not.

"Right. I will try and talk to this slore, woman to whore. Try and be really calm. Cool. And I'm going to ask her when she discovered Kendu was married—before or after she became the stalking-ass sidepiece. Because maybe, maybe she didn't know." Milan paid the toll. "You know how niggahs do. Lie and shit. Deny their whole damn family for some pussy. And maybe, maybe this blonde bimbo has been under a rock. You know how white girls get. Dizzy-ass shit. Don't know a damn thing. Think all black folks look alike. So maybe she didn't know that Kendu was married. But"—she exited the highway— "if she gets flip at the lip and admits that she knew he was married, babeeeeeee, I'ma grip her by her blonde-ass scalp and teach her ass about trying to up her pussy mileage off my husband! And you can put five on that!"

Milan parked her car on the tree-lined street. "Oh, this here home wrecker is straight up cookie-cutter middle America. White picket fences, dog over there in the yard. And if I'm not mistaken"—Milan walked up the front path and peeked around the side of the large colonial—"that's that damn baby she's been taunting me with. Is Kendu paying for this cunt to be tucked away in the burbs? He has to be, 'cause Charlie said she was a Z-list actress. Lowballin'. And everybody knows those hos are broke."

Milan pushed the bell and then she could hear the sound traveling through the house.

"I'm coming!" a happy valley-girl voice said from inside before she opened the door and cocked her neck to the side.

"Yeah, bitch," Milan said, sticking her foot in between the door and the doorpost. "It's me."

"What are you doing here?!"

"Oh, you know what the fuck I'm doing here! Don't be scared. Were you scared when you were stalking me all over New York? Were you scared when you were fuckin' my husband? Hell no. You weren't scared. But you're scared because I'm at your door!"

"What do you want?"

"Well, Susan," Milan said in perfect sarcastic diction, "shall we start with did you know that Kendu was married?"

Susan frowned and snickered. "Are you serious right now?

What are you? Stupid? Of course I knew he was married. He's a football legend. An ESPN commentator on the number-one sports show in the country. He's been on reality TV for three seasons. Not to mention he is fine as hell. And you're asking me if I knew he was married? How silly. The real question is did it matter? And that answer would be no. Now what you'd better do is get out of here, go back home, and watch me work as I continue to take your man!"

POW! BAM! WHAP! BOOM! AHHHHHH!!!!

Milan dragged Susan out of her doorway and slapped her so hard that the strike against her skin made the sound of wet leather. Susan was able to grip Milan by the hair, but that didn't stop Milan from punching her in the face. "I will kill you!" Milan roared as she and Susan scrambled across the grass.

"Get off me!" Susan yelled.

Milan right hooked her and Susan swung, but missed. "It's gon' be more than me on you. It's gon' be six feet worth of dirt on your ass!"

"Stop it! What are you two doing?!" Two men pulled the clawing women apart.

"Let me go!" Susan yelled.

"Yeah," Milan said, waving her hand for Susan to come near. "Let her ass go so I can stomp that hooker's face in. You stalk me and fuck my husband! Make a fool out of me and think you won't get your ass beat! Bitch, please!"

"I'm not sleeping with your husband, you dumb broad! Stupid ass!"

"Lying ass."

"Bipolar slut! I was hired! You lunatic! Bridget hired me!"

"Liar!"

"She did! She told me your ass was boring and she wanted me to help you spice things up. But I didn't sign up for this! Tell Bridget that I quit! I'm done! You've come to my house where I live! My children are in the backyard and you've attacked me! Oh, you will see me in court!"

"You pretended to be my husband's mistress?!" Milan clawed at the air because she couldn't get around the man holding her back. "You ruined my marriage and act like you're the victim! You'd better watch your back, because the first opportunity I get I'ma snatch your scalp off and beat your goddamn face in!" Milan stormed toward her car, got in, and took off.

CHAPTER 42

VERA

*D*ear *God, why?*

What the hell am I going to say to this man?

Just tell him.

Tell him what? "I'm your sister. You need to come and meet your mother because she snorted the wrong bag of dope and will probably die"?

I need to go home.

Vera slid her keys back into her Range Rover's ignition.

I can't do this.

What if she dies!

Then die, damn it! I'm soooo tired of always being worried about her. On edge. Not sure if today's the day she's going to go back to using. Can I trust her now? Can I . . . ? I'm tired of being the junkie's kid who just wants a mother . . . a mother! She's been clean for years and in one night, she throws away her whole life. One night!

She pounded her fist on the steering wheel.

Fuck!

Tears filled her eyes.

A brother. She has a son. Who the hell leaves her baby in the hospital to go and get high? My mother, that's who. God, what the hell do you want me to do?! Why'd she have to dump this shit on me?!

"I'm not doing this," Vera said to no one in particular as

she picked up her cell phone and dialed a number. "Aunt Cookie, I can't do it. I can't. I'm tired. I'm confused. And I can't go in here and tell this man that I'm his damn sister and Rowanda is his mother. He's going to think I'm crazy! Hell, *I* think I'm crazy!"

"You know what, baby girl? I love you like I gave birth to you, but sometimes I wonder if I kicked your li'l ass enough as a child! And it's your Uncle Boy's fault 'cause he helped me to raise a selfish, spoiled, and self-centered damn brat. What the hell is wrong with you?! Your mother is on her dying bed and you are contemplating not telling this man, who knows he was a foster child, who knows he was adopted, who he really is. I could halfway understand it if it was a secret, but it's not. Now your mother asked you to tell him and you need to do that!"

"She should've never left him!"

"Well, she did! She was a junkie. Hell, she *is* a junkie, and you are expecting her to act and think sober. She couldn't do that at the time. You have to stop trying to make your mother someone else and accept her for who she is. No one wants a mother who gets high, but this is your damn life. Now work with it!"

"Suppose he doesn't go to the hospital?"

"That's not your problem. Now go in there and tell him!"

"Aunt Cookie—"

"Vera Bennett! Get off this phone and go talk to your brother now!"

Click.

Vera looked up at Milan and Kendu's house and shook her head.

Fuck it. She grabbed her purse and rushed out of her X-6 before she changed her mind.

Here goes. She sighed as she rang the doorbell. She could see the hanging mic and the cameraman's shadow as someone approached the door. *Damn it. The camera.*

Kendu opened the door. "Vera, hey. How are you doing?"

Vera could tell by the creases in his face that he was upset. She stared into his eyes and for the first time, she realized they had the same almond-shaped eyes, full bottom lip, and mole in the center of their left cheek.

"Are you okay?" he asked her.

"Huh, what?" she said, startled. "What did you ask me?"

"I asked if you were okay. You're just standing there staring at me."

"Oh, I'm sorry. Umm . . . Is your wife here?"

"No."

"Do you know when she'll be back?"

"Vera, believe me, I don't mean to be rude, but given the last few days that I've had, the last thing I want to do is stand here and answer a million questions. So what you can do is call Milan tomorrow."

"Look, I don't want to be here either, trust. But I really don't need to speak to Milan. I really need to speak to you."

"Me? About what?"

"Can we step inside for a moment?"

Kendu hesitated.

"It won't take long," Vera said, looking into the camera. "Can you please turn that damn thing off and give us a minute. Damn."

The crew, who were trained not to respond to the cast, didn't say a word. They simply kept recording.

Aggravated, Kendu said, "Vera, would you just say what you have to say?"

This motherfucker here . . .

"Look here." Vera handed Kendu the picture of him that Rowanda gave her.

Kendu's gaze sank down into the picture and Vera could see the reflection in his eyes of the red Transformers' sweatshirt he'd had on in the photo. He looked back at Vera, confused. "Where'd you get this from?"

"Our mother gave it to me."

Kendu stared at Vera and she could see a million emotions running through his eyes. She wondered if he noticed that, with the exception of their complexions, they had the same face. He walked up close to Vera and said, "Our mother? What are you talking about . . . our mother?"

Unwanted tears streamed down Vera's face. "You're my brother. Rowanda Wright is our mother. She left you in the hospital at birth."

"Rowanda Wright, the woman you brought with you to my birthday party?"

"Yes. She didn't know you were her son until after she came here, heard your story, and saw pictures of you as a child. She knew then."

"What? She's not my mother. My mother abandoned me when I was born. She was a junkie, a fiend, and she's probably dead somewhere in the damn street."

"She's not dead, Kendu. Look at me. We have the same mother. You are my baby brother. I was nine and living with my Aunt Cookie. I had no idea that Rowanda had a baby until last night." She wiped tears. "And, no, she's not perfect. She's not. But she's all we have. She couldn't take care of you or me. And I know it's hard and it's hurtful, but it is what it is."

"After all of these years? Man, please. Fuck that. I'm good and I don't want shit to do with her."

"She's in the hospital dying!"

"From what? AIDS or an overdose?"

"That's fucked up!"

"No. What's fucked up is leaving your newborn in the damn hospital so you can get high, and instead of getting your ass together you continue to get high, and now you want to come and dump this shit on me? Hell no. I was never her damn priority and she damn sure isn't one of mine. So if she dies, then oh well." He shrugged. "Shit, she's already been dead to me."

"You know what? Let me leave here before I mess your big ass up!"

Kendu's eyes dropped down nine inches. "Yeah, okay."

"I didn't want to come here in the first damn place. If you don't want to accept her or come see her before she dies, then don't. You have to live with that! Not my damn problem. All I know is that she gave us what she could, which wasn't much. Now either you stay here and pout like some mad-ass little boy or you be a damn man and get your ass to the hospital and see your mother!"

"I don't have a mother!"

"And maybe you don't!"

CHAPTER 43

BRIDGET

"This is going to be the best season yet," I said to a boardroom full of executives. "All of the women are on top of their game. Which is why I called this meeting. I think now would be the perfect time to add *Millionaire Wives Club LA* to the lineup. I can see it now. We'll have an entire franchise sweeping the nation. And if I may toot my own horn, I believe I deserve—"

WHAP! WHAP! WHAP-WHAP!

Suddenly my face was on fire and all I could see were stars. For a moment, I thought I was back in the convent and had gotten caught by Mother Superior giving the Father a blow job.

I was wrong. Because when the stars floated away, there was Milan being held back by security.

"Oh, baby!" I grinned, stepping out of my heels. "You have slapped the right one now! I've been wanting to kick your ass. Bad. I swear I can taste your blood in my mouth!"

"Bring it, bitch!" Milan invited Bridget. "You hired some actress to play my husband's mistress."

As the executives looked on in shock, I chuckled and said, "Oh, you found out about that, did you?"

"You ruined my marriage!"

"Trick, you need to thank me! Thank me for revamping your career and making you the star you are! You were a raggedy-ass mess and I turned things around for you!" Bridget took a quick peek in the mirror. "Dear God, you have ruined my makeup!"

"I'm going to ruin more than that!"

"You are incredibly ungrateful! Here I've made you a star and this is how you repay me! You'd better find your damn self, mind your manners, and kiss the screen instead of trying to fight me!"

"I didn't sign up for you to ruin my life!"

"You're on reality TV! Your life belongs to me!"

"My marriage is off the table!"

"Please! Spare me!"

"I quit."

"Quit. But you'll be back. You're a fame whore, and as much as you hate them, you need the cameras in your face because you don't have any talents. You have a degree you don't use and a life you aren't happy with—unless there's a camera around. And if all it took was for me to hire an actress to get your ass goin' then I would do it again! Now go!" Bridget pointed toward the door. "Before I order the guards to ax your head off!"

"Fuck you, Bridget!"

"You already said that! Now get out!"

CHAPTER 44

MILAN

Milan walked into the living room and immediately noticed Kendu sitting on the sofa with his head tilted back, his eyes closed, and the camera zoomed in on him.

The room was silent. She knew him well enough to recognize that he was in deep thought and whatever thought he'd settled in on was one that rocked him to the core.

I know I pushed him away, but please . . .

Milan walked over to Kendu and sat beside him. "Knott . . ."

"Milan, let me tell you something right fuckin' now," he said sternly, never once holding his head up or opening his eyes. "If you want to leave me, then pack your shit and go. I'm done with this. Fuckin' finished. I'm sick of trying to convince you that I don't know that trick and that I love you. Because obviously you never trusted me to begin with."

"Knott . . ."

"Shut. The. Fuck. Up." He held his head up and the moment he opened his eyes, tears rolled down his cheeks. "Stop cutting me off."

Milan's heart sank. She'd never seen her man in tears. Not even when he was a little boy with nowhere to go.

Kendu continued, "I have loved you too fuckin' long for

you to let some strange-ass chick step to you and tell you any-thing about me. You—"

"Knott, she was an actress."

"Didn't I tell you to stop cuttin' me off—what did you just say to me?"

"You've been telling me the truth the whole time. Bridget hired her for a goddamn story line!"

"What?"

"Yes. When we first started taping, she said I was boring and needed to spice things up. Well, she took it upon herself to hire this actress to pretend to be your mistress!"

Kendu shook his head in disbelief. "An actress? She hired an actress? What the hell?!"

"Yes. Can you believe it?"

"Yeah, I can believe that. Because Bridget is grimy as hell. But what I can't believe is that you, my wife, the woman I love more than anyone and anything, took my ass through hell. Cussing me out publicly. Humiliating me. Feeding me rabbits and shit."

"I didn't cook the rabbit."

"I know you didn't, because the damn nanny found his ass hopping around in the garden. But that's not the point! The point is that you would let anyone come between us and make these last few months hell!"

"Knott, I'm so, so sorry. I am. Please believe me. I'll never doubt you again. Whatever you want and whatever you need, I'm here. Nothing and no one will ever get between us. I'm done with reality TV. Things have gone too far. I'm finished."

"This shit is crazy."

"I know, but I beat that damn actress's and Bridget's ass in the same damn day!"

Kendu looked at Milan like she was insane. "Fuck them." Tears glimmered in his eyes.

"What's wrong with you?" she asked. "It's something, and whatever it is doesn't have a damn thing to do with reality TV."

He handed Milan the picture Vera left behind and Milan smiled. "Look at you looking like our son. How old were you? You look like you were about three. I thought you didn't have any pictures of yourself before the age of ten. Where are you? In a playground somewhere?"

"I didn't have any photos. I got this from my sister."

Milan blinked. "What? Your sister? What sister?"

"The one who came over here today."

"Wait, wait—start from the beginning. Who is this person and how do you know she is really your sister? For all we know, Bridget could've hired her."

"Bridget did hire her."

"I'm confused."

"Milan, Vera is my sister."

Milan blinked. "What do you mean?"

"She came over here a little while ago in tears and she told me that we had the same mother."

"Vera's mother. The lady who came with her to your birthday party?"

"Yeah. Oh, my God . . ." He shook his head. "My mother."

"Which makes Vera your sister."

"My sister." Tears streamed from his eyes. "And I'm so fuckin' mad!" He pounded his fist on the glass coffee table, sending a crack straight through it. "I'm pissed. I'm angry. I'm hurt." His voice cracked. He cleared his throat. "I used to dream that my mother would come and get me when I was in foster care. And I used to wait and pray and shit, that my mother would come, and she never did. 'Cause she was too busy in the damn streets getting high."

"She's not anymore though, Knott."

"Milan, Vera told me that she's in the hospital right now on her deathbed from an overdose. So now I finally know who my mother is and she's getting ready to fuckin' die on me!"

Milan's eyes popped open wide. "Don't let her die. Let's go to the hospital now and you walk into her room and you tell her, "Don't fuckin' die on me! I've been waiting all of my life to be loved by you and you'd better not fuckin' die on me! I need you.' "

"I can't do that."

"I tried." Vera sat at Rowanda's bedside and held her hand. "I told him and that's all I could do. I couldn't make him come. Okay. I kept my part of the bargain and now I need you to keep yours and don't fuckin' die on me. Get your shit together and fight." Vera pushed her head into the side of her mother's hip. "Please . . ." She cried. "Please."

"I need you, too," Kendu said as he walked slowly into the hospital room.

Vera raised her head in surprise as Kendu walked around Rowanda's hospital bed and squeezed her hand. "I don't know what to say or what to do. All I know is that I have loved you all of my life and I've waited for the day when you would love me back. Now don't take that shit from me." He cried. "Don't!"

Beep . . . beep . . . beep . . . .

"Everybody out of the room!" a doctor yelled as a team of doctors and nurses rushed in. "Everybody out!"

A nurse screamed, "We're losing her!"

CHAPTER 45

CHAUNCI

*J*ust *act normal . . .*
  No guilt.
  Damn. I keep smelling Grant's cologne.
  Relax.
  And I keep feeling his touch.
  Chaunci closed her eyes as a vision danced before her of Grant lifting her breasts and slipping first one nipple into his mouth and then the other.

  "Chaunci, do you hear me?" Emory said, waving his hand in her face.

  "Huh? What? What did you say, baby?"

  "I was asking you if you wanted white or red wine with your pizza."

  "Red, sweetie."

  "You've got it."

  You'd better get it together. It happened once. . . . No. It happened five times over a weekend. You can shake this. Emory is the man you need to marry.

  Yes, he is.

  Chaunci smiled at Emory as he placed two glasses of wine on the table.

"How was the party, babe?" Emory asked, taking a bite of his slice.

Chaunci hesitated. *What party?* "Umm . . ."

"Kendu's party."

Chaunci's eyes grew bright. "Right. Kendu's party. It was really nice."

"Why didn't you come home that night?"

Think. "Now you know I was with Milan and whenever we get together we have a little too much to drink. I tell you. I'm going to hate to see that footage." She gulped her wine in one shot.

"Yeah, me too. So why didn't you come home the next night?"

Think. "Same thing. Got carried away with Milan."

"You couldn't call?"

"Umm . . . You know what? I should've called. I'm really sorry about that. Anyway, honey, let's talk about this movie you have planned for us to watch. We haven't had a pizza and movie night in a long time." She placed her left hand on his knee and squeezed.

Emory's eyes dropped to Chaunci's hand. "Where's your ring?"

Chaunci looked down at her finger. *Where's my fuckin' ring? Think. Think. Think. I don't know.* "I took it off this morning when I was oiling my skin. I must've left it on the vanity."

"Okay. If you say so."

"What is that supposed to mean?"

"Should it mean something?"

"You tell me."

"Chaunci, relax. I didn't mean anything by it. Like you said, we haven't had a pizza and movie night in a while and I think you'll especially like this movie. So let's just sit back and enjoy, okay?"

"All right." *Relax.* "What's the name of the movie, baby?"

"Whores."

"What kind of movie is that? A documentary?"

"Yeah, something like that."

Chaunci refreshed her glass of wine. "Put the movie in and let's see what this is about."

"Let's."

The movie lit up the television screen with a view of the ocean. Crystal clear water sparkled under the moonlight. The camera panned to a yacht's upper deck as two bodies, one chocolate and one cream, made love on a massive white sofa.

What the hell . . . ?

I can't breathe. . . .

Chaunci's fantasy weekend came to life as Grant sucked her breasts and his scrotum smacked her pussy lips.

"WHAT THE FUCK IS THIS?!" Chaunci screamed, jumping up and spilling her wine everywhere. "What kind of sick shit are you on!"

"Me? You're the sick bitch!"

"Bitch! Don't you ever call me a bitch!"

"A bitch! A whore! An unfaithful ass-lying slut! Up there fuckin' some white ass punk! What? Was I too black for you?!"

"That's ridiculous!"

"No, what's ridiculous is that the same motherfucker who stole your company you laying up there fuckin'! Lying about Kendu's party! You weren't even there!"

"I was there!"

"Why the hell are you still lying?! You weren't there because I was there and your ass was nowhere to be found!"

"Let me explain."

"You can't explain a damn thing to me! But what you can do is get your shit and get the fuck outta here before I beat your ass! God knows I'm a good man, but I'm not a saint, so you'd better get the hell away from me! Oh, and your goddamn ring is not on your vanity! It's right here!" Emory pulled it from his pocket. " 'Cause along with the video, that motherfucker sent it back to me!"

"Emory." Chaunci reached for his hand.

"Chaunci, I swear to God if you don't leave I may kill you."

Say something.

I can't.

Chaunci picked up her purse and took one last glance at Emory. "Emory."

He grabbed her by the arm and roughly walked her to the door. "I'm done with you! And I don't ever want to see you again! Whore!"

CHAPTER 46

VERA

The Next Day

The sidewalk leading to the courthouse was filled with news reporters, bloggers, and photographers all looking for a quick interview, a word or two, or to snap a quick picture to sell to the highest bidder.

Vera stood next to her attorney doing her best not to make eye contact with any of the news cameras.

"No comment. No comment," Vera heard repeated again and again as her attorney waved off the reporters' questions. The sheriff led Vera and her attorney into the courtroom, where Taj and his attorney sat in the back waiting.

Taj looked Vera over from her hair draping over her shoulders to her red bottoms. She wore a black pencil skirt, starched white Chanel blouse, and around her neck a three-strand pearl necklace. She wondered what his thoughts were and started to ask, but quickly changed her mind.

After all, considering today would be the last day they would share last names, she no longer had a right to ask him what his thoughts were.

Vera sat down on the opposite side of the courtroom, as her attorney walked over to Taj's attorney and asked to see him in the hallway.

Don't think.

Don't look at his ass.

Don't do anything but listen to these two dumb motherfuckers standing before the judge fighting for custody and visitation rights to a dog.

Dear God.

"Listen, Mr. and Mrs. Frank," the judge said. "I'm going to set a new date for the two of you to come back. You need to meet on your own and try to figure who the dog should go to." The judge walked off the bench.

"Next case," the bailiff announced. "Bennett versus Bennett."

Vera and Taj stood up while their attorneys rushed in and made their way to their respective clients.

"They refused to settle on anything," Vera's attorney, Matthew, whispered. "They said dropping the restraining order was enough. Taj refuses to settle for anything less than half."

"All rise!" the bailiff said as the judge walked onto the bench.

"You may be seated," the bailiff stated as the judge took his seat.

"Have the parties reached any agreements?" the judge asked, looking toward Vera's attorney.

"No, Your Honor. Please review the settlement we have submitted to the court."

"Have you copied the respondent?"

"Yes, Your Honor."

The judge looked toward Taj and his attorney. "Have you reviewed it?"

"Yes."

"And?"

"We will not accept and will instead accept whatever decision Your Honor makes."

"Wait," Vera said, standing. "Can I please say something?"

"Have you consulted your counsel?"

"No, she hasn't," Vera's attorney said.

"I don't need to speak to you on this," Vera said, looking back toward the judge.

"Well, what would like to say, Mrs. Bennett?"

"Your Honor, I have spent so much time being mad and pissed, and trying to seek revenge on my husband for hurting me, that I never stopped to see what I was doing to myself. To us. To him. My life has suddenly gone crazy. I have a brother whom I never knew I had. My mother is in a coma, and my husband, my best friend . . . I have completely pushed him away from me. I don't want to go forward with the divorce at this time."

Tears covered her face as she sat down and closed her eyes, doing her best to ignore the buzzing of the people in the courtroom.

The next few minutes felt like hell as Taj didn't say a word, and instead his attorney asked for a brief recess.

"I think one is needed," the judge agreed.

"Vera," Matthew said, "Taj would like to speak with you. The bailiff said that you two can step into the break room and close the door."

Vera walked into the room and there was Taj leaning against the orange Formica countertop, dressed in a double-breasted tan suit and loose tie. "You know what, Vera?" Taj said. "It took everything in me not to ask the judge to grant the divorce anyway."

"What?"

"You stood up there and said all that shit to the judge and you never once looked at me!"

"To whom did you think I was apologizing?"

"I don't know! Damn sure not me. This isn't a damn romance novel and you can't confess your love to me all melodramatically and think I'll just run over to you and scream, 'I love you!' Hell no. This is real life and that damn stunt you just pulled pissed me off! You don't need to be telling the judge shit. You need to be speaking to me. Your husband. And if you can't do that, then our business as a couple is done. Now you've got five minutes and then I'm out of here."

Vera bit her bottom lip. Her heart raced as her palms started to sweat. She wanted to take the easy way out by telling Taj, "Fuck it! We're done." But the thought alone awakened a pain in her belly so strong that she knew spewing the words would knock her off her feet.

"You only have five minutes and you've already used up two of them."

"Taj, you know how I feel."

"No, I don't. I know that you filed for divorce. I know that you tore up my penthouse, took back my car, cussed me out, cut me off, and refused to accept my son. A son I didn't even know about until last year. And instead of you being by my side, you flipped into this cold, scared, and hard-acting witch that I didn't even recognize. I know that I love you to death, but as of right now, I'm not so sure that I like you at all. That's what I know."

"You know what? To hell with it."

"Cool. Then let's go and get divorced."

"No." Vera ran over and blocked the door.

Just say it.

She locked into his eyes. "You and Skyy are my life. My everything. You complete me. I miss you. I miss your smile. Your laugh. Your quirks. I miss you complaining about me leaving all the lights on and making the bill too high. Even though we had enough money to own the damn electric company. I miss you leaving the toilet seat up and watching sports every time I turned around. I miss your cologne. Your smile. Your scent on our sheets. I miss waking up to you in the morning and going to sleep with you at night. I miss having a man who knows me better that I know myself at times. I miss my best friend, and if you will have me as your wife"—Vera pulled her wedding and engagement rings from her skirt pocket and put them in Taj's hands—"I promise to never take you for granted again. I promise to love you and put you first. I promise to be the best stepmother I can be to our son, Aidan. I promise to cook every night—"

"Now you're going too far." Taj chuckled.

"I promise to never, ever shut you out again. Just say you'll stay my husband."

Taj looked down at Vera's rings in his hands. He took her left hand and said, "Repeat after me. For better or worse."

"For better or worse."

"For richer or for poorer."

"For richer or for poorer."

"To honor and obey."

"Obey?" Vera curled her top lip. "What kind of obey are we talking about?"

"Do you trust me?"

"Yes."

"Then say it."

"Honor and obey."

"In sickness and in health."

"In sickness and in health."

"Until death do us part." He slid her rings back onto her finger. "I love you, Mrs. Bennett."

"I love you more," Vera said, as they began to kiss passionately.

CHAPTER 47

CHAUNCI

*L*isten. *You're going to have to calm down.*

I don't believe he did that.

I just can't believe it.

"The motherfucker sent me the ring . . . along with the video. . . ." Chaunci did her best to shake Emory's voice.

Dear God.

Calm down.

Don't worry, he'll be here and you'll be able to serve his ass.

Chaunci tapped her stilettos as she sat in the wing chair facing Grant's desk. She'd been sitting at his desk since six a.m. doing her all to erase the thoughts that told her to slice his throat.

It wasn't that she regretted sleeping with him. The regret was him ruining her life with the shit. She'd already settled on marrying Emory. Fucking Grant was to be a one-time event. An affair that she was set to carry to her grave, not have played for her fiancé.

You can't kill him.

"Now isn't this something?" came from the doorway.

Chaunci's heart dropped. Xavier.

I should've locked the damn door.

Xavier stood before her dressed in a black suit, flicking his chin.

"What are you doing here?!"

He walked over and pointed into her face. "You know what the fuck I'm doing here! It's been over a month and I want my money or I will own this company of yours!"

"Actually, you can have the son of a bitch!" She grabbed a piece of paper and scribbled, 'Co-owner of Preston Publishing formerly known as Morgan Enterprises.' "All yours! I no longer want it! I'm finished."

"Don't fuck with me, Chaunci! Trust me, you're not finished, but you will be if you don't get me my money by the end of the day!" He turned toward the door and roughly brushed past Grant, who was now standing there.

"What was that lowlife doing here again?" Grant squinted.

"He wants to be your new business partner," Chaunci snapped as Grant walked over and kissed her on the forehead.

"You look lovely as usual." He smiled as he removed his cell phone from his pocket, dialed a number, and a few seconds later spoke into the phone, "Mr. Mayor, how are you this morning?" He paused. "Great. Great. Great. Of course I know you're running for governor. You know my father and I will contribute greatly to your campaign. I'm calling because I want to remind you about that favor you owe me. Yeah. Xavier Dupree. I need you to do that for me today. A routine traffic stop will be perfect. Have a great day." Grant hung up the phone and looked back over at Chaunci. He tilted his head to the side. "Why are you looking at me like that? Are you pissed off at me? You're far too beautiful to be so mad. I just helped you out."

"No, you just ruined my life!"

"Ruined your life? I just did you a favor. A big damn favor."

"I didn't need you to do a damn thing for me!"

"Sweetie, are we talking about the same thing?"

"I'm not your damn sweetie and you know what the fuck I'm talking about!"

A smile ran across Grant's face. "My package." He laughed. "I take it your janitor received it."

I should slap the shit out of him. "You think this is funny?! You're laughing! Are you crazy?! How could you do something like that?! What the fuck is wrong with you?!"

"Look. I should've told you I was videoing you. Forgive me," he said nonchalantly.

"Not only did you video me without my permission, you took my damn ring and sent it back to my fiancé. How dare you do some shit like that?!"

"I'm a selfish bastard and sharing is not my forte." He shrugged. "What do you want me to do? Apologize to Emory? Well, I won't. As you can see, I don't give a damn about him." He paused. "Actually, he got off easy, because I could've called his loan officer, especially since my family's bank finances his business, and had his damn loan taken away. But I didn't. I figured taking you was enough."

"What the hell?!" She pounded a fist on his desk. "I don't belong to you."

"So you say."

Tears glimmered in Chaunci's eyes. "This is a fuckin' game to you! You ruined my life because you wanted to enter a pissing contest with Emory and measure dicks! I can't believe you did this to me!"

"Oh, please, knock off the victim shit. You're much too smart for that. You were a willing participant. I didn't have a gun to your head and I told you that you were free to leave at any moment. You made a choice, which was my bed. You wanted me and you wanted to be there. Now whatever the hell you're trying to prove to me is not working. You don't love Emory. He doesn't even turn you on. And you know it.

When you got your ass on that plane, it was because you wanted to be there. So don't game me with the bullshit. Be real with me because I've always been that with you."

"Really?" came from the doorway. "So then what have you been with me?"

Chaunci and Grant looked over at a tall, thin, white woman, with flawless peach-colored skin and brunette hair that hung over her shoulders.

Chaunci could tell by the look in Grant's emerald eyes that he'd been caught by surprise.

The woman walked into the office and over to Chaunci. "I'm Marissa. Grant's wife. And you are?"

A smile spread across Chaunci's face as her eyes landed on Grant.

I could kill this bastard.

She held out her hand and looked back to the woman. "I'm Chaunci. Grant's mistress."

CHAPTER 48

JOURNEE

Journee wore a long, black, fitted dress with a low, scoop neck. On her head she wore a black hat with a veil that hung to her chin and every few minutes, one of her black satin-gloved hands would ease beneath her veil and dab dry tears.

Xavier walked into the attorney's office and sat next to her. He looked up at the attorney and said, "My daddy's gone!!" He cried and his shoulders shook. "My daddy! He's gone! Why didn't he take me! My daddy was a good man. We used to talk all the time at dinner. Stay up late nights . . . and the stories he used to tell." He shuddered. "I don't know how I'll go on. I just don't know!"

Journee squeezed his hand as hard as she could. "That. Is. Not. Needed," she mumbled, as the lawyer looked at the two of them in amazement.

"Umm, perhaps we should do this in a few days," Chad, the attorney said. "I'm thinking this may be too soon for you two. If you need a little time to collect yourselves, that'll be fine."

Xavier sat up straight. "Nawl, we don't need any more time. I got a plane to catch." He cleared his throat. "I meant I'll be okay."

"Umm-hmm," Journee mumbled, shaking her head. *I promise you I can't stand this goddamn idiot. A fierce dick and a snake for a tongue is all he has. But when he opens his mouth . . .*
Relax.
You've got this.
"Let's just get down to business," Xavier said. "My dearly departed daddy's business, of course. God bless the dead."
Journee shot him a look that clearly said, "Shut the fuck up."
"If you insist," Chad said. "I just want you to know that Zachary changed his will and did one by way of video." He walked over to the flat screen television that hung on the wall and pushed in a DVD.
"He did what?" Journee asked, her heart dropping out of her chest. She closed her eyes.
You have to keep it together.
Ten . . .
Nine . . .
Eight . . .
That no good motherfucker!
"Of course," Journee said, opening her eyes. "Granddaddy told me about that."
The attorney pressed play and Zachary's face filled the television screen. "If you are seeing this video, that has to mean I have already met my . . . demise."
"Oh, Daddeeeeee!" Xavier screamed, looking up toward the heavens. "Why did you have to take him, Lord?! You were wrong for that, José—"
"It's Jesus."
"That's what I said."
Journee was completely disgusted.
The DVD played. "My dearest Journee. I was so happy when I married you. To have a woman so young and so beautiful was amazing."
Journee smiled. *Too bad I couldn't stand your greasy old ass.*
The video continued, "My son. My dear, dear son. I always

regretted missing so much of your life. I'm glad that in the end we were able to get close and be a family."

"Oh, Daddy!" Xavier cried.

"Shut the fuck up!" Journee pounded her fist on the coffee table. "Just shut your ass up! I'm tired of you now!"

Chad paused the DVD. "Is everything okay?"

"I'm sorry," Journee said. "I'm just upset right now."

Xavier looked Journee over. "Make that the last time you tell me to shut up."

Chad pressed play and Zachary continued to speak. "My beautiful wife and my son."

This motherfucker hasn't run out of breath or fallen asleep mid-sentence yet. I've never heard him speak this clear.

He continued, "Thank you for showing me and the video cameras that I had planted all over the house—"

Cameras? Did he say cameras?

"Yeah, I said cameras," Zachary said as if he predicted Journee's thoughts. "Thanks to my cameras, I was able to see that you two were two big-ass piles of horseshit."

"Horseshit?!" Journee and Xavier spat simultaneously.

"And, Journee, I watched you ride his dick every night and call his name. In my damn house!"

"What the hell is this?!" Journee peered at the attorney.

He didn't answer as the video continued. "You dirty bitch you. And, Xavier, I never thought you were my damn son. 'Cause your mama was some damn slut monkey who swung from scrotum to scrotum."

"Slut monkey?" Xavier repeated in disbelief.

"Yeah, I said it. A slut monkey!" The video continued, "Hell, as far as your mama knows, your damn daddy is Waldo! And nobody can find that motherfucker!"

"Oh, hell no! He just cussed my mama!"

"She stayed drunk half the damn time, so God only knows who your damn daddy is. If I meet him on my way to hell, I'll be sure to tell him to haunt yo' ass. You two stayed in my house and thought you were going to sucker me. Did you really think I spoke that goddamn slow? Hell no. You are two of the dumbest motherfuckers. Now, I've already given the house manager, Mary, instructions to burn every goddamn bed and all the sheets after I'm dead, 'cause ain't no need for her to catch y'all nasty motherfuckin' disease in her new house."

"Her house?" Journee looked at Chad. "What does he mean, her house?"

The video went on, "Mary owns the island now and she already has y'all shit packed and waiting at the goddamn pier. And as far as my money, it's all going to charity. Every bit of it! Now both of y'all can kiss my dead ass! Bitches."

Breathe . . .

Breathe . . .

There was nothing to say. There was nothing Journee could say. She just wanted out of Chad's office. It felt hot and stifling. She couldn't breathe. She could hear him talking to her, but she couldn't make out what he was saying.

Journee rose from the chair, tucked her purse under her arm, and walked out of the attorney's office. She could hear Xavier on her heels as she walked outside and slid into the backseat of the black Lincoln town car.

"Phillip," Journee said to her driver as she slid her bumble bee Chanels over her eyes. "I just need you to drive. Just drive. I don't care where you go. Just go."

She tilted her head back, resting it against the seat.

"Well, while you're trying to figure shit out," Xavier said, "I'm getting ready to run over to Millionaires' Row and knock Mary off."

"You getting ready to do what?"

"Fuck that. That bitch is going down! I will drown that ho before she gets my daddy's damn house!"

"You don't know if he was your damn daddy!" Journee screamed. "All you did was bring your ass back here and ruin everything for me! Everything! And now what do I have?!

Nothing but two goddamn strip clubs that I signed over to yo' ass!"

"Well, that's too motherfuckin' bad, bitch! I took the rap for you and your slutty-ass girlfriend. I didn't rob that bank by myself and I damn sure didn't shoot that security guard. But I was the only one who spent ten years in prison!"

"You were a junkie-ass piece of nothing, motherfucker! You deserved those ten years and I hoped you dropped the soap and somebody bust yo' ass!"

"I don't believe you said some shit like that!" He pushed her.

"You don't put your hands on me, motherfucker!" Journee slapped Xavier so hard that spit flew from his mouth, and seconds later, they were wrapped in a backseat brawl.

"Stop it!" The driver swerved to the side of the street, the rear of the car running onto the crowded New York City curb, missing by inches the people who'd been standing there. People were scattering and screaming as the driver tossed the car in park and snatched open the passenger-side back door, doing his best to break up Journee and Xavier.

"Bitch!"

"Bastard!"

"Motherfucker!"

They scrambled.

"What is going on here?!" Two officers approached the car. They looked in the backseat and saw Journee and Xavier engaged in World War III.

"Please help!" the driver said desperately.

The officers walked to opposite sides of the car. One pulled Journee and the other yanked Xavier out of the car.

Journee's hair was everywhere and her dress was hiked up, exposing her thong. "I'm going to kill him!" she screamed.

"Let's go, bitch!" Xavier yelled, as the officer slammed him against the car. His face was marked with fresh, bloody scratches. His left eye was swollen and his bottom lip was busted.

"Are you Mrs. Dupree?" the lead officer asked.

"Yes! I'm Journee Dupree. And I want his ass arrested! Right now!"

"And I want that bitch arrested too!" Xavier yelled.

"Calm down," the officer said, looking at Journee as she pulled her dress down. "Relax. And stand here."

Journee was in total shock as people gawked and took pictures of her standing center stage. She looked up and saw Bridget and the *Millionaire Wives Club* cameras zoomed in on her. She patted the sides of her dress and pulled her hair back.

"Tell the camera what's going on." Bridget smiled.

"That motherfucker attacked me!" Journee huffed.

"Where are you two coming from?"

Journee hesitated. "We had to take care of some family business. And while I was meditating and trying to clear my thoughts, he attacked me! Out of nowhere. He's nothing! He's finished!"

"Is that why they are arresting him?" Bridget asked.

Journee whipped toward the action and saw Xavier pressed up against the side of the car and the officer waving a plastic bag with a white powdery substance in it.

"That's not mine!" Xavier screamed. "I didn't have that shit!"

"I knew it!" Journee said, disgusted. "You junkie motherfucker! You're back to getting high again?!"

"Cuff him!" the lead officer said as his partner placed handcuffs on him and read him his Miranda rights.

"Journee!" Xavier cried. "Come on, baby, I need you. I need you to call the attorney! Have him meet me at the station!"

"I'll call the attorney all right. Call him and have him press charges on your paroled ass!"

One of the officers pushed Xavier into the backseat of the police car while the other officer said, "I apologize you had to go through this, Mrs. Dupree." He handed her his card. "If ever you want to talk about this, call me." And he pulled off.

I must be dreaming. She pinched herself. *That shit was real.*

"Bridget," she said, "I have to go!"

She got back into her car, and her driver, who was visibly upset, got behind the wheel. "Lose them," Journee ordered. "And then take me back to the attorney's office."

After a few ducks, dodges, and dances through traffic, the driver was able to shake the cameras and could safely park in front of the attorney's Park Avenue building.

Journee's heels clicked loudly as she hurried into Chad's office and closed the door.

Chad looked up from his computer and raised a brow. "What the hell happened to you?"

"Xavier. I tried to kill him."

"Is he still alive?"

"He's in jail."

"You had him arrested?"

"Yes and no. The cops broke up the fight and while they searched him, they found some damn dope in his pocket."

"Are you serious?"

"As serious as the kidney failure that finally killed Zachary's ass."

"So that's why you're back so soon." Chad smiled and walked over to Journee, placing his hands around her waist.

"You can call off the hit now," she said.

"Or we can have the hit happen in prison."

"Good idea."

A smile spread across Journee's face. "It's been a long four years."

"It sure has." He kissed her softly on the lips.

"Now tell me, what the hell was with that video will?"

"Don't worry about that." He kissed her again. "Not only did I not file it. I've already destroyed it."

CHAPTER 49

BRIDGET

Reunion

These bitches were winners! They'd sung a drama-filled lullaby for the third season in a row, making my baby, *Millionaire Wives Club,* a huge success. And yeah, they all ended the season hating me—except Journee—but I didn't give a damn. After all, this was never personal. Even Milan charging into the office and backhanding me wasn't personal. It was always business.

The reunion was taking place in the ballroom of the Ty Warner hotel. The room was a shimmering white, with two white leather couches and an exquisite chandelier hanging from the ceiling.

Vera, Jaise, and Journee sat on one couch while Milan and Chaunci sat on the other. Each was dressed in a fabulous roaring twenties ball gown and limited edition heels.

Their jewels reflected in the light and they all appeared to have their own sparkling hue, as they looked out into the audience and watched their host walk up the center aisle, pose, and smile.

All of their jaws dropped and I just about pissed in my pants.

I swear I just loved these hos.

Their host was none other than Al-Taniesha Richardson, a former star of the show, who had moved on to star in my other hit production, *A Preacher's Wife*.

Al-Taniesha sauntered onto the stage wearing a purple leather dress and silver gladiator platform heels that lit up like Christmas lights with every step.

She took her seat and crossed her legs. "Umm-hmm, it's me. First Lady Niesha. Al-Taniesha Chardonnay Richardson, as most of you know." She looked into the camera. "The star of my own hit reality show. You can catch me every Thursday night at ten. Or every Sunday morning at Heathen No More Tabernacle, on Grove Street, Hotlanta, USA. " She gave a small wave and then turned back to the cast. "Chile, y'all bitches begged for your supper this goddamn season! Oh, hell yes, y'all did!" She slapped a thigh. "And to think you called *me* ghetto. Now had y'all been in the projects, you would've been called hood rats, but change the zip code to Fifth Avenue and without further ado . . . I present to you the *Millionaire Wives Club*."

The audience clapped and after the applause simmered down, Al-Taniesha held up a blue index card and said, "This question is from Taylor in Jersey, and it's for you, Jaise. She wants to know how you are feeling since the death of your son."

Jaise dabbed the corner of her eye. "It gets better every day, Al-Taniesha."

Vera patted Jaise's back, while Journee touched her hand and Milan and Chaunci said almost in unison, "I'm so sorry that happened to you."

"Thank you," Jaise said. "Everyone has been so supportive. I still miss my baby though."

"I can imagine you have to," Al-Taniesha said. " 'Cause I know my daughter misses his damn child support." She looked into the camera. "For those who don't know, my daughter, Christina, and Jaise's son had a baby together two years ago. The baby is doing well. But I'm tired of Chrissy begging me for money. Dat ass knows I don't believe in taking care of grown children. No, ma'am. I'm young. Vibrant. Sexy. And I just don't do that. That's how you ruin 'em. And the next thing you know they all fucked up and dead somewhere. No offense, Jaise. I'm just making a point. But anyway, you wanna tell the audience about your new bundle of joy?"

Jaise mustered up a smile and ran a hand over her stomach. "Who would've ever thought?"

"Damn sure not me," Al-Taniesha said as Milan and Chaunci chuckled and agreed. "A baby," she continued. "And you're damn near forty? No, honey, that's when you need to adopt a dog or a damn monkey. But anyway, hallelujah! What a blessing."

"Yes. My baby is a blessing," Jaise said, pissed. "I'm five months pregnant and I can do without your comments!" She gawked at Milan and Chaunci. "So instead of being worried about me and my pregnancy, you need to be concerned with your raggedy-ass relationships. Tell us, Chaunci, did sleeping with the boss pay off?"

Journee and Vera laughed.

"Good question, Jaise," Vera said.

"That's a damn good question!" Al-Taniesha stood up and gave Jaise a high five. "Bitch, that mouth has always been slick. That's what made me want to always boom-cock you in the face, because of some of the shit you would say. But anyway, before we move on, Jaise . . ." Al-Taniesha retook her seat and picked up another index card. "Sydney from Iowa wants to know how Bilal is doing and what's the state of your marriage."

"We're still separated. And I guess he's fine."

"Does he know about the baby?"

"After today he will."

"Damn! He doesn't even know you're pregnant? You are really giving it to his ass. And let me tell you when you kicked him out of the house, the only thing missing from that scene was you coming down the stairs, lighting a cigarette, and setting his shit on fire!"

"KABOOM!" Lollipop, Al-Taniesha's husband, who was dressed in a white patent leather catsuit, screamed from the audience.

"But you did well," Al-Taniesha continued. " 'Cause I would've busted four caps in his skull. Yeah, Jabril was sorry, and triflin', and you should've done a better job teaching him how to be a man, but he was my grandson's father. Bilal could've let him live in the basement."

"Al-Taniesha, I think you need to move on," Jaise said.

"Okay, okay, okay. Now on to Chaunci. Girlfriend, you did that shit. You owned this season, baby! My mouth hit the floor when it came out that you were doing the panty drop with Grant. When Emory leaked that damn video to the media, chile, I almost died! So what do you have to say about that?"

"I'm not going to discuss that," Chaunci said.

"What the hell?" Al-Taniesha's mouth dropped open. "Don't you think folks wanna know?"

"I know I'd like to know," Vera added. "Because I saw the video, and wow!"

"I really think you need to stay in your lane." Chaunci pointed at Vera.

"Or what?" Vera pushed.

"Let me just pause it right there, ladies," Al-Taniesha said, and looked at Chaunci. "Don't get fucked up during commercial break. You already know that hood ho will slice your ass down to the marrow."

Chaunci sucked her teeth. "Whatever. Next question."

Al-Taniesha continued, "Kenya from Alabama wants to know, what's the state of your company?"

"I am still co-owner with Grant Preston."

"Oh, damn." Al-Taniesha laughed. "So, umm, have you been back to the creamalicious side of things?"

"I'm doing well and my daughter is fantastic." Chaunci changed the subject.

"Excuse you, I'm the host here. I'll change the subject. Bitches kill me! Shit, you were on reality TV and if you were going to get on the reunion and act like you're too good to discuss your drama, then you shouldn't have done the bullshit during the season. Everybody wants to know about you and sexy ass and this is what you pull? Shade? As Bridget says, 'Bitch, you'd better get into it.' "

Al–Taniesha turned toward Vera. "You know phony hos work me over, which is why I always fucked with you, Vera. But I must say this season you and Taj went through some hell. Are you truly back together or not? 'Cause you know last reunion you lied and said you were one happy family and the truth was you hated his ass. Now what's the deal?"

"We are more in love than ever. He's back home and it's a beautiful thing."

"Girl, you'd better keep that black man happy. 'Cause I had a few church ushers and nurses lined up. And I told 'em right after that divorce scene, 'we'll see how this goes, and if she acts stupid, I'll put you on him.' But you turned it around and I'm proud of you! You did that shit. You are my kind of bitch, Vera. And I'm so glad you got your mind right. 'Cause you know that little boy ain't do shit to you. You and Taj were broken up and he slid over to another chick real quick. That's life. And the lesson for him is to wrap it up. He's a doctor and he ought to know better than that. He had a blood test, right?"

"Yes. And like I've already said, we're happy."

"Now, how is your mother and how is it having a brother?"

"My mother is still in the hospital and things are touch and go. As far as Kendu being my brother . . . it's been different. I've never had any siblings, so I'm learning how to be a sister. We spend time together. He comes over—"

"Does he bring his wife?"

"Sometimes."

"Girl, I'd love to be a fly on that damn wall. Do you two get along now?"

"It's a process."

"It sure is," Milan remarked.

Vera pointed at Milan. "As long as my brother, my nephew, and my niece are there, you don't ever have to come. Ever!"

"Oh, hell!" Al-Taniesha laughed. "Y'all whores are related. Oh, damn, I would love to be around come Christmastime!" She turned to Journee. "Now, Journee, the new chick on the scene. You turned out to be a fan fave."

"Yes. I did." Journee smiled and waved at the audience.

"But I have to know, what in the hell did you see in Granddaddy? It had to be the money, honey. 'Cause all I could imagine was a short and stumpy dingaling!"

A chorus of "ewww" traveled through the audience.

"I loved my husband," Journee insisted.

"Chile, please. Now were you doing his son? Admit it. Were you?"

"No. I was not."

"Girrrrrl!" Al-Taniesha yelled. "You have better coochie control than me, 'cause I would've hit him off a few times. I understand you were trying to be a stand-up woman. But that husband of yours, chile. He reminded me of a sick dog who needed to be euthanized! Now, Kai from Oklahoma wants to know what's going on with his son."

"He was killed in prison," Journee answered.

"Whaaaaat? Somebody shanked him to death?! Wow!"

"Yeah, pretty sad," Journee said. "Next question."

"I don't have any more for you, boo. You just blew me out the water with telling me that Xavier was dead. He said he wanted to be with his daddy, so I guess he is."

"Now on to you, Ms. Milan. So somebody finally beat Bridget's ass and it happened to be you!"

"Yes. I tried to bury her in the carpet, but security wouldn't let me. Needless to say, this will be the last time you'll see me on reality TV."

Lies.

"Fuck Bridget."

We all know you don't mean that.

Milan continued, "She hired an actress to ruin my marriage. I'm done!"

"Any advice you'd give anyone who wants to be a part of reality TV?"

"Yes. That karma is not a bitch; reality TV is."

"Carl!" I looked over at him. "She's a fuckin' genius. Make sure that line is her intro for next season."

"You got it."

"I tell ya, Carl"—I wiped tears—"for the next few months, I'm gonna miss these hos."

RICH GIRL PROBLEMS

Tu-Shonda L. Whitaker

About This Guide

The discussion questions that follow are included to
enhance your group's reading of the book.

Discussion Questions

1. How much of a role do you believe the cameras played in the characters' lives? Had there been no cameras, would their lives have been the same?

2. Do you believe that Bridget acted the way all reality show producers behave? If so, in what way? If not, then how is she different?

3. What did you think of Vera's struggle to accept Taj's son? Was it truly about him having a child outside their marriage? Or do you believe their marriage was affected by other factors? If yes, what might those factors be?

4. Rowanda had a long history of drug abuse. Can you believe she will ever change?

5. How do you feel about Kendu and Vera being siblings? Do you believe that this could happen in real life? Do you know someone with similar family dynamics? How did they handle it? How would you handle it?

6. Jaise struggled with choosing between her husband and her son. Do you think she made the right choice? If not, why not? Would your opinion be different if Jabril had not been killed?

7. How do you feel about Bridget hiring an actress to spice up Milan's drama? Do you think Milan not trusting her husband was about the actress or about her own insecurities?

8. Do you believe that Chaunci truly loved her fiancé?

9. How did you feel about Grant having a wife? How do you imagine things will unfold?

10. Journee was the newcomer to the show. How do you think the story would be different if she were not a part of the cast?

Meet these dramatic divas for the first time in

Millionaire Wives Club

Available wherever books and ebooks are sold

Turn the page for an excerpt from *Millionaire Wives Club* . . .

The Club

Millions of dollars in premier fashions and champagne diamonds were on display at Manhattan's 40/40 Club as four ultrarich and ubersuccessful women—America's newest addition to reality TV—strolled the red carpet and smiled at the flashing lights of the paparazzi. The clicking of their designer stilettos was like exquisite steel-pan beats as they crossed the club's threshold, and the sultry sounds of Maxwell's live performance filled the air. Despite their individual insecurities and doubts, at this moment as they sauntered into the sunrise of superstardom, what mattered most was that they'd gotten their own piece of the latest in rich bitch candy.

"Ladies, ladies," a reporter from *E! News* said, motioning for the four of them to come together and meet him across the room. "Can you all tell us a little about yourselves?" He looked at the woman to his left. "May we start with you?"

"I'm Milan Starks, wife of the great Yusef 'Da Truef' Starks, number twenty-three on the New York Knicks." A lovely mix of her cinnamon brown Dominican father and golden-skinned African American mother, Milan had an effortless beauty that didn't require makeup or facials to be perfect. She had a Marilyn Monroe mole on the corner of her top lip, hazel eyes, her Beyoncé-like hips were a size ten—twelve at most—and she had a true apple bottom.

"Wasn't he suspended?" Evan Malik said and then quickly covered her mouth. "Oh, my apologies, I didn't mean to say that."

"He was suspended," the reporter said, following up on Evan's comment. "Do you want to tell us how you feel about that?" he asked Milan.

"My husband is a great man." Milan smiled. "Sure, he hit a rough patch, but he's on his way back and will be better than ever."

"Thank you, Mrs. Starks, now on to you, Mrs. Malik," he said to Evan. "Is it true that you were the first to be cast for the show?"

Milan shifted her weight from one Christian Louboutin python pump to the other, praying the nausea she felt as she sized up Evan would go away. Evan stood five eleven, fabulously slender, a figure-eight shape, and skin the color of butterscotch. Her hair was cut in a short and spiky Halle Berry–inspired 'do with touches of honey blond that glimmered in the spotlights.

Milan hated that she and Evan had ended up in the same circle, because every time she saw Evan, heard Evan's voice, and was in her presence, Milan was forced to deal with the fact that Evan had won. Evan had ended up with the only man who made Milan feel true love was obtainable: Kendu. But since image was everything in this business, Milan planned to do her damnedest and pretend that they were all friends, even if the knife she had for Evan's back weighed down her Chloé clutch.

"Why of course, sweetie," Evan said. "Who wouldn't want to start with me?" She winked.

"It's been five minutes," Chaunci Morgan, Milan's neighbor and one of the four costars, whispered to Milan while maintaining a smile, "and already I'm sick of this bitch. Did she forget that she was a video ho?"

"Seems so," Milan whispered back.

"Excuse you." Jaise Williams, Evan's friend and their costar, turned toward Milan and then eyed Chaunci. "What did you just say?" she snapped.

"I said that she looks fabulous." Milan smiled at Evan. "She gives retired video hos, I mean vixens, a good name."

"Umm-hmm," Chaunci added, snapping her fingers in a Z motion. "A true fashionista. You better work it, girl."

"So, Mrs. Malik," the reporter said, "tell the world who you are and what it means to be on the show."

Evan paused. The microphone pointed toward her and the spotlights shining in her face caused her to draw a blank. There was no way she could say, "*Millionaire Wives Club* is a last-ditch effort to save my life, something to keep me busy and silence the self-destructive thoughts running through my mind." And she definitely couldn't say, "I may be married to Kendu Malik, linebacker for the New York Giants, but it's an unending struggle holding on to the motherfucker."

"Mrs. Malik," the reporter interrupted her thoughts, "is everything okay? Do you want to fill us in?"

Evan blinked and shot him a Barbie-doll smile. "I am a beautiful wife"—she arched her eyebrows—"an outstanding mother, and I have the talent and the foresight to seize the moment. And being on the show will allow all women to see what it takes to be me."

"And what exactly does that mean?" the reporter probed.

"What she means," Chaunci mumbled to Milan, "is that she thinks us peons are pissed that we didn't hit the same groupies party that she did."

Milan tried not to laugh, but then couldn't hold it in any longer, and when she looked at Chaunci they both cracked up, neither one of them stopping until they noticed everyone standing around them was silent.

"Oh," the producer, Bridget, said to them, batting her eyes, "don't stop on the boom mic's accord. For ratings' sake, carry on."

Milan was embarrassed; the last thing she wanted was for her and Chaunci to be seen as the troublemaking pair. "I'ma ummm"—Milan pointed to the bar—"go and have a drink."

"I'll join you," Chaunci said, as Bridget motioned for the camera guy, Carl, to follow them.

Once they were at the bar and had ordered their drinks, Carl tapped Chaunci on the shoulder. Both she and Milan turned around. "When I cut the camera on, tell us what happened over there. Why'd you say those things?"

He turned the camera on and pointed it at them. "Evan works my nerves," Chaunci said, popping her lips. "I've known her for three days, since we met at the studio, and already she's been in my life too long." She shot Milan a high five. "And believe me, as editor in chief of *Nubian Diva* magazine everyone knows that I'm too classy to lose my cool, but trust me, I will not hesitate to tap dat ass." She pointed toward Evan.

"But since this is a nice place," Milan interrupted as she sipped her drink, "we're not gon' tear it up."

"So we're just going to sit here." Chaunci crossed her legs.

"And enjoy our evening," Milan added.

"Thanks, ladies." Carl smiled and turned away.

Jaise stared at the *E! News* reporter, wondering how she should introduce herself to the world. Should she tell people the made-for-TV parts of her life story or should she lower the boom, let 'em know the truth, and maybe, just maybe, some sanity-teetering superwoman somewhere would understand that this single-mother-doing-her-thing bullshit was overrated?

She stood next to Evan and her eyes shifted from the people mingling across the room to the reporter standing before them. Her open-toed pencil heels were aching her feet, and she wondered why she had committed to doing reality TV, especially when her postdivorce resolution was no drama. Yet here she was drowning in it. All because she and Evan had sworn that cable's *Millionaire Wives Club* was the new bling they needed to rock.

It was public knowledge that Jaise had married and divorced ex–heavyweight champion Lawrence Williams, but she wondered if anyone knew how much she had suffered in silence during their marriage. She'd been slapped, punched, kicked, and humiliated, almost daily, by her ex. And if people didn't know it, would revealing it make hers a story of empowerment or weakness?

Then again, maybe she would look like a shero if she revealed how she had walked out on Lawrence by placing a sedative in his nightly shot of Hennessey, waited for him to drift to sleep, grabbed her son, and then escaped to a battered woman's shelter.

But she had been married to him for seven years and never once publicly complained. There was no way she could now admit before the world that a man with money had clouded her judgment. And since some shit was better left unsaid, Jaise stood there, waited for Evan to finish, and when the reporter turned to her she had her intro down pat.

"Mrs. Williams," the reporter said, "can you tell us a little about yourself? We hear that you're superwoman. A single mom, the owner of the online Shabby Chic antique business— you seem to be doing it all."

"Superwoman," Jaise responded, laughing, "is a myth." She flung her emerald-and-rhodium-draped wrist. "But I am handling money and power quite well." She chuckled a bit. "I'm just so excited to be in the company of some remarkable women."

Once Jaise was done the reporter shook the ladies' hands and said, "Good interview, ladies. Now I need to go and speak to your costars."

As he turned away Jaise let out a sigh of relief. She sat down at one of the tables and lit a cigarette, and Evan sat across from her. As Jaise eased her feet from her four-inch heels, she said, "I hope I can survive this shit." She looked at Evan and took a pull. "I keep thinking and rethinking what to say and what not to say." She let out the smoke. "I swear somebody is going to think I'm crazy."

"Girl," Evan said, as she watched Milan and Chaunci laugh and converse at the bar, "just be yourself."

"Be myself?" Jaise smirked. "Yeah, right."

"No seriously, I mean, hell, I have no problems being me. I meant what I said to the reporter."

"Well, I'm not that put together. I'm stressed and sometimes I feel beat down. And you know that's too real for TV."

"It's *reality TV*," Evan insisted. "Speak to the camera as if you were talking to me."

Jaise laughed. "Okay, I'ma relax this bill collector's voice, put on my Brooklyn-mami twang, and say, 'I'm so goddamn tired of faking the funk. The truth is my sixteen-year-old son needs a man to call daddy and, hell, I do too.'"

Evan laughed, but her eyes were on Milan. She couldn't help but wonder what Milan had that she didn't. Why had Kendu chosen Milan for his best friend and why was Milan able to touch places and parts of Kendu that he wouldn't dare let Evan into? Kendu's rejection of her had steadily become Evan's obsession.

"What are you thinking about?" Jaise asked Evan once she realized she'd lost her attention. Jaise followed Evan's gaze to Chaunci and Milan. "Fuck them."

"That's it!" Bridget unexpectedly walked over to their table and said, "That's the spirit. Fuck them, and just so you know, they just finished calling you two a buncha rats' asses."

"What?" Jaise said, slipping her shoes back on. "They don't even know me."

"And from the sound of it," Bridget said, "they don't want to."

"Let's go and straighten this out." Jaise looked at Evan as she rose from her chair.

"Sit down," Evan warned Jaise. "I wouldn't give those low-budget bitches the satisfaction."

"Low-budget"—Bridget grabbed a napkin and a pen and scribbled down what Evan had just said—"bitch-es."

"I thought most producers didn't get involved with the cast," Evan snapped.

Bridget, who resembled a redheaded Heidi Klum, smiled and tossed her red hair over her shoulders. "Meet the new and improved way to produce."

"Anyway," Evan said, looking back at Jaise, "we have more going for us than to argue with a pair of half-dollar hos."

"So what makes you different from all the other women?" the *E! News* reporter asked Chaunci.

Chaunci did her best to hold a steady smile and act sober considering she and Milan had had one too many shots of Patrón and glasses of white wine. Milan smiled sweetly, knowing that if her friend said even one word it was sure to be slurred.

"Well," Chaunci attempted to speak in a steady tone, although her being tipsy was evident, "what makes me different is that I have my own, and all the rest of these women are uppity skeezers on the stroll." She turned to Milan: "No offense." Turning back toward the reporter she continued, "I'm not upset with them, though, not one bit. What woman wouldn't want to marry well?"

"But then they'd have to worry about groupies," Milan managed to add without slurring.

"Any advice about that?" the reporter asked.

Chaunci laughed. "Certainly, I have some advice. As soon as some groupie comes shakin' it around your man, bust a cap in her ass and then put one in him. Shit, I can't say he won't cheat, but make sure he's a handicap motherfucker doin' it. Alright." She and Milan exchanged high fives again.

"So what do you think people will learn from the show?" the reporter asked Chaunci.

"That when these Jones come down"—she sipped her drink with one hand and pointed her index finger with the other—"it's gon' be a motherfucker."

"And there you have it." The *E! News* reporter turned to face the camera. "I present to you the ladies of *Millionaire Wives Club*. Stay tuned!"